THOUGH THE MOUNTAINS MAY FALL

THOUGH THE MOUNTAINS MAY FALL

The story of the great Johnstown Flood of
1889

T. William Evans

Writers Club Press
New York Lincoln Shanghai

Though The Mountains May Fall

The story of the great Johnstown Flood of 1889

Writers Club Press
an imprint of iUniverse, Inc.

For information address:
iUniverse, Inc.
2021 Pine Lake Road, Suite 100
Lincoln, NE 68512
www.iuniverse.com

This novel is a work of fiction. While it is based on the actual events leading up to and including the great Johnstown Flood of 1889, and includes many of the people, famous and common who faced that horrific time, the main characters are fictional. Any similarities between these fictitious characters and events with actual persons and events are merely coincidental but are central to the flow of the story.

ISBN: 0-595-26172-8 (pbk)
ISBN: 0-595-65545-9 (cloth)

Printed in the United States of America

To the people of Johnstown—
Those from the past
Those from the present
And those yet to be

And to my Mary…

"Though the mountains may fall, and the hills turn to dust,
Yet the love of the Lord will stand,
As a shelter for all who will call upon His Name."

—*Though the Mountains May Fall*
By Dan Schutte

CONTENTS

▼

Acknowledgments

So many people have contributed to this book that I fear I should let someone out. First and foremost are my family, my relatives and my friends. Without their words of encouragement, their continued support and counsel, this book would not have happened. I must though single out my wife and daughter for their patience in editing and reading the many versions and shapes this book has traversed. I appreciate my son for his solid support and for use of the computer. My brother also must be acknowledged for assisting me in the critical process of making the book exciting and hopefully capturing the reader right from the start. Lastly, I thank my dear friend Lynne Storer for her patient reading of my first draft.

I have included a bibliography at the rear of the book so that people may research and learn more about the flood and the events surrounding that horrific time. However, I do feel it necessary to single out several references for people interested in learning more about the flood. David McCullough's *The Johnstown Flood*, the ultimate reference point and starting point for any serious endeavor on the flood. I found Anwei Law's book *The Great Flood*, fascinating and the description of Anna Fenn (Maxwell) and her family's loss to be riveting. Victor Heiser's colorful descriptions of his own experiences recounted in his book, *An American Doctor's Odyssey* told from an eyewitness the terrible toll of this great flood. I must acknowledge Martha Frick Symington Sanger's book on her great grandfather, *Henry Clay Frick, an intimate portrait.* In her book, I found a much more complex man than previously envisioned. I hope that I am able to convey this image in these pages.

I would be remiss if I did not acknowledge the wonderful visual and materials offered by three sites central to the flood story. The National Flood Memorial site offered much research material and information regarding the flood. The Flood Museum in Johnstown, donated by Andrew Carnegie after the flood (as a library), was also significant in the artifacts and information provided there from the flood and its destruction. Then there is St. Michael and the 1889 South Fork Fishing and Hunting Club Historic Preservation Society. They were so helpful and led us on a tour of the clubhouse, even including showing us some of the rooms on the second floor. Please visit these sites, read the books sited above and in the bibliography. And always, trust and place your hope in God.

The Aftermath

The date is May 31, 1889 around four twenty P.M. The place is just north of Johnstown Pa. The makeshift raft floats more slowly now moving away from the stone bridge and the devastation there. The cries of agony and unspeakable horror are still heard, although fading, as the distance lengthens between the raft and the bridge. Mary Mihelic releases her fierce grip on the raft, really nothing more than a slice of a split roof, and guides the small beaten craft to the newly defined shoreline.

She steps off onto the first solid ground since being swept away in the flood. Shaking, she falls to her knees and cries. She is soaked through and her clothing clings to her skin. Not much is left of her clothing, however, just her long petticoat. Even it is torn in places and bright red splotches indicate cuts. Her dark brown hair hangs limply over her face. Even with this stark reality, her natural beauty shines through the mud, blood and the water.

Mary stays there crying for what seems like hours to her. It is only minutes.

"I have lost everything. Everything. James, everyone, all gone. Why? My darling, why didn't you stay with me? Why did this happen? Please, can someone tell me why?"

She looks up at the heavens as if expecting an answer from there. None comes, only rain. She climbs unsteadily to her feet. She looks back on the devastation and the town that only minutes ago existed but is now a flooded plain. She hears the continuing cries for help from the distant bridge. The stone bridge crosses what used to be the Conemaugh River and is, or was used by trains coming from Pittsburgh.

Mary is drawn slowly back towards that stone bridge. She shivers, though not from the cold. Her chills are the result of the terror she has faced and from that which she is about to face. Bone tired she walks, climbing over debris and wreckage, to get back to the Johnstown side of the bridge. As she gets nearer the screams of terror and the cries for help get louder. She finds herself listening carefully.

James, are you one of those poor souls? I am coming dearest.

When she arrives at the stone bridge, she is struck by the havoc there. The bridge and its stone supports have acted as a barrier to all that is carried there by the raging waters. Train cars, entire houses, lumber, wires, and people all crammed together. In just the short time that she and James had made their break for the culvert, the amount of wreckage had more than tripled. The mass of debris left little escape for those now being rushed into it by the swirling waters.

Mary starts to climb out on the wreckage looking for James. She feels an arm reach out and grab her.

"Ma'am, I don't think you should be here. This is very dangerous. There's fuel in there that is going to catch fire at any second. Besides, you need attention."

Mary smiles at the would-be rescuer.

"You don't understand. Someone I love may be in there. But thank you so much."

The man doesn't release his grip on Mary. Instead he thinks for a moment, and then says, "I can't let you go, miss. Here take this blanket. Please."

He wraps a blanket around her to shield her from the chill. She continues to shiver.

"Thank you," she mumbles.

"I'll go. Who am I looking for?"

"James Peyton, my fiancé. We're going to be married. He's about six feet tall with light brown hair and blue eyes. He was wearing a white shirt. I believe it may be torn." Mary pauses here trying to recall all of the events, which swirl in her mind. Her face squints up and she turns her head as if reflecting on her description. She continues, "He is wearing brown pants, with stripes, a part of his suit." Mary wanted to continue but the man places his hands on her lips.

"That's enough ma'am. I can find him from that description."

"Yes. You see we were separated. Please find him."

Mary slips to the ground, catching herself with her hand, then watches as the man climbs out over the wreckage. She watches intently from her knees as he makes his way through the rubble of Johnstown.

Bodies are everywhere. Arms reaching out for help, others lying there presumably dead. The man reaches down and pulls one small boy to safety. He tries to help a woman to safety next. She is so tangled in the wire that he can't get her loose. After trying several times, he moves on. She clings to his arm.

"Don't go. Please, please don't leave me."

"I'll come back. I have someone I have to find now."

"Save me! Please!"

He pulls away and moves forward searching for anyone fitting the description of James Peyton.

Suddenly, there is a deafening roar followed by another loud blast. Boom! Smoke billows up into the night air in sharp contrast to the swirling waters and the still driving rain. Mary ducks from the blast and the flying debris. When the dust settles she turns back, looking frantically for the man who had aided her.

He is gone. Dear God, he is gone.

Shooting flames and smoke now billow up into the air where he last stood. Mary cries out, "No! No, it cannot be. Oh God no!"

The screaming of the people trapped in the wreckage now rises to a deadly panic. People are literally being cooked in the raging fires. Mary gets up from her knees. Dropping her blanket, she rushes out onto the twisted debris. Stepping hurriedly and with little regard for her safety she soon arrives at the lady ensnarled in the wires. The wires look like thin cables that could have been from one of the Johnstown steel mills.

The lady screams out.

"Help Me! For God's sake, save me!"

Mary Mihelic stops short and looks down at the lady.

I must find James. If I leave her, she will die. God, she is so trapped.

Mary reaches in and starts to separate the wires. The sharp wires cut into her hands as she moves to free the woman. The woman is screaming now. The blaze was now in full force and moving towards the two women. The woman's eyes dart back and forth between the growing fire and her rescuer. Finally, she cries out, "Save yourself. I am going to die here. Go!"

Mary does not listen. Something inside of her keeps her at her task. Her hands now bloody pull on one wire. It gives way. Another and yet another loosens, as slowly the woman is able to move. The woman thrashes around now trying to aid the process. The heat is overwhelming. Mary keeps at her work, not looking up to see the approaching fire.

Mary stares at the still entangled lady. Even with her work, the wires are twisted in her clothing and offer little chance at escape. Mary Mihelic looks into the eyes of the lady and says firmly, "You have to get out of your clothes. It's our only chance."

The woman's panicked gaze stares back at Mary.

"I-I can't. I mean…it's not proper. I am a lady. Only women of ill-repute…"

She stops short as she sees Mary kneeling before her in torn undergarments and bloody hands. Mary sighs, exasperated at the lady's insistence on propriety. They both face certain death. The lady quickly recovers and says, "Oh, I don't mean you. It's just…"

Mary stops her with a wave of her hand and resumes pulling at the wires, tearing the clothing where necessary. The woman suddenly screams out as the flames catch the arm of her dress and quickly burns through to the flesh. Mary pats the arm and quiets the fire.

The two women share a look of understanding. Together, they start to remove the remainder of her bulky dress, ripping and tearing in a race against the fire. The last parcel free, the lady suddenly pushes Mary away from her and climbs out of the entrapment. She crawls to the shore, retrieving the blanket there and covering herself. She mumbles some thanks to Mary and in her confusion, and embarrassment continues to climb to safety up the hill.

Mary sits there reclining backwards, supported by her elbows on the rubble. She continues to watch the lady scramble to safety for a brief time, then just stares at the progressing fire.

I am done now. It is over. I am coming James. Wait for me.

Something inside of her refuses to let it be. She finds herself crawling to the shoreline, back over the devastation. Reaching solid ground once more, exhausted, she sits and brings her knees up to her chest.

She stares out over the debris and she watches. The blaze is now in full force. People are rushing everywhere and pushing past her on their quests either to help those still entrapped in the wreckage or to save themselves. She remains steadfast there gazing. Sometimes she turns one way or the other as if looking for someone. Mostly she just stares. The fire and the screams slowly die out to be replaced by the putrid smell of burnt flesh. The raging waters are now slowly calming and receding as they flow through the newly defined creek beds. Mary remains there until morning and then slowly makes her way back, back to the main part of what used to be the city of Johnstown.

CHAPTER I

▼

SPRING BLOSSOMS

Back in the spring of 1883, the events that will transpire on that horrible Friday in May 1889 are far in the future. Today the flowers blossom forth from the recent rains. The sun is shining.

A covered carriage rides up the street and turns left onto the wide tree-lined Main Street of Johnstown. Trees stretch forth over both sides of the road and for as far as the eye can see. Further on, mountains leap up from the earth and appear to reach the sky. In fact mountains rise up on all sides of the quiet town in the valley and offer a feeling of quiet protection. The carriage pulls to a stop next to the largest house on the street. Including the yard, the imposing white frame house takes up a full city block.

The driver, Ben Huffman, jumps down and opens the carriage door. He removes his top hat and assists a stunningly beautiful lady out first. She is wearing a floral silk bonnet, which matches her powder blue dress. She smiles at the driver and opens her parasol to protect her delicate face against the searing sun. Her broad dress swirls in the slight breeze. Next out is a large man, well over six feet tall. Scowling and obviously frustrated, he puts on his derby hat and looks about to get his bearings. Then he takes the lady's arm and looks back to the door of the carriage. The last person to descend from the carriage is a boy, about twelve years of age. He is wearing a straw hat, a white shirt with brown suspenders and dark blue knickers. His eyes narrow as he enters the sun's glare and looks out onto the field across the street.

"Hurry up James. We're late." James does not hear his father. His eyes remain focused on the field facing Main Street by the river. There, some kids are playing baseball. "James! Come now." The boy takes one last glance and then hurries to catch up to his parents who are now on the porch of the house.

The door opens and they are led into a foyer. The butler, stiff and formal, says, "Please wait here, Mr. Morrell has company at this time." He turns and moves off leaving the family waiting there in the foyer.

"I don't know why I had to come father. I could be fishing." James' father leans down towards his truculent child and in a quiet voice says, "Please son, we have discussed this already. I want you to start learning the steel business." His mother reaches over, brushes James brown hair and smiles. She whispers into his ear, "Don't frown James, there will still be time for fishing later." The butler returns to say that Mr. Morrell will see them shortly, and directs them into the living room just as a knock is heard at the door.

Through the door, they hear the booming voice of Andrew Carnegie. The butler and he are in an animated conversation when the parlor door opens and in steps Dan Morrell, leader of the Cambria Iron Works. Behind him is another man, larger than Dan Morrell, and beside him trails a small girl. The Peytons arise from the plush sofa and return to the entranceway just in time for the greetings.

"Ah, Andrew, how are you? And John Peyton, great to see you both!" Dan Morrell reaches out his hand to shake first Andrew Carnegie's then John Peyton's. He then turns to the lady and child standing next to John Peyton. John Peyton quickly steps in and says, "Dan, this is my wife, Fiona and my son James." Fiona curtsies to Dan Morrell's half-bow and James offers his hand, which is accepted with a hearty laugh.

The large man who had entered the room behind Dan Morrell now moves forward to speak. "Mr. Morrell, we'll be off now. Thank you for your time."

"Nonsense Charles, please stay. I could use your help here if these two gang up on me," Dan Morrell says and chuckles at the impression. "Of course, Andrew may try to steal you from me like he did Capt. Dave Jones. Charles here is the best coke man in the business, but you're too late anyway Andrew because he is going back to farming." Dan pats the large man on the back and smiles slyly. "Oh yes, and I believe he is to be a neighbor of yours. Charles is moving to South Fork, up near that lake you have." Andrew Carnegie stares intently at first Dan Morrell and then at Charles Mihelic but says nothing. After a lingering silence, John Peyton speaks up and says, "Let's meet. We have much to discuss."

Dan Morrell strokes his chin and then says, "I don't believe Mrs. Peyton or the children would find our talk exciting. Why don't you children go outside and play. Mrs. Peyton, Fiona, I am sure Martha can show you around our home." With that Dan turns towards the hallway and not waiting for the butler, calls out, "Martha! Please come here."

James Peyton looks panic stricken at his father pleading for relief. What once sounded horrible, sitting in a boring meeting has been supplanted by an even more dastardly possibility. John Peyton nervously speaks up. "Dan, I don't think…"

He is interrupted by the appearance of Martha Morrell from the back of the house.

Dan says, "Ah, there you are. Martha this is Fiona Peyton. Fiona, my wife Martha. Can you show Mrs. Peyton our fine home while we businessmen talk my dear?"

Martha Morrell nods her head and takes a reluctant Fiona Peyton by the arm. Fiona is about to speak when Dan Morrell reaches out and points to the little girl standing quietly by her father. "This is Mary Mihelic, Charles' daughter. You children go outside and play now."

John is about to rebut the request when Andrew quickly speaks up.

"Good. Excellent. Can we now get to our meeting?"

Fiona Peyton moves off with Martha holding her arm gently. She looks back first at her son James then to her husband, John. Neither one acknowledges her frantic look of concern as they are both dealing with the unexpected changes to their courses of action.

On the doorstep to the grand home the two children are quiet at first. The brisk spring air is invigorating but their hearts are already pumping wildly. James stares off into the distance at the baseball game being played across the street.

The girl, Mary, follows his stare and smiling says, "Do you like to play ball? I know those fellows over there. That tall lanky fellow is Victor Heiser. Those two boys standing over there are Harry and Will Hoffman. They are the sons of the hack that drove you and your parents over here. And…"

She would have continued but James stopped her.

"I don't want to play any ball." He emphasizes 'ball' to note his frustration. "Can't you see that I am not dressed for playing ball?" He shakes his head as if in wonder at why she would even ask such a question. Mary looks at him and has to agree with his logic. The straw hat cocked to one side is one thing but the starched shirt and wool pants would not last long in the dust and tumble of a pick up baseball game. She shrugs her shoulders and they resume their silence.

James walks down the steps to get a better view of the field. Mary follows not watching the field as much as the people walking up and down Main Street.

"Oh look. What have we here?"

James turns around at the sudden noise. He sees Mary hugging a little puppy close to her. The dog has flowers sticking out of his mouth and an inquisitive look of innocence. James laughs in spite of himself.

"Looks like we have a flower lover here," He says now patting the dog on the head.

Mary gently takes the flowers from the dog's mouth and says, "This is Mr. Morley's puppy."

She continues. "I don't know how he got way down here. Mr. Morley lives up there."

She says pointing up the street. Mary pauses for a brief second and then starts walking briskly up the street.

James yells out. "Where are you going? I think we are supposed to stay here."

Mary Mihelic looks over her shoulder and says, "I have to get this puppy home. Come if you wish, or stay if you wish."

She turns back and continues walking but intently listening she hears James running towards them. She smiles.

James catches up to her and inquires.

"How far is it we have to go?"

"Not far, up past the park and down an alley."

James Peyton rolls his eyes and looks back towards the Morrell house. *Should I go back? Nah.* Now he is committed to the adventure and leans down to pat the puppy's head once more. Mary looks more closely at her companion now noticing him in a different light.

A short walk later, they find themselves in a small alleyway. There is a fence there and a recently dug hole where the dog had made his escape. Mary grabs James' arm.

"Shish. We have got to be quiet. If Mr. Morley hears us he might get mad at the poor puppy." Mary brings her hand to her lips as she says this. James nods his head in agreement moving more quietly towards the gate. The gate creaks as it is opened. The children jump back in alarm. Peering in they notice no movement. Mary hands the dog to James and pulls up her dress so that she can move more freely. They enter the yard and look around spotting a broken rope tied to the porch.

Rushing up to the rope Mary fashions a quick knot and they tie up the dog. A door opens above them and a loud voice is heard.

"What's going on here?"

Mary finishes tying the dog hurriedly. They both pat him on the head and make a headlong rush for the gate.

"Hey, you kids get out of here! What are you doing to my dog? Ga-won, get out now." They run laughing down the street and into central park.

"That was scary Mary." James says, using her name for the first time.

Mary nods her head then bolts forward. James follows quickly.

Mary stops abruptly and turns to James.

"Don't you just find this park beautiful?"

Before he can answer, she says, "I do. I bet this is the most beautiful park in all the world."

James looks around at the small park. It is filled with trees and several small paths wind through it connecting to the streets on each side. But it is small, no more than a city block. Not at all like some of the Pittsburgh parks he is more familiar with. He decides not to answer her question.

Mary runs behind a tree and hides. James pretends that he can't find her at first then goes straight to the tree where she is. He peers around it but just as he does she moves to one side. "Hey!" he says and moves further around the large Elm tree. But she moves further and now has once more grabbed her dress and raised the hem from the ground. Soon they are laughing and chasing each other around the Elm tree. Mary stops finally as she is out of breath. James holds onto the tree and taking his straw hat off, wipes his brow from the sweat.

Mary sits on the ground and her smile fades as she looks out towards the Main Street. James notices her changed look and wonders what to do. Should he sit down beside her? Or should he remain standing? Why, he wonders, are simple decisions so difficult when in the company of girls? Mary finally relieves his quandary by gesturing for him to sit beside her.

There follows a long silence. James is quite content to let her alone with her feelings. He takes a new look at this girl named Mary. She is slightly taller than he is and slender of figure. Her hair is a dark brown, long and curly, hanging off her shoulders. Her skin is soft; creamy with a glow from the air that brightens her cheeks. Her eyes are green or are they more hazel? Regardless of color, they sparkle with an intensity that James finds different from other girls he has known.

Mary Mihelic leans down and picks at the grass beside her. Finally she speaks. "I don't want to leave here. I love this town. It's so pretty and the folks are so nice." James replies, "Then don't. I am sure your father would listen to you." Mary frowns. "You don't understand. Papa is so good. He has worked in the mill for so long and now it is making him weak. That is why we were at Dan Morrell's house today. Papa was asking him for a loan so he could buy farmland. Mr. Morrell is so kind to everyone. Papa just can't work any longer in the mill. We have to move."

James places a hand on her shoulder. She looks at him and he shyly withdraws it to his side. She starts to cry, not a wail, but tears just seem to form in her eyes and travel down her cheeks. James nervously seeks to comfort her.

"It's not like your moving far away. Heck, South Fork is just up the mountain apiece. And as Mr. Morrell said, we'll practically be neighbors. I get up to Lake Conemaugh often during the summer." He brushed off his pants and rose as he finished that statement.

He reached out his hand to Mary to assist her in rising. She brushed away the tears and accepted his hand. They walked in silence back to the Morrell's place.

John and Fiona Peyton come out of the Morrell residence looking tired and worn. Andrew Carnegie, a short fellow with a white beard and determined eyes follows them. His face is broad and he is smiling. His countenance changes to an intense stare as soon as they reach the street. He looks at John Peyton and inquires, "What about the dam John? Dan Morrell seemed more interested in that then in our proposal for linking Johnstown steel more closely to our Pittsburgh operations."

"Andrew, I flat out don't understand these Johnstowners. I really don't. Sometimes they are so damned inventive it makes you blink. Other times, they can't seem to keep their minds on business. I tell you this Andrew. As long as I am treasurer of our club, that dam will stand."

Andrew patted John Peyton on the back and his smile returned.

"Good show Peyton! I will see you back at the clubhouse. We have more work to do now. Good day Fiona. I am so glad you came with John. You brighten any conversation."

Fiona smiled and curtsied, "Thank you Andrew." She wondered at his comments as he moved away realizing that she had been whisked away by Martha Morrell before the business was discussed. Just as well, she reflected, I enjoyed Martha's tour of the house.

Andrew turned up Main Street, off to a meeting with the local papers. He had expected to announce the deal, but now would need to think of something else to tell them.

John shook his head and turned to Fiona.

"I can't believe that Morrell took up most of the time discussing our club and lake. I came here expecting to sign that partnership. He just rambled on and on. What a colossal waste of time! And what was that Mihelic fellow doing there anyway? He contributed nothing to the talk. I always say, don't mix the help in with business."

Fiona looked at her husband and smiled. He was always strictly business at which he was very good.

The door opened behind them and Charles Mihelic comes through. He nods to the Peytons and looks around.

"Where is Mary? Have you seen her?"

Fiona's smile drops to a frown. She raises her hand to her lips as her brow furrows.

"Where is James?"

John Peyton throws up his arms in the air in obvious frustration.

Just as they are about to run off in search of the missing children, Charles Mihelic spots Mary and James walking towards them on the other side of the street.

"Mary, where have you been? You had us scared to death here."

Fiona eyed the large man beside her and found his concern so opposite to his physical presence that she almost commented on it. John Peyton spoke up and any chance to talk became mute.

"There's the hack. Let's go now. Young man we will deal with you later. Mr. Mihelic, good day."

Without further comment the Peytons enter the carriage. Charles and Mary Mihelic stand by the side until they depart. Then, they turn and walk up Main Street to their home.

James can feel the tension thick in the air. He says, "I'm sorry father, mother. I guess I lost track of time." His father fixes James with an intent stare, pausing only for a second, he replies.

"You bet you're sorry. What in God's name were you thinking going off like that?"

His father wanted to say more but Fiona placed a gentle hand on his arm. John Peyton still couldn't resist one last comment.

"Well let's get on home. I swear that the sooner I leave this town the better."

The rest of the ride to the train station was quiet. James fell asleep on the train ride up to the lake. Fiona looked at him and stroked his hair.

My precious one, I think you are growing up faster than we expect.

CHAPTER 2

▼

THE BAIT IS CAST

James didn't see Mary Mihelic again for almost a year. His father no longer stopped in Johnstown when the train passed through on its way to South Fork. His last experience there had soured his taste for the town. Furthermore, John Peyton was busy working on stocking the lake with fish and increasing the membership in the Pittsburgh exclusive club. The South Fork Fishing and Hunting Club had been formed and organized five years earlier in 1879. Its purpose was to provide a place of respite and relaxation for its limited and select membership. In that it had been singularly successful.

Walking along the breast of the dam, two young boys laugh with the joyful exuberance of youth.

"James, my man, we are going to have some fun today. Yes, I am always so excited when we get to come to the Lake, aren't you?"

"Yes, Robert," answered James smiling back at his friend.

"Just look at that water, I'll bet that is the best fishing lake in the whole country."

James reached up and placed his arm around his friend's shoulder. Soon they were pushing and shoving, seeing who was going into the water at the lake's edge. James was the shorter of the two with sandy blonde hair. Robert had rich black curly hair. Laughing, they moved forward pitching rocks into the lake watching them glide across the surface and break up the sun's reflection. Shortly Robert nudged his friend.

"See there, over there?"

"What?" asked James, turning to look in the direction to where Robert was pointing? He shaded his eyes with his hand, but still failed to see what Robert was pointing at.

"There, there is one of them local people stealing our fish again. Over there!"

Before James could say anything Robert was off, yelling to the person ahead to stop fishing. James looked to where his friend was heading and shook his head.

What in the heck has gotten into Robert now?

He shrugged his shoulders and ran after his erstwhile friend.

Robert was pointing to someone ahead of them by the lake and yelling, "You! Who are you and what are you doing here? Can't you read the signs? 'For members only?' Violators will be prosecuted. That is meant for you."

By the time he had finished yelling, he had reached the interloper. He reached down and yanked the young would be fisherman to his feet.

"Ouch! You're hurting me!" Yelled the fisherman whose cap fell off revealing that the fisherman was a fisher girl.

"My, My, My, and what have we here, a naughty girl stealing our fish. Well little one I am sorry but you shall have to face the punishment for your ways. Come with me!"

"Please! You are hurting me, please. I didn't mean to steal and there are so many fish. What can it mean to you? Ow."

"Ha! That is what you say now, but if one is allowed many will follow. You must pay the price for your thievery and I for one can't wait. Come on now. Off we go!"

James had caught up to his friend and looked first at him and then at the young girl that Robert had by the arm. She was about his age. Her hair was long and curly, brunette in color hanging gently off her shoulders. She was dressed as a boy, in wool knickers with a shirt half tucked in and half hanging out. Her cap, which was lying at her side, was that worn by the local baseball players.

James' face paled. On the other hand, Robert could hardly contain himself. He stuck out his chest and held onto the fisher-girl by the arm.

"Look James, a poacher! Won't our fathers be happy? Low-class locals, thinking to steal our fish! Now we shall see an example set, isn't that right my little poacher?"

"Robert, let her go."

James gaze was fixed on his friend, Robert. He could feel himself getting beet red and silently wished his emotions did not show so easily. Still he stood there burning with anger at his friend. His hands clenched and then unclenched. Robert turned from the 'poacher' and scrunching up his face cried out to his friend, "What? Let her go. Are you crazy? She was poaching James, pure and simple. Oh, I am loving this; father will be so happy. He was just saying the other day how the locals are getting too curious about our private matters. This little one will serve notice that we mean to protect our land!"

"Leave her be, Robert. I-I know her. Let her go."

He and Robert locked eyes. Robert sneered at James.

"You know her?" He asked, wondering why James had gotten involved with the locals. However, Robert didn't wait for an answer. He persisted, "No. I'm taking her to father."

He had barely finished the sentence when he found himself sprawled on the ground. James had pushed him and was surprised when Robert fell. He had just meant to get him to let go of the girl. Robert got up off the ground and brushed off the dirt from his pants.

"What the heck was that for? Shoot James, that hurt! Ow! I am going to tell your father! You're a fool!"

With that said Robert ran off back in the direction from where they had come.

"I'm sorry for my friend. He means well. I hope he didn't hurt you."

The girl wiped tears from her cheeks and rubbed her arm where Robert had gripped it so tight. "Nah, he didn't scare me. Thanks for your help."

Still wincing from the pain in her arm, she manages to twist her head inquisitively and smiling she says, "Nice to meet you again Mr. Peyton."

She laughs, and then just as quickly stops as a stab of pain shoots up from her arm. He blushes at her remembering his name. For the life of him, he cannot remember hers. She continues not waiting for his response.

"I was only fishing for some food. Fishing is so much fun, and this lake, well it has got the best fish in all the waters around."

She continued talking about how the fish in this lake were so much bigger, and better than the scrawny fish that you found downstream.

As she described the sport of fishing, he looked at this would be sports person. She was not like the girls that he saw, always giggling and playing with dolls. No, she was not in a frilly dress with those big bustles so in style now. From a distance, he reckoned, she would have appeared to be a boy. Still up close, there was no mistaking that she was a girl. Yes, she was a girl and very pretty. Pretty, thought James who here to fore had found girls somewhat bearable but never in any sense 'pretty'. A piece of wild grass was caught in her hair and James reached up to retrieve it, which broke into her speech on the fine art of fishing.

"Oh, thanks. Once more, that is. Well, I guess I had better be going. Your friend was none too happy and I don't want you to get into trouble."

James heart was pumping wildly. He held up his arm to stop her.

"Wait!"

"What?" She said.

"You surely haven't finished fishing yet, have you?"

Laughter escaped from her lips once more, this time full and hearty.

James found she looked even prettier when laughing.

I must see her laugh more.

"I thought that I was the evil poacher. Grrrr. Taking all of the poor fish away from you."

"Ah, come on, that was my friend talking. Even so, now you are with me, and I can let anyone I want fish here."

He stuck out his chest as if to emphasize his authority. The girl looked at James intently. She was about to say one thing but then changed her mind.

"Alright, let's fish. Name is Mary in case ya forgot."

Again the smile.

"Nah, I didn't forget. James Peyton here, at your service."

He bowed and waved his arm in a flourish. Then he suddenly realized his earlier blunder in offering to fish. He shrugged his shoulders.

"I forgot my reel so I guess I won't be able to fish after all."

He laughed but he felt his cheeks redden at the obvious stupidity of his earlier invitation.

She laughed again and her smile was dazzling. She shook her head and touched his arm. James felt the gentle touch and the shock went zipping up to his head. *This is truly crazy.*

"You're such a silly goose. Look at my pole. It is a twig from a tree. Here I'll get you a pole and then we can get to some serious fishing."

Mary reached up to a suitable sapling and cut off a nice long branch.

"There. This one is good, not too loose and not too stiff. You have to give them fish some room to move."

James took his new 'pole' in hand thinking it quite different from the new reel his father had bought him just for this trip. Still he liked it and watched as Mary took some string to tie onto the end of the pole.

"Now we are ready for some fishing!"

Laughing the two went over to the edge of the lake and sat down. They talked and laughed the whole afternoon away and James could not remember a better time.

The afternoon wore on. Reluctantly, Mary indicated that she really had to leave now. Her mother would be worrying about her and besides these fish needed cleaning before dinner. James let out a sigh and agreed. He did not want the afternoon to ever end. He got up from their perch at the shoreline and then helped Mary to her feet.

"Well, thank you again, James. It appears that I'm always thanking you. Are you a knight in shining armor?"

She laughed again and ruffled his sandy blonde hair. Without waiting an answer from the blushing youth she turned and went skipping off down the hill to the town of South Fork.

"Nice fishin' with ya," He called after her.

She looked over her shoulder and called back to him, "You too."

He watched until she turned the corner and disappeared from his sight. Then he turned and started the trek back to the clubhouse. If anyone had seen him at that point in time, they would have wondered at the large smile on his face and the lilt in his step.

He was lost in the memories of the day until he approached the breast of the dam that held in Lake Conemaugh. There standing at the breast overlooking the dam was his father, John Peyton and a couple of folks he did not recognize. Then he saw Robert. Had he really waited there all this time? Had he told his father about the fishing girl? What would his father say? He slowed his pace as he got nearer. Even so, it seemed the distance between him and the group was closing all too fast. Now his heart was pumping wildly once more, but this time he knew the feeling, it was one of fear.

His father was intent on the conversation going on and did not notice him until he was almost up to the group. Then he turned to James, and fixed him in his tracks with a stern angry gaze.

"I'm busy now James, but we will talk. Go to the clubhouse and await my return."

He pointed off to the distant side of the lake. James was about to protest but his father had already turned back to the conversation.

Dejected, he moved past the group to an awaiting Robert.

"I told your father! He is mad. You're really going to get it too. You shouldn't have knocked me down James." Robert smiled as he pictured the awaiting punishment.

"Sorry I knocked you down Robert. I didn't mean to. But you were wrong, wrong, wrong. That girl was just doing some fishing. She wasn't hurting anybody."

"Well, now we shall see won't we? Let's see what you father says about it."

However, Robert did not wait for a response. Instead, he ran on ahead, skipping and laughing, singing a song derogatory to the local residents. James just hung his head and started to go to the clubhouse to await the return of his father.

James turned back to his father and the men. He wondered what they were discussing. He strained to hear what they were saying.

"Dammit, Fulton don't be so cantankerous! This dam is safe and you know it! We used only the best engineering talent on it and it is built to last."

"Mr. Peyton, I am withholding judgment until my report to Mr. Morrell but I can tell you this dam is unsafe!"

John Fulton, the man speaking, was much shorter than John Peyton was. However, Fulton looked him in the eye and stuck his chin out in defiance. This gesture only served to irritate John Peyton more. He turned beet red. Wiping his head with a handkerchief, he looked directly at John Fulton and said, "You have spent all day up here looking around, investigating. You took me from my family and our brief time of relaxation together. You had me walk all over this bloody dam. After that, all you can say is your report will say the dam is unsafe? Then so be it! My time with you is done Fulton. Please find your way out. And since we are finished please leave soon."

John Peyton looked about and saw his son out of the corner of his eye.

"You still here? Get up to the clubhouse. I will deal with you later. Dammit! What in hell is going on around here?"

He didn't turn back towards Fulton but continued watching as James made his way across the breast of the dam. John Fulton took that as an indication that further discussion was fruitless.

"Good day, Mr. Peyton. I thank you for your time."

James watched from the clubhouse as his father walked back, trying to judge his mood once more. Looking out he saw Mr. Frick walk up to his father from the clubhouse he looked serious.

"Peyton, how did it go with those locals?"

"Not good I am afraid. They sent me all day around that dam looking for anything to note as a concern. I fear they won't be satisfied until we fix it to their liking."

"Well I don't want them snooping around here time and again. Solve it Peyton. Get them out of here."

"I know Henry, it's just we have so many items needing work, the boathouse, the clubhouse annex, the…"

He would have continued but Henry Frick waved him off with a wave of his hand.

"You are the treasurer of this club. It is your job to balance our needs. All I know is I don't want the local people meddling in our club business. Get it done."

"Yes, Henry, don't worry about that."

James saw Mr. Frick walk away and his father step up the porch of the clubhouse. He decided it would be best to put off their discussion and ran up to his room hoping that his father had forgotten their earlier encounter. He had not. As he entered the clubhouse, he called out, "James, son, come here."

"Yes, father," answered James. He hurried back down the stairs to find his father standing in front of the large window looking out on the lake.

John Peyton paused for a minute. He gazed out onto the tranquil lake. Turning quickly, he held one hand on the curtain and spoke to James.

"Robert told me a story today that frankly I find hard to believe. You know how hard we have worked on this place, to make it beautiful and a place so serene that all the members can enjoy. Look outside here."

John Peyton pointed to the outside and the sun now setting over the lake. James came up closer and peered out. "It's nice father, I know that."

"Well son, to enjoy it the place must be preserved. We can't let the local folks in to mess it up, trampling it up and taking out the few fish that we have imported for our enjoyment."

John Peyton walked away from the window. He threw his hands up in the air in frustration, and then continued.

"I just spent most of my day here trudging all over the dam and for what, I ask you? To prove to some local yokels that the dam is safe? Safe, by God! I'll give you safe. We have paid for this land, developed it, and the dam. If I had my way, they wouldn't even be let in here!"

James didn't comment. He wished the discussion would end soon. He continued to stare out the front window. Then he turned, hoping to see that his father had left. He hadn't. James looked at his father, John Peyton. His white shirt was dripping with sweat. His thinning blonde hair was matted down, both from the derby but more from walking around the dam on a hot summer day. His wool pants, usually so neat and clean had a tear in them. *Once he notices that, he's going to get really angry.* His father continued, "James, we are fortunate to be in this club. We are now a part of an elite group. We must act and work as a team to keep what is ours safe and around for the next generations. I don't mean to speak less of these people. Many of them are fine people, and a lot of them work here and help to keep this place clean. Nevertheless, we mustn't let our vision be clouded by that. You must surround yourself with friends like the members of this club. They will be able to help you in your future. These commoners will not. I have a dream for you son and I intend to see it come true."

James shuffled his feet. He knew it would be better just to agree and let it be done with. Something within him said no. He kept his face down, knowing if he looked at his father, he could not say what he needed to say. He took a deep breath and then quickly spilled out the words he couldn't keep in.

"Father, I understand what you are saying but I find it hard to accept. You remember the girl we met last year? At the Morrell's? She's nice and her name is Mary, Mary Mihelic. Mary isn't going to harm us or this club. No way. She just wanted to catch a little fish for her family and well I think we should let the local people fish."

James breathed in again. He wanted to say more, to talk of Robert's bad behavior but he didn't get the chance. John Peyton had turned livid. The events of the day had proven too much.

"Listen to me, James, and listen well. If I ever catch you with that girl again, you will be whipped until you can't sit down. Do you hear me? Do you understand?"

James started to protest but then thought the best of it. His father was not in the mood for further discussion. "Yes, father, may I be excused now?"

"Yes. Go now. Remember my words; make friends with those that are like you. We need to keep to our own kind."

"I will remember father. Goodnight."

James bent down and kissed his father's cheek. He wondered at his father's strange lecture. In the past, he had always viewed his father as right and all. He reflected on that as he walked up the back stairs to his room. *I am sure he is right here too. She just seemed so...nice.*

Shrugging his shoulders, he rushed up the stairs. Remembering his father's admonition against seeing the girl again, he thought wistfully. *I do wish I could see her again.* Then he shook his head and laughed.

What are the chances of seeing her again anyway?

As father says, 'We are from different worlds'.

Still, the little fisher girl stayed on his mind the rest of the time there at the lake.

CHAPTER 3

▼

THE FUNERAL

James had been right, at least as another year flew past. Mary Mihelic and fishing were far from James' mind. He had just finished the annual Regatta Races and he and Robert had won in the schooner race. The locals who had viewed these races often commented on "the sailboats on the mountain".

"Wasn't that something Mother? Robert and I were really moving there. I don't know where that last burst came from. I was sure that those new boys had us beat."

Fiona Peyton smiled at her son but seemed preoccupied. She said, "Yes dear that was really something." James was a good son who looked like his father but was more like his mother in personality.

"James, please come here," Fiona said as she turned in the chair to face him.

"What do you want mother? Robert is waiting for me outside?"

Fiona smiled once more, and then said, "You can go play for now. Your father and I have to attend the viewing for Mr. Morrell. He died this past Tuesday. You remember meeting him two years ago, at his house in Johnstown?"

"Vaguely, a big white house and he was big if I remember, although not as big as father."

Fiona nodded her head. "That's him, well he passed away and we need to pay our respects".

"Don't worry about me. I'll be all right."

James didn't wait to hear more and was soon rushing down the broad steps out onto the porch to meet a waiting Robert. Fiona closed the fan she had used to cool her face, set it on the small table beside her and rose from the lounge chair. *There is time enough for her son to learn of these duties. Let him stay a child for now.*

The viewing had been tiring. The lines were long and it seemed as if everyone knew the Morrells and stopped to chat with Mrs. Morrell. Dan Morrell had been sick for a long while. Still, his death struck the town of Johnstown hard. The Peytons paid their respects and made the long carriage ride back to the Club arriving tired and ready for bed.

Janie burst into their room crying. Janie, James' sister, had lost her race earlier that day when her boat capsized. She was at that awkward age for girls, taller than boys her age were and skinny as a rail. Her blonde hair was pulled back into a tight bun. Her green eyes were large and almost circular in shape. Right now, they were filled with tears.

Her lower lip quivered as she spoke. She could not be consoled.

"I failed mother. I was in the lead but I just got excited. Now I will never win. I don't even know if I will race again. I was so mortified."

"Now Janie dear, it is all right. You did well and you will get better. It takes time."

Just then James bound into the room. Hearing Janie's lament he was about to tease her with some disparaging statement about her lack of sailing expertise. Fiona's stern gaze stopped the words in his mouth as he heard her say.

"James didn't always win either, did you James?"

Janie continued to cry loudly but now looked at her older brother for reassurance.

James inhaled slowly and said, "Mother's right Janie. I had some tough times too. Keep working and you will win."

"I'll never win! I could just die. I quit," and with that, Janie stomped off to bed.

"James you had best be getting off to bed too. We need to get up early for the funeral service."

"Funeral Service? I thought that was today! I can't stand it. Well I'm not going, that's that!"

John Peyton, who had been reading up until this point, slammed down the book and looked sternly at his son.

"Son, you are going to the funeral and now you're going to bed."

"But father, I didn't have any free time today and now another day will be wasted. We hardly knew this Morrell person. Can't I stay home with Robert and his family? Please?"

"No son. It's important that the whole family is there. Remember we're also representing the club."

"Mother, please tell him. I don't want to go. Take Janie. They'll never know."

John Peyton turned a bright shade of red. He was tired and had a long and trying day.

"James! Go to bed now!"

James looked at his mother for support but finding none left and went to his room upstairs.

Fiona watched her son climb the stairs and waited until she heard his room shut. She turned to her husband and said, "John, you shouldn't have been so rough. They are just children and don't know about these duties that we have."

"Don't you start in on me. It's about time they learned Fiona. It's about damn time they learned."

At the Mihelic farm a somewhat different scene was being played out.

"Good night kochanka" said Charles Mihelic to his daughter Mary. "Kochanka" was Charles Mihelic's affectionate nickname for Mary.

Loosely translated it meant "favorite pet". His use of it never failed to bring a smile to her face and a gleam to his own eye.

"Papa, why did Mr. Morrell have to die? He was such a good man."

"That he was, kochanka, that he was."

"He helped found the Cambria Iron works and it is because of him that Johnstown is growing into a great city. He helped me to get this farm too. It seemed that at one time or another he just about helped everyone."

"I guess that is the reason for all of those crowds today. I'll pray for him tonight. Good night papa"

Mary kissed her father and turned to sleep.

"That is good," Charles Mihelic said as he slipped from his daughter's room.

The morning of August 24, 1885 was bright and clear. The sun was shining through the white clouds and the birds were chirping their sweet songs. Some would later say it was just like Dan to order up a great day for his funeral. Everyone in town showed up. Those not in the funeral procession to the Sandyvale cemetery were lined up in the streets. If you didn't know it was a funeral, you would have sworn it was a parade, a grand one at that. All would miss Dan Morrell.

"There he is!"

John Fulton yelled to his rotund companion, Cyrus Elder. Before Cyrus could reply, John Fulton ran up to John Peyton, grabbed him by the arm and said, "I can't believe you folks showed up here. You helped put him in that grave."

"Fulton, you're crazy. Let go of my arm."

Fulton was not about to be deterred. He let go of John Peyton's arm but continued to block his way. "You, and all those high and mighty Pittsburghers, plotting up there on the hill. Building a dam that has no business being built, threatening our very lives!"

John Peyton looked at the shorter lean man in front of him, his own anger growing.

"I am here to pay my respects. Please let me and my family by."

By this time, Cyrus Elder had arrived and tried to restrain John Fulton. It was to no avail. John Fulton pushed the pudgy Cyrus back, and continued to block the Peyton's way.

"You think it's over now, don't you? With Dan Morrell dead, you think no one will care what you do. Well, I care and I will stop you."

John Peyton moved to face the shorter Fulton directly in front of him. Staring intently at the smaller fellow, he said, "Look Fulton, Dan Morrell was a member of "that club" as you call us. We have nothing to hide."

Then he pointed his finger right into John Fulton's face to make his next point even clearer.

"I vow to you today, Fulton, that dam will last. Now get out of my way."

John Peyton pushed past Fulton and moved his family on. Cyrus Elder held onto John Fulton who was clearly ready to give chase. James Peyton looked back to see the chubbier fellow holding onto the 'mean' man that had spoke so disparagingly to his father. Fiona Peyton grabbed her husband's hand more tightly and with concern, said.

"John, please, let him go. There will be time enough for those battles. Let's pay our respects to Dan."

"All right Fiona. I just plain don't understand these folks. I just don't."

James Peyton wondered at this strange event.

Why would anyone doubt my father's word? I too, will watch over the lake. Johnstowners, you will be safe, us Peytons never go back on our word.

Looking up at his dad and feeling proud, James gripped his father's large hand and walked to the gravesite.

At the graveyard, the Rev. Chapman spoke words of sympathy and compassion. James Peyton was bored. *I can't believe that I am here watching this dumb funeral. These people don't even like us if that fellow back there is to be believed.* Then, James caught sight of a dog bounding towards the resting-place. The dog was running straight towards them as if on a mission. James' eyes widened as he saw the gap shorten between the dog and the funeral.

Just when it seemed the dog would crash into everyone he slowed to a walk. He moved up through the crowd slowly and stopped in front of the burial area. He sat down there and looked at the funeral bier as if it was a fallen master. Not many in the crowd even noticed him there. James did and so did one other person standing almost opposite James. She smiled.

James Peyton started to squirm until his father put a hand on his shoulder and squeezed. *Well, at least that dog brought some excitement.* He was anxious to get back to the lake and do some fishing. Heck, do anything. Still lost in his thoughts he looked around at the gathered crowd. So many people just standing here watching a burial. As he scanned the gathering, his eyes caught sight of someone in particular. She was smiling, smiling at him no less.

The girl was in a dark black dress, with a bustle befitting the somber occasion. She had a parasol over her shoulder, which she twirled slowly. It too was black with a frilly edge. Her dark brown hair fell from her shoulders in long flowing curls. A small lace covered her head in delicate brocade. Even with the plain dress and the large crowd, Mary Mihelic stood out as a rare gem among common stones.

James decided then and there to go over and talk to her. *I have to find out if it's her.* Just then, he was jostled. He turned to see that the service was over and the people were leaving. His mother took his hand and the Peytons began the walk back to their carriage. He glanced over his shoulder hoping to catch sight of Mary once more. She was gone.

Dang it, not now! Why does she have this stupid effect on me? I must see her again, but how? Where did she go?

John Peyton was pleased that James had finally gotten quiet and quit complaining. Still, he wondered at the smile that appeared on his son's face. Strange to be smiling, coming from a funeral, he thought.

CHAPTER 4

▼

REACQUAINTED

James did not see Mary after the funeral. In fact another year and one half would pass before their paths crossed again. Mary had spotted James several times coming in on the train from Pittsburgh. She had wanted to go up and talk to him, but James' father was always present. Mr. Peyton doesn't seem to like me, she thought and then she remembered the incident at the Regatta last year. John Peyton had come upon Mary and her family watching the Lantern Procession held after the sailing Regatta. He had chased them away.

Why did he have to do that? Does he really think we are that much different? Maybe we are. Oh well, it was only a foolish dream to begin with.

The winter of 1886 and early 1887 was cruel and cold; bitter cold. Nevertheless, the snow brought its own sense of beauty on the land and Lake Conemaugh. The lake was frozen as it often was during the winter. The trees were sparkling with ice hanging from the branches. The weather lately had warmed and the icicles dropped little beads of water to the ground.

A lone figure provides a silhouette against the white background of the lake and the trees. He skates with a vigor and speed as if the devil were in pursuit. Across the frozen lake he moves, both graceful and fluid, challenging the skates to carry him ever faster.

On the other side of the lake and down from the breast of the dam, a girl was walking towards the lake and enjoying the radiant winter weather. The girl was pulling a toboggan. Inside was a smaller girl sliding her hands along the snow. Both were bundled against the cold air wearing overcoats over their full dresses.

"Mary, why do we always head this way? I do think that the sledding is much better on the other side of town and much closer too!"

"Hush Grace, I know what I am doing! Momma told me I had to take you with me, but she didn't say that I had to take you where YOU wanted to go. Anyways, the sledding is always better here, and less hazardous. Besides there are less people too."

"Yea, that's because it's not good to sled here!" Grace smiled knowing she had topped her sister once more.

"Grrr, can't you just keep quiet?"

"Nope" said Grace, "and besides I know why you want to come up here."

"Oh, you do, do you, miss smarty. Well why don't you enlighten me hmm?"

"You want to see if you can catch sight of that rich boy from the lake. That's it, isn't it?"

"No, you little devil you. I don't like boys, and especially the high and mighty boys from Lake Conemaugh. Ugh!"

"Yes you do" and she let the "do" drag out in a slight whistling voice.

Mary looked at her sister sternly, and said firmly, "I do not"

"Do too."

"Not"

Sticking her chin out, the young Grace was determined to have the last word.

"Oh, my, yes you do dear Mary. I can see why though. He is handsome, and if you don't take him than I shall."

"Grace! If you don't stop this nonsense you WON'T live to see tomorrow!"

Mary turned and pulled hard on the toboggan, which knocked her sister Grace back. That should keep her quiet at least for a while. *Was it that obvious?* A smile came on her face. Mary tugged on the toboggan once more and knocked Grace backwards again. Grace adjusted her hat pulling it tighter around her face to protect against the cold. She rubbed her back where it had hit the toboggan.

"Hey, Mary, come on! That hurts!"

"Sorry Grace I'll be more careful."

They continued up the hill near Colonel Unger's home. The hill there made for nice sledding regardless of what her sister Grace had said. Colonel Unger was a member of the club and watched over the lake. Being local to the area, he was not as reserved towards the local people.

Once up at the top of the hill, Mary looked back over the lake. It was so resplendent with the mist just rising and the frozen trees providing just the right addition to complete the scene. She was about to slide down the gentle sloping hill when she caught sight of someone skating through the mists. Her heart skipped a beat.

Could it be him?

She told herself to calm down.

You're being silly Mary.

Still her eyes strained to make out the figure moving very quickly towards the dam. She figured she could get a closer look at the mysterious skater if she slides down the slope and then took the long way back. Just then, her sister said.

"Let's go Mary. I am ready to zoom down the hill. Yippee!"

"Ready?" Mary said, "Hang on tight now."

They practically flew down the hill, as the now slick snow was patted down and smooth.

When they got to the bottom, Grace threw her arms up and yelled, "You were right Mary! That was great! Let's go again. Hey, where are you going?"

Mary had grabbed the sled and headed off to the dam.

"I, oh, I want to see how the lake is doing. You know, is it frozen and all?"

"Sure, but wait up. I am coming too."

Mary was about to complain but thought better of it since Grace had not questioned her desire to see the lake.

"Gee, every year it seems that the lake is getting bigger. It scares me sometimes. Does it scare you Mary?"

Mary was focused on the lake. It was harder to see out over the lake now that they were almost at the level of the breast of the dam. She could not see the skater as of yet. The morning fog had yet to lift off the lake.

"What Grace? The lake is beautiful, isn't it?"

Then, all at once she spotted him, skating fast. It was James Peyton. She had known it even from afar.

Look at him go.

Grace had spotted him also and was transfixed by the speeding figure skating across the lake.

A loud crack was heard and the skater disappeared beneath the ice.

"Oh my gosh Mary, he went into the lake."

Mary didn't hear the last comment as she had already taken off running. She held high her skirt and rushed towards the lake. *Oh please don't let him drown. Why was he going so fast? Oh God please let him live.*

When she neared the shore, she could see where he had fallen in and she could see that the ice was thin all through this area. *If I go out on that ice, we will both go under.* Dressed as she was, she might fall in and never come back up. She made a quick decision. Quickly she slipped out of her heavy overcoat. Still, she felt encumbered.

Why must women dress like this?

She slipped out of her dress and the bustle attached around her waist. It was so cold that she shivered involuntarily. *Slowly now.* She inched her way out close to where the break was in the ice. Each step was followed by a pause, listening for sounds of breaking ice. *It's cracking. Oh, I'm going to go in.* Then, she slipped down onto her knees. She laid out flat on the ice to more equalize her weight. She listened for signs of further cracking.

"God it's cold."

Her heart was pumping and the cold ice cut through her body. *How am I to get him out of here? I've got to. I've just got to.* She found him there in the water, floating head down. *He must have hit his head falling in.* She reached into the frigid water and caught him under the arms. The pull of his weight was awful. The pain racked through her body but on she pulled. *If I can just get him up onto the ice, I can make it.* With one mighty heave, she pulled. He lay half on the ice and half in the water but still unconscious. She had to rest a while before trying to get him further out. The chill of the air brought a chattering to her teeth. The whole length of her body was now wet with the ice and the water. James and her would need help soon, if they both were to survive.

Grace had at last arrived at the edge of the shore.

"Wow, Mary, how did you do that? And what're you doing with no dress on? I'm telling momma!"

"Grace, there isn't time for that now. Listen. I need you to go up to Colonel Unger's house and see if we can get some help here. Please, I don't know if I can get him out. He is hurt and freezing. Please go get help!"

"All right Mary, I will go, but be careful yourself!"

"I will Grace, now go! Hurry."

Mary found herself smiling at her sweet sister. Sometimes Grace could drive her mad, but yes she did care about her older sister.

I can't last much longer. I'll freeze to death.

Grace took off for the hills and for a brief time, Mary watched her go. Then she turned to the boy in the lake. As cold as she was she knew that he must be even colder. He would not last long in the frozen water. She had to get him out now. She tried to get hold of his belt and tug him up but that did not work. She was too exhausted from her earlier efforts. She sagged back and her concern grew. She looked at the young man in front of her. The eyes were closed but she could see long eyelashes now crusted with ice. His face was pale but even so, she could see his rugged good looks. She bent over and kissed his cheek softly. He stirred.

"What? Where am I?"

Her heart beat wildly. He was awake.

"You fell in the lake, please help me get you out of there! Hurry!"

Between her pulling and his lifting, they managed to free him from the lake. The strain had taken its toll on James, however. He again passed out.

Great, now what am I to do? She couldn't lift him since he was much larger than she was. She found that by sliding him along the slippery ice she was able to get him to the lake's edge. Her back ached from the effort and she found herself chilled by the icy lake surface. Her focus however, remained on James. She took her dress which had remained dry and wiped off his face and warmed his hands. She wrapped her overcoat around his shoulders. Then, she pulled on her dress to cover herself. Little warmth was provided. She continued to shake uncontrollably.

Colonel Unger came upon the two by the lakeshore, running down from his house.

"My God, are you alright girl?"

Mary stood there shivering but answered Elias Unger in a firm voice.

"Yes Colonel Unger, I'm fine, but I'm not sure about him. He must have hit his head when he fell in. He was skating awfully fast out there."

"Well let's get you both up to the house and into some warm clothes."

Elias Unger took off his coat and replaced Mary's overcoat with his own. He handed her well-worn coat back to her. She promptly put it on but it seemed nothing could stop the awful cold feeling in her bones.

"If it's all right Colonel Unger my sister and I can make it home. I just live down the hill there in South Fork."

"Let's get up to the house first. I can get one of my hands to take you home. You can't make it as cold as you are."

James was loaded onto the toboggan and the trio headed up the hill to the Unger's home. Mary thought they would never make it there. Her teeth continued chattering as the cold air bit into her body. Grace kept saying, "Mary, are you all right?"

Mary would just nod her head and continue walking unsteadily up the hill to the Unger home. Elias called out to John Clark, the young Engineer who worked at the lake. "John, please get the carriage for these young ladies and take them down to South Fork. Hurry! I have to get James Peyton inside and notify his parents."

John Clark nodded his head and went to fetch the carriage.

Colonel Unger turned to Mary and once more observed her fragile condition.

"Come inside and get warm. You can't wait out here."

Mary wanted to protest but instead just nodded her head and followed Colonel Unger inside.

Mrs. Unger rushed up as soon as they entered the house. Her hand went to her face.

"Oh my, dear me, Elias, place James in our bedroom. And you, young lady, follow me. What is your name?"

"Mary." Grace answered for her sister, nervously looking up to her as she stood there shaking. Then she added, keeping her eyes on her sister, "I am Grace Mihelic, we live down in South Fork."

Colonel Unger stopped in his rushing about and looked at the two young girls.

"Why yes, I know your father well. Helped me with that fence building last year. Good man. It appears he has fathered two fine ladies, heroines no less."

Mrs. Unger led Mary to the back bedroom. Grace followed. Mrs. Unger grabbed a dress from her room and gave it to Grace. "Help your sister out of those wet clothes. She needs to get something dry on lest she freeze. I will go and make some hot soup. Hurry now."

Mrs. Unger rushed from the room. Grace assisted her sister who was turning a ghostly pale.

"Mary, maybe you ought to lie down. Are you sure you are all right?" Grace asked nervously biting on her fingernails. Mary nodded her head in the affirmative.

"I just want to go home, Grace. Can we go home now?"

"You wait here Mary, I will see." Once more Mary nodded her head and lay back on the bed.

Mrs. Unger knocked on the door of the bedroom. Mary had almost fallen asleep but leaped up at the noise. Sitting up, she brushed her hair and said, "Come in."

"Here is some soup. I insist you drink this before you go. It will take some of that chill out of you."

Mary smiled wanly and inquired, "How is James…err…the boy?"

"James is very lucky you came along. He is doing fine. Quite a bump he has on his head, but he is resting comfortably as you should."

The soup was delicious and revived Mary somewhat. Still, she wished nothing more than to get home to her own bed.

"Thank you so much for the soup and the dress. I will return it as soon as possible."

"Don't be silly my dear. Please keep it. It looks better on you anyway."

Mary rose unsteadily to her feet. Mrs. Unger rushed to her side and supported her.

"Are you sure you can make it home? Why don't you let me get a doctor to look at you?"

Mary stood up straight and smiled.

"I am fine, really. Grace and I had better be going now. Momma will be worried."

At that time, John Clark rushed in announcing the carriage was ready. Grace grabbed Mary's arm and helped her out to the awaiting conveyance. Mary looked back at the Unger house as they rode off. She wondered how James was doing, whether he was awake, and if he knew who had saved him. She hoped that he felt better than she did. Grace pulled the blanket up for Mary to cut down on the cold air.

"Thanks Grace. I am all right now. We are almost home."

Colonel Unger made sure James was recovered and that he had no lingering injuries.

"I'm fine, Colonel Unger, really I am."

"I am sure you are James, but you need to be checked out by a doctor. Let's get you home now."

Then he took him in a carriage across the breast of the dam and to the clubhouse where Fiona and John were staying. They were shocked as Colonel Unger and James described the events. James wanted to go immediately and thank Mary Mihelic. John Peyton said, "Don't be ridiculous. You need your rest now. There will be time enough for thanks. We've got to get you back to Pittsburgh and have you checked out by Doc Stevens."

James was too weak to argue. Fiona took him up to bed staying with him until he drifted off to sleep.

She closed the door to his room gently and walked down the back-stairs to the clubhouse meeting room. John Peyton stood by the fire-place and turned to the steps when he heard the light rustle of her dress as Fiona descended the stairs. John cupped his hand to his chin. Then tapping his chin slightly he said, "Fiona, don't you think it odd that this girl is always finding a way to be near James?"

Fiona looked at him in shock.

"John Peyton, my God! She saved our boy's life! Are you wishing she hadn't been there?"

John scowled and shook his head.

"No, of course not. It's just she keeps showing up at the oddest times."

He thought of the Regatta incident and quickly shook his head.

Fiona continued to straighten up the room but then turned to John Peyton.

"I am sure that it is all coincidence and I really don't care what reason she may have had. I just thank God she appeared when she did."

John continued to stare at the fire.

Fiona went to the stairwell and turned once more to her husband.

"Let's get to bed John. Tomorrow is going to be a long day. We need to stop by at South Fork to offer our thanks and check on the girl and then onto Pittsburgh and see Doctor Stevens for James."

"I'll be right there Fiona. I'm going outside to smoke a cigar."

John Peyton walked out onto the broad porch of the clubhouse. He lit a long cigar and took a big puff. *I still find it odd, I do.* He paced back and forth awhile mulling the coincidences in his mind. Finally, he looked at the cigar, which tonight was not relaxing him as at other times. He crushed it on the porch and flicked it into the grass beyond the house. *Time to go to bed, Fiona is right. Tomorrow will be a long day.*

The next day hurried good-byes were said to the few houseguests there and preparations for the trip to South Fork and the train ride back to Pittsburgh were made.

John Peyton made one last effort to avoid the side trip to the Mihelic's place.

"Fiona, I really don't think James is up to any side trip. We should wait till a better time. I am sure…the girl is also not feeling too well either."

Fiona Peyton would not hear of it. She placed her hands on her hips and tapped her foot.

"John Peyton we need to thank that young lady and that is that. Now please, get the carriage." Fiona propped James up in the bed kissing him on the forehead. John looked at Fiona wanting to say more but realizing his cause was hopeless. James stood by smiling largely, even though he had a bandage on his head and was still lying in bed. John Peyton caught James' eye and said, "What are you smiling at? Let's get this over with."

The road to South Fork from the lake was rather rough and narrow, but fairly well maintained. Still, with the snow the road was dangerous. Fiona clung to her husband as the driver made his way through the woods and down the tight road. James lay in the back of the carriage and looked up at the snow-covered trees. *I wonder how Mary is? I wish I could talk to her alone. I have so much to say.* Shortly, South Fork appeared out of the woods. It was a small town built into the side of the mountain with even smaller homes dotting the hillside. Against the snow the town appeared as if a small village in the Alps. The Mihelic home was on the outskirts of South Fork and on the small area of the town not on the hill.

The carriage pulled to a stop outside the little frame house. A large man stood in the doorway. He wiped his head with a handkerchief sweating even though the temperature had to be in the forties.

"Hello. Good afternoon. What is your business?"

The strong Austrian accent came through as the large man approached the carriage outside the home.

John Peyton sprung from the carriage and then assisted Fiona down. James, still weak from his ordeal, waited looking up at Mary's father from the back of the carriage. John Peyton held out his hand to the large man.

"Good day sir. I am looking for the Mihelic home. Our son, James, was rescued by a Mary Mihelic and we've come to thank her."

Charles Mihelic looked at the people closely and with some degree of skepticism. He recognized John Peyton from their two brief encounters, first at Dan Morrell's place and then at the Regatta. He was certain that Mr. Peyton did not recognize him. Finally, he broke the chilly air with an even chillier greeting.

"I am Charles Mihelic. Mary is my daughter. She is too weak to see anyone."

He turned and started back into the house without shaking hands. John Peyton let his outstretched hand dropped to his side awkwardly, then looked to his wife for guidance.

Fiona Peyton raised her arm towards Mr. Mihelic. "Wait. Please."

Charles Mihelic stopped. He then turned slowly to face the Peytons once more.

"Yes."

"Can you tell us, is she all right? If you or she need anything, please do not hesitate to ask."

"She is strong girl and will recover. We need nothing."

Thwarted once more, Fiona decided that perhaps another day would be better for this meeting. She smiled a warm smile at Charles Mihelic, which had an effect on the man. He relaxed and the tension briefly went out of his face. His square jaw remained jutting out in defiance however.

"Please, give your daughter our warmest regards. And really, if you or she require anything, it would be our pleasure to provide, truly."

Charles Mihelic face lit up with the smallest of smiles. He nodded his head in the affirmative, and said, "Thank you ma'am. That is good."

James leaned up in the carriage and called out.

"Mr. Mihelic! Wait, please come here, as I cannot get there."

Fiona turned quickly and was surprised to see her son lifting himself up.

"James do be careful, don't overdo it. You are still weak."

Charles Mihelic stiffened up but walked over to the reclining James.

James reached out his hand from the carriage and extended it to Mr. Mihelic.

"James Peyton sir. Your daughter saved my life. It indeed would be my personal pleasure to offer those thanks in person once Mary is up and about."

Charles Mihelic stopped, looked at the young man in front of him closely, and then tentatively held out his hand. They locked grips and shook heartily.

"I am glad to meet you boy."

The Peyton's departed the Mihelics' home and headed on into South Fork to catch the train to Pittsburgh. The trip and the train ride were quiet as each Peyton pondered the last day's events and the impact on their lives.

Jennie Mihelic, Charles' wife, a small round woman with white hair swirled in a bun behind her head, had observed the brief encounter from inside. She didn't wait long to question Charles on his manners. She turned to him with a stern look and a frown.

"Now, Charles, what is the matter with you? Mary was so excited to see them come up to the house. Why did you not let them in to see her and thank her?"

Charles stood there, shaking his head back and forth.

"It is not good. Not good, I tell you. They are different people. The less we see of them the better. Besides, Mary is sick because of them."

"Oh Charles. Sometimes you upset me so." Jennie Mihelic looked at her husband and his stubborn manners and then threw her arms in the air. She slammed shut the door as she re-entered the house and went back into the room where her daughter lay.

"Momma, how were they? What did they say? Was their son with them?"

The questions leapt from Mary and for the first time, Jennie suspected that the chance meeting at the lake was less chance than she had originally thought.

"They are gone Mary. The Peytons are very nice. Their son James is handsome don't you think?"

Without thinking Mary Mihelic responded. "Yes. Momma! And so big. I thought I would die trying to get him out of that ice."

Jennie smiled, patting her daughter's legs beneath the blanket.

"Well now you get your rest. I am brewing some nice warm tea for you to drink. Maybe it would be good to have them down to dinner sometime. What do you think of that?"

"Yes, Mother, oh yes. Let's." Mary said, trying not to appear too eager.

"Good now get some rest. Grace, you come with me and help with the tea."

Jennie rose from the bed and adjusted the waist on her plain cotton dress. Grace bounded up to follow while still complaining.

"Auwww Momma, I want to stay and talk with Mary."

Grace looked at her mother with a frown on her face. It was no use. Jennie firmly said, "You let Mary rest now. Come child."

"Sure." Said Grace. Her frown turned to a smile as she let loose one last comment for her sister. "Momma, you do know that Mary loves that boy? Yes she does!"

Mary reached up and tried to grab Grace but could not reach her. Grace had anticipated that the last statement would rouse her sister and had already darted from the room. She rushed past her mother who pretended not to have heard the incriminating remark.

CHAPTER 5

▼

A TRIP TO TOWN

It would be a couple of weeks until they met again. James was hurt more than he would let on. Doctor Stevens kept him in bed for a week. Then he had schoolwork to catch up on. However, the girl in South Fork was never far from his mind. He pleaded with his parents to make a trip to the lake. Finally, they acquiesced.

Robert, James' old friend was there and rushed up to greet them when they arrived.

"James, how great that you are here. Let's go shoot some duck."

James smiled wanly.

"Oh, I forgot. You are still recovering from being saved by a girl."

Robert emphasized 'girl' and rolled his eyes.

James brow furrowed in thought, then he said.

"She didn't save me at all. I just let her think she did, that's all."

He leaned up on his elbows when he said this so that he could see his friend's reaction.

Robert nodded his head in sage agreement.

"I knew you wouldn't let a girl save you or anything like that. What a tale that would make, 'James Peyton saved from ice by a local girl.' Quite embarrassing you must agree?"

James eyes darted back and forth as his thoughts bounded back and forth between Mary and his friend Robert. Finally he said, "I am tired now Robert. Perhaps tomorrow we can hunt some duck."

Robert's smile quickly turned to a frown. "All right then. Perhaps we should invite that local girl along in case you need her to hold your rifle?"

James' face turned bright red and his friend Robert decided that the last joke had gone too far. "I was only kidding you James. See you tomorrow!"

He turned around and left the room. James heard his feet bounding down the club house stairs two at a time. As the front door slammed, James thought on what he had said until he tiredly fell back to sleep.

The next morning James was up early and confident that he could get away before anyone saw him. He walked slowly down the back stairs trying to not make noise on the creaking steps. No one had heard him. He opened the front door to the clubhouse.

"James! What in the devil are you doing up so early?"

"Hi Father. I ah, was just wanting to take an early ride, perhaps into town."

"Um, fine. I will ride with you. Nothing like a morning ride to invigorate the senses."

James frowned. *Why did his father have to be here now?*

"Would you mind father if I went alone? I just want to get away for a while. I haven't been feeling well for so long now."

"No problem son. I understand. I do have to meet with Mr. Mellon here on some banking information anyway. I probably would need to cut short our ride. I will let your mother know you are gone. Don't be gone too long, your mother will worry so."

John Peyton patted his son James on the back and bounded up the steps to the porch.

He watched James walk off towards the dam breast.

James rode slowly towards the breast of the dam. Thoughts swirled through his head as the horse trotted on the well-worn path. A carriage entered from the other side. James found himself appreciating the low-ering of the dam's breast to permit two lanes. He had always found it aggravating to wait for the slow carriage crossings. He tipped his hat to the club members heading up to the cottages as he continued his jour-ney. After crossing the breast of the dam, he turned down to the path that led to the town of South Fork.

Mary came out of the house just as the rider arrived.

"James Peyton, I do declare. What a pleasant surprise?"

James resisted the urge to smile. He collected himself and speaking rather formally, he said, "Good day to you, Mary Mihelic."

Mary smile left her face. She had pictured this moment differently. The silence seemed to hang in the crisp winter air.

Finally, James spoke, shifting nervously from one leg to the other.

"I just wanted you to know that while I appreciate your efforts that day at the lake, they really were not necessary."

Mary wondered at these comments. She decided that it might be best just to make light of them.

"All right. But if I hadn't have come along, you would have frozen in that ice quicker than a snowball."

"Would not! I could have gotten myself out."

"Would too!"

Now Mary was upset. *Why was he talking this way? This is not the way I pictured this. How can this be happening?*

She wanted to say more and calm her own rushing blood but it seemed James had his own sense of urgency and purpose.

"I guess you feel I am obligated to you now. That I owe you some-thing."

Mary's mouth opened in shock at these words. Her mouth tight-ened and the words flowed quickly from her lips.

"Wait just a minute Mr. Peyton. You owe me nothing, nothing at all. You know what? I should have left you in that ice! And if you are through now, would you please leave?"

She pointed up towards the lake. James Peyton paused as if undecided on a course of action. Then he tipped his hat, rose up on his horse and galloped away. But he headed not back to the lake. Instead he headed on towards Johnstown.

Mary was steaming. She paced back and forth her hands clenching and unclenching as she moved. *It's not like I needed a "thank you" or anything. Why did he even come down here, if that is all he had to say? He is so pompous. You know what. I am going to tell him that. I let him off too easily. Yes, that is what I will do. Pompous pickaninny!*

She rushed into the barn and hooked up the carriage. She started out and hesitated. Sighing, she got down from the carriage and went up to the small house. Opening the door, she saw her mother coming in from the kitchen wiping her hands. "Momma, I am going to town for some fabric. I shouldn't be longer than two hours."

"All right Mary but be careful. And please be back before nightfall."

Mary replied "Yes" confidently and leapt the three steps from the porch to the ground. "Mary! They put steps there for a reason," she heard her mother call after her. She did not answer but instead leapt into the carriage and whipped the horse forward, onto Johnstown.

The trip to town took about one hour. The hills are steep and the roads rough. Still, the scenery of the countryside was beautiful. The sun popped out from behind the clouds to further enhance the day. The snow continued to melt and green could be seen in patches everywhere.

Down the steep Frankstown hill and into the main part of Johnstown she went. She knew that James had quite a head start on her. She began to wonder if she was being foolish. After all, James could have been going anywhere's and even if she did meet him, what was she going to say to him? Slowly a smile came across her face. She urged the horses on.

The town was bustling as it always was on a weekend day. People greeted each other with smiles and small talk whether friend, neighbor, or just someone passing bye. Shops were popping up everywhere and the town was continuing to grow. Johnstown had two Opera houses, a beautiful park in the center of the city, and many fine churches for the faithful. Of course, it also had its share of saloons for the men folk to wet their whistles after a hard day at work.

Mary was not smiling when she slowed her horse down on Clinton Street. *This is so stupid*, she thought. *I will just get the fabric I needed anyway and head home.* She pulled the carriage to the curb and climbed down. Drawing a deep breath to calm her emotions, she turned to go into the Quinn Dry Goods Store just as another person coming up the street turned to go in from the other side. They crashed.

"Ow! You! Are you following me?" asked a bewildered James.

"Following you? I am not following you Mr. Peyton. Do not presume you are that attractive. I am merely going into Quinn's, that is if you will kindly move to the side."

James' face turned beet red and he stepped to the side to let Mary pass. She walked past him quickly and hurried to the fabrics. *Grrr! I must get that fabric quick and get out of here. What was I ever thinking that he was special, different?*

James stood stunned in the doorway. He watched Mary move purposely through the store. He had wanted to look at the new rifles the store had ordered for his father. But there was another man there with Mr. Quinn and both were deep in conversation.

He saw Mary over by the fabrics. He walked over to her and touched her on the shoulder. She turned around abruptly and stared into his eyes, which once more caused him to hesitate. Once Mary saw it was James she started to turn back to the fabrics, when he found his voice. "Wait! Please."

"What do you want Mr. Peyton? To help me select fabric, are you as good at that as you are at ice skating?"

James looked down, then raised his eyes to meet Mary's stony stare.

"I deserve that Mary. Please, let me finish."

Mary's face remained stern as she let the fabric drop back on the table. "Alright, what is it?"

James Peyton was suddenly knocked forward before he could reply. A hand had been placed strongly on his shoulder.

"Excuse me, aren't you John Peyton's son?"

He turned to see a man he recognized from the past, from the funeral. His body stiffened at the memory. "Yes, I am James Peyton, why do you ask?"

"I'm John Fulton, Chief Engineer for the Cambria Iron Works". He held out his hand, which James shook. It was a strong grip and hearty as if old friends.

"Look, I realize that your father and I got off on a bad footing. It's just that I know that dam is a large problem waiting to happen. Can you please relay that to him? Have him check into it and take action now, before something happens?"

James was listening to John Fulton but his mind was on Mary Mihelic and what he had to tell her. He nodded his head in the affirmative and turned to see Mary had moved a ways down still looking at fabric.

John Fulton patted James' back and smiled, "Thank you boy, thank you."

"Sure, Mr. Fulton." James said and moved away.

James Quinn called out to John Fulton, "John, leave the boy alone. He's just a child." John waved off his friend, looked to where James had gone then turned and went out the door.

"Mary?"

"James, I thought you had gotten involved in other matters?" Mary said with a disinterested voice as she picked among the fabrics.

"No, no. I don't know what he wanted, something about the dam, I think. Mary…"

Once more they were interrupted, this time when a woman appeared from the backroom. She was a broad woman with dark hair pulled into a bun. "Mary Mihelic, I do declare. How is your mother?"

Mary smiled in recognition and grabbed James' arm. "Hello Mrs. Quinn, she is fine, thank you."

"And who is this fine gentleman here, a new boyfriend?"

Mrs. Quinn smiled broadly at this and continued, "You make a lovely couple."

"No. I mean yes. I mean we are just friends."

Mary looked at James with a plea not to talk and dropped her hold on his arm.

Mrs. Quinn smiled even broader.

"Well good. I have always had a desire that you would like my son Vincent. He was just in here awhile ago." Mrs. Quinn looked around the store as if in expectation of seeing her son.

You two should talk."

James shifted nervously on his feet. He looked from Mary to Mrs. Quinn, wondering what he should do. Mrs. Quinn continued to discuss both fabrics and her son.

James waited a bit but then turned and walked out the door. Mary stole a glance and wondered whether to call out to him but then decided that would be improper.

"Oh dear, your friend has left. I do hope I didn't scare him off."

Mrs. Quinn let out a hearty laugh. Mary shook her head no.

She picked up the fabric they had been discussing.

"I believe I will take this if you wouldn't mind ringing it up for me."

Mrs. Quinn took the fabric and moved to the register to make the sale. She began to ring up the sale but then turned to Mary.

"Why don't you go outside? Perhaps down the street to the park. I can wrap this and have it waiting for you. You might even catch your friend."

Mary's face brightened.

"Thank you Mrs. Quinn! I believe I will"

She raced out the door. James was nowhere in sight.

She walked down the street to the park. It had been a long time since she had been there but all looked the same, beautiful. She remembered the time that she and James met there. *Was it all a silly dream?*

As if to punctuate her thoughts a large dog bounded from an alley-way and headed straight towards her. She shook her head and tamped her foot. The dog stopped at her feet and looked up sheepishly. "Did you escape again? How do you do it?"

The dogs tail wagged and his head turned to one side as if straining to hear the young girl's words. "You know, I do believe you are one smart dog. Yes I do." The wagging increased and it seemed his whole body was in motion as he jumped side to side in playful gestures. "Yes. You went to Mr. Morrell's funeral too. I saw you there." The dog stopped at the mention of Dan Morrell's name. He looked around quickly as if he would see him soon.

Mary reached down, patting the dog on the head and reaching for what was left of the lead rope. "No boy, Mr. Morrell isn't coming here. Sorry. Now, let's get you back to Mr. Morley. I am sure he will be wor-ried."

She walked back the alleyway and opened the gate. Mr. Morley was walking down the steps.

"Ah, so there he is. Thank you Mary for bringing him home. I don't know what gets into that dog."

Mary smiled and handed the rope lead over to Mr. Morley.

"I guess I had better be going."

"Bye," she said more to the dog than to Mr. Morley.

Mr. Morley called out after her. "Good-bye Mary! Tell your father we need him at the mill. Production is down and the boss ain't happy."

Mary thought on what Mr. Morley had said as she headed back to the park. If her poppa would move back to town she could see the park everyday like it used to be. *But I can't tell him that. He is so happy now farming.*

Mary sat down on one of the benches in the park. Looking up she saw Mrs. Anna Fenn walking towards her with her five children in tow. "Good-day Mrs. Fenn," said Mary smiling.

"Why good-day to you Mary. How is your family now? Living up in South Fork right?"

"Yes Mrs. Fenn. They are fine."

"Good. Good. Please tell your mother to stop bye the next time you are in town. We get so few visitors now a days."

"Oh, I will Mrs. Fenn. With the farm and all, we just don't get to Johnstown as often as we used to."

"Mary!"

A voice came from behind and Mary swirled to see James Peyton rushing towards her.

"I just took a hunch that you would come here! I'm so glad you did!"

James grabbed Mary's hands. "I have to talk to you."

For the first time James noticed the woman standing by the path with her five children. Mary looked between Mrs. Fenn and James, breathing in, she said. "Mrs. Fenn, this is James Peyton. He is from Pittsburgh and stays up at the lake."

Mrs. Fenn looked closely at James. Her face showed a mix of skepticism and concern. Her manner, which had been so open and jovial, turned cool.

"Nice to meet you Mr. Peyton. Well, I must be going; these children get rambunctious if they are not fed on time. Good day Mary."

Mary waved at the now departing Mrs. Fenn; happy that she and James could talk she didn't take notice of Mrs. Fenn's changing tone and manner.

James also watched her go. Such a pretty lady, he thought. *I wonder why she was so cool towards me?* Mary dropped his hand, which broke him from his reverie.

"Mary, I am so sorry about this whole day. I've been acting stupid. Of course I'm thankful you came along that day and saved my life."

Before he could continue Mary stepped in. "Then why did you act that way James? I don't understand and I didn't appreciate it."

James nodded his head and shrugged his shoulders.

"I can't explain it. Can we just let it go? I do know that I want to be with you. We have such fun and I don't want that to end. Am I forgiven? Please."

Mary smiled. "All right Mr. Peyton, I shall forgive you, but now you will have to be my eternal slave."

James looked into her eyes and at first expressed surprise. Then laughing he said, "all right." Bowing deeply, he said, "and what is your wish my lady fair?"

"See that house over there." Mary said, pointing across the park through some trees to a large house facing the park. Ironically, the house happened to be John Fulton's.

"I want someday to live in that house, or any house downtown. I really miss this town."

"It's a nice house, I guess. I would rather live in Pittsburgh."

"Well Mr. Peyton, we have got a problem there," said Mary smiling while she placed her hand on a nearby tree.

"We do?" he inquired twisting his face as he asked.

"Yes. How can you serve me when you are so far away?"

She ran off laughing as James caught onto her latest joke and chased after her.

He caught her and twirled her around to face him. They looked into each other's eyes. Their lips were so close. The day felt warmer all of a sudden.

"Children!"

James and Mary were startled and turned to find Reverend Beale racing up to them.

"Mary, I know you. I can't believe you are here acting like that. It is a disgrace. Your father would be embarrassed. Please young man, take her home and act like a gentleman! I will pray for you both."

He turned on his heel and was gone. Mary and James looked at each other sheepishly. The spell was broken. They walked slowly and quietly back to the carriage. James helped Mary up into the carriage and they made the trip back to South Fork after picking up the fabric at the Quinn's store.

Once there, Mary jumped down from the carriage and James dismounted his horse. Again they found themselves face-to-face but mindful of the last time, they parted quickly and waved to each other. James remounted the horse and galloped off.

Mary pranced up the steps to her home not noticing Charles Mihelic watching from the window of the house. As she entered the house, Charles turned to her. "What were you doing young lady?"

Mary was stunned to see her father and her mouth dropped in shock.

"Papa, hi! I thought you were downtown?"

"I was. What are you doing with that boy?"

"I-I was just doing some shopping. I met him there. He just wanted to thank me for saving him from the lake."

"Stay away from him Mary. It isn't good I tell you."

"Oh Papa! You don't know him. He's…"

Her father waved his hand shook his head and turning quickly he went out the door banging it shut behind him. Mary wondered at what her father had said. *I am so confused.* She walked back to her room slowly, a smile creeping back on her face.

James rushed into the clubhouse beaming from ear to ear.

"So what are you so happy about young man?" Asked John Peyton.

"I went downtown. Did some shopping."

"Did you get that new rifle? We are having a sporting event up here next weekend and I want you to have the best weapon. You will need it. There will be some real marksmen there."

"No father, I didn't. I…"

He hesitated to tell his father of seeing the man from the funeral. Fortunately his father intervened. "Good! I wanted to get you a special one, like that one I saw in Philadelphia."

He patted James on the back and returned to his reading. James breathed a sigh of relief and rushed up stairs to his room.

The next day as she cleaned up the dishes Mary told her mother of the shopping trip with James.

"Oh Momma, it was so nice to be back in town. We walked in the park. Oh, I saw Mrs. Fenn. Did you know they have five children now? She still looks wonderful. She said to tell you 'Hi'".

"It does appear you had a good time Mary. I do wish you had not gone off alone with that Peyton boy, James isn't it?"

"Yes momma, James, why?" Mary braced herself for another lecture on rich folks-poor folks. Her mother paused as if thinking of her own youth. She said, "Well, sometimes it doesn't look right to people. We really should meet him and his parents, don't you agree?"

"Momma that would be wonderful! We could cook up a great supper!"

Then a frown came to her face. "I think they have left for Pittsburgh already."

Patting her daughter's hand, Mrs. Mihelic smiled, "Don't you worry none. I know some of the ladies who work up at the lake. I am sure I can get the Peyton's address and send them a note."

"Would you mother, that would be grand?"

"We'll see child. Now, let's get these dishes done."

As it turned out the Peyton's were still up at the lake so the invitation was delivered by one of the local boys. John Peyton read the note and frowned. He patted the note on his open hand as he thought. Finally, shaking his head, he ascended the stairs to their bedroom where Fiona was waiting.

He showed the invitation to her. She read slowly as was her way, taking in each word carefully. John paced the floor waiting for her to finish. She looked up at him inquisitively. He spoke.

"Fiona, what are we to do? I really don't want to visit with them. What could we talk about? Is there a polite way to decline? Perhaps we could ask them to come here?"

Fiona smiled at her husband. *Will he ever learn the social graces?*

"John, we must accept the invitation and go to the Mihelics' home. We cannot now turn to them and say that we want them to come here. We must be gracious and accept the invitation. Actually, I look forward to it, they seem like such nice people."

John Peyton frowned.

"I don't know. To be truly honest I am uncomfortable around them. I mean, they are not our type at all, don't you agree?"

Fiona placed her hands on her hips.

"And John, just who are 'our type'?"

"Oh, you know what I mean."

He knew better than to challenge his wife further. John quietly set the invitation on the bureau for his wife and left to rejoin his fellow club members for a cigar and talk of steel. *Steel was much easier to discuss than people. Well, Fiona will see. We should not mix together.* He stopped at the top of the stairs. His brow furrowed. *Why did they invite us down there?*

Fiona Peyton sat down and wrote a brief note in response to the invitation.

> *We would be delighted to accept your warm invitation for dinner. If there is anything you would like us to bring or to prepare please let James know and we would welcome the opportunity.*
> *Thank you so much for thinking of us,*
>
> *John and Fiona Peyton*

"There. Complete. Now to find James."

As if on queue, she heard a bounding up the stairs and her son bolted into the room.

"Mother!"

"What is it James?"

"Would you tell Janie to please leave me and Robert be! We're fishing and she's throwing rocks. If you don't tell her to stop, I do believe I shall strangle her."

Fiona was quick to respond. She pointed her finger at James and said, "James! Now stop that talk. Even if you're kidding as I know you are."

"Yes mother," the frown on his face betrayed that the statement, while gentle teasing, did reflect his current view of his sister.

Fiona arose from her writing chair gracefully smoothing out her skirt. She picked the letter off the desk and handed it to James saying, "Besides, I have this letter I wish you to deliver to the Mihelics. They have invited us to a dinner this Saturday and we are accepting."

"Great mother. I'll take it down now."

"Good," his mother answered and gave him the letter. She is somewhat puzzled at his prompt acceptance, particularly since he had just said how much he was enjoying fishing with his longtime friend Robert. There and then, she decided to be more observant of her growing son.

James dashed off to let Robert know of his duty. Janie was still there plopping rocks in the water and running when Robert threatened her. James yelled at his sister who was still running away from them, although she kept looking back to see if she was being chased.

"Janie, mother says to stop throwing those rocks now!"

Janie stopped running. Her brow squiggled into a knit.

"You told mother? You're a tattler James! Tattle-tale James tattle-tale James"

James face reddened and he chased his sister off once more so that he could talk to Robert.

"I have an errand to run Robert. Mother has asked me to deliver a letter to the Mihelics down in South Fork."

"Down there? What the hell are you doin' goin' down there? Shit James, we just haven't had that much fishin' time this summer. You always seem to be rushing off anymore. And today, cripes are they biting. If it wasn't for Janie!"

"I know, but they'll still be biting tomorrow and Friday."

His friend Robert had to agree. The fish were really plentiful this year after the spring stocking.

Robert picked up his gear and turned to James. "Fine, let's go."

"You don't need to come Robert. After all, it is not good that both of us should miss out on the fishing."

Robert looked at his friend curiously. It used to be that they did almost everything together. Lately James seemed to be more aloof, independent. Was he growing tired of their friendship?

What in the heck is going on here?

He was determined to learn more but not now. There would be time later to see what James was up to. He sat down again and acted disinterested.

"Fine James. See you later."

James breathed a sigh of relief. Anxious to be off, he turned to go, but wanted to ease his friend's feelings of desertion.

"Yes. Tomorrow Robert. We shall catch many fish, bigger and better ones then!"

James waved a quick good-bye and skipped off to get a horse for the trek down to South Fork.

Janie returned with rocks in her hands looking around cautiously. She said, "Hey where did James go?" Robert placed his pole down and smiled. He motioned towards the dam and said, "Janie, James went down to South Fork. Do you know why he would go there?"

James loved to ride. He had a gift with horses that few could master. Horse and rider seemed to be one as they moved in one smooth motion. James loved the way the wind would blow in his face and he could feel the power of the animal moving beneath him and over the land. He thought of Mary as he rode.

He slowed the horse down and now as he neared the house, he grew more tentative. *What would he say? What would she say?*

His stomach began to churn. Then he heard her voice call out.

"James! What are you doing here? Hello!"

She ran up and hugged him and all his worries passed away except one. Why did this girl have this crazy effect on him? Mary held onto his hand and beaming she said, "I was so looking forward to seeing you. I asked Mother to invite your folks for dinner Saturday. Are you coming? Is that it?"

"Yes we're coming! I have with me my mother's reply. I just had to see you again."

"You did, did you?"

Then she smiled that smile, the one that made James heart rush up to his throat. *How could she be so pretty and so charming at the same time?*

James looked at his feet. He fumbled with an answer.

"Well, you know, I mean, I did want to see you and all."

"But of course you did you silly goose. This will be wonderful!"

Mary's excitement was catching. James smiled. Mary continued with her thoughts.

"Our parents will get to know each other and oh it is going to be so great. Momma is a great cook. Just wait."

James nodded his head.

"Yes. We will have an absolutely magnificent time. Your folks, my folks, and us."

"Come James, let's take a walk."

She grabbed his hand and off they went like old friends. They chatted and laughed at each other's jokes. Sometimes they would poke at each other playfully, not hard, but more to touch and to feel the person that you were with.

Ultimately, as the day turned to dusk, the time to part had arrived.

"Well we'll see you this Saturday, Miss Mary."

"Oh dear, so formal now Master James?"

She laughed to take away his nervousness. Funny how she was able to keep him guessing and yet provide him relief when needed. She touched his arm, and then laughing said, "I know what you meant you silly bean. Now off with you, for us ladies must prepare for the feast."

He leaped onto the horse and proceeded off at a gallop. He knew that he looked dashing there riding that horse or so he hoped. Off he flew back to the clubhouse.

Mary went back into the house with a glow in her cheeks. Practically dancing she handed the response from the Peyton's to her mother.

CHAPTER 6

▼

THE DINNER

James let his mother adjust his tie. He wanted it to look just right. His striped trousers were dark blue and sharp looking. The suspenders added to the look. He knew that. Girls at school looked at him when he wore them. His shirt was white, with the black tie his mother was now straightening, hanging down just right. He looked into the mirror.

Yes, Mr. Peyton, you are one fine looking fellow.

His mother interrupted his interlude.

"James, hurry downstairs now. Tell your father I will be there shortly. I have to check in on Janie."

"Mother, is Janie going to get better soon? I have never seen her so down. Maybe we should not go?"

Fiona Peyton had had the same thoughts as her son.

John had not wanted to go anyway. He even volunteered to stay back with Janie, God bless his soul.

In the end, she had decided to go. Something inside her said that it was important to go tonight. She was sure it had to do with the changes in her son.

Is there more to this friendship with Mary Mihelic? Tonight we shall see.

"She will be just fine son. Now go down to your father."

"All right mother." He kissed her on the cheek and burst off and down the stairs.

"Janie, sweetheart, we are going."

"Mother," Janie coughed, "I will be fine, really. I did so want to go. To see James make mushy with Mary."

She started to laugh but then all at once began coughing uncontrollably. Fiona rushed to her side and tapped her back to ease the congestion.

"That does it! I'm staying. I can't leave you here, sick like this."

"Mother, there's almost a full house here. Mrs. Frick will watch over me. Her baby is sick also. She'll take care of me for tonight. Don't worry. I'll be all right. I'm feeling better already."

Janie felt another cough coming on but held it in as her mother tucked in the covers, and kissed her forehead.

"Well we won't stay too long. And if anything happens I am going to tell Mrs. Frick to send Robert down to get us."

"Mother nothing is going to happen. Now scoot off."

Janie, my precious little lady, are you now going to grow up like your brother? Please do not grow too soon. I love you both so.

She then stood up from the bed and turning off the light left the room to go downstairs.

John Peyton was off talking to Henry Clay Frick. The two men were seated opposite each other. The conversation was very intense. Their heads were close together and they spoke quietly as if concerned that someone might overhear what they were saying. Every now and then, one or the other would nod in agreement. Since Ben Ruff, founder of the club, had passed away it seemed that John and Henry had become close. Fiona Peyton never liked Mr. Frick much. He seemed so secretive, even cold-hearted. A frown crossed Fiona' face. Was her husband becoming more like Henry Clay Frick? *Impossible!*

But then, am I reading Henry wrong? John is usually such a good judge of character.

She walked up to the two men and slipped her arm into her husband's.

"Hello Henry. Nice to see you but I am afraid I must drag my husband away or we shall be late for a dinner engagement."

Henry Clay Frick looked at Fiona Peyton and thought to say something but then just bowed gracefully and walked over to the bar.

"Fiona, Henry and I were talking of the Steel Mills."

"Why does that not surprise me?"

"Point well taken. Let's go, shall we. I sent James off to get the carriage. He should be back by now."

As if on a schedule, James arrived with the carriage and they departed. No matter how many times they made this trip away from the clubhouse, down to the dam, and across the very breast, Fiona Peyton never tired of it. The road leading to the breast of the dam was lined with trees and the cottages of the members. On the other side of the road lay the clear lake often reflecting the glow of the moon across its surface. Once the face of the dam was reached, she would have James, or John if he were driving, stop the carriage so that they could enjoy the spectacular view. When the carriage reached the center of the dam, she would ask them to stop. Then she would look out over the green lush valley.

The dam was man's creation, but the valley, that was God at work.

Today it looked especially grand. The late day sun shone down on the trees and the lake. "Isn't this beautiful John? We are so fortunate to be here."

"Yes Fiona, This mountain is surely paradise. So much abundance in one place."

"Mother. Father, shouldn't we be going? I don't want us to be late for dinner."

John Peyton looked at his son sharply.

"James, how unlike you? You always liked this spot almost as much as your mother?"

Fiona Peyton touched John's arm and said, "John, James is right. We shan't be late. It wouldn't be proper."

John Peyton mumbled under his breath.

"Well I would just as soon as not go at all. That's what I am thinking."

"John Peyton, I heard that. Now you be good tonight. Remember the Mihelics are good people."

James Peyton jolted the horses to life and they continued their journey, each lost in their thoughts of the coming evening.

Tonight will be great. Mary is so pretty. I am sure once we get together the two families will just hit it off swell.

I wonder how Janie is doing? I should have stayed home. James is truly anxious tonight. I hope it goes well.

Disaster. I could be back at the club playing cards. Instead, I am going off to South Fork to meet the Mihelics. They are just not high-type people, but how do you explain that to Fiona? You don't. It can't go well.

The trip down to South Fork was well known since they made it each time they came to the lake. South Fork had the last train stop and then you took a carriage or a horse up the final miles to the lake. The remainder of the trip did not take too long and they arrived at their destination. The smell from the house was most pleasing and even John Peyton felt his stomach doing flip-flops at the fragrance of warm well-cooked food. *Maybe I spoke too hastily earlier. The smell coming from the house is positively enchanting.*

Mary greeted them at the door. She had an apron on over a long blue dress, and her hair hung loosely on her shoulders. John Peyton was stunned by what he observed. He had expected a younger girl, not one so mature.

So, this is the girl that saved James? My God, she is pretty! I expected, well I don't quite know what I expected. Not this, that is for certain. He observed Fiona and James moving forward to the door. *This could be more difficult than I had thought especially if James is taken in by her obvious charms.* His reverie was interrupted by Mary's smile and outstretched hand.

"Hello and welcome. I am Mary Mihelic. I am so glad you could come."

Although she talked to them all it was apparent that she was addressing James. Fiona looked at the girl in the doorway closely.

It is plain to see that James likes her. She seems so much more mature. I do so hope he is not hurt. This should be one interesting evening.

"Thank you so much my dear. You know James of course. This person to my left standing so quiet is my husband John, and I am Fiona. Last time we met you were so young, I was not sure you would remember us."

Mary smiled and then said "I remember meeting you at the Morrell's place, such a dear man." She didn't mention the incident at the Regatta although she wondered if Mr. Peyton recalled it. "Please do come in. Mother is cooking in the kitchen. I'll go get her."

They entered the small living area. The furniture while plain and simple was quite comfortable. The whole house had the smell of fresh flowers. That smell plus the smell of the food cooking was almost too much to take. Mary led John and Fiona Peyton over to the sofa.

"Please do sit down. I shall be right back. James you can sit there."

She pointed to a stiff chair next to the sofa.

Mary left and went into the room from which the fragrant cooking smells had emerged. Soon she returned with an older version of herself. It was easy to see where she got her beauty. The introductions were again made. Besides beauty, both ladies possessed incredible charm. John Peyton was struck by the singular gentleness in the mother. That seemed the only difference. *Mary is pretty and definitely charming but she doesn't appear to have her mother's softness. Yes, Mary is a lady to be reckoned with.*

"Good day," a loud voice boomed from the entrance.

"Papa!"

Mary ran to the person filling the door. John Peyton was a big man in his own right but this man standing in the door was a small mountain. John Peyton rose to greet his host.

"Mr. Mihelic. Nice to meet you again. John Peyton here. This is my wife Fiona and I believe you know my son James."

"Yes I know James. It is nice to meet you. I am hungry. Are you?"

"I can smell it already. I can't wait."

"Well if you all will excuse me, I must get washed up now."

Mary led her guests through the other door into a small dining room. The table was in the center of the room and chairs for eight were placed around it. On the one wall was hung a lovely quilt with a pattern of alternating squares. The stitching was meticulous. A large painting of a country scene hung on the other wall. There was a small cottage there with a woman waving to someone off in the distance.

"That is a remarkable painting. Would you be willing to part with it?"

"John!"

"What? I am only asking. I admire good painters and I don't believe I recognize this style but the quality is extraordinary."

Mr. Mihelic stared at the picture and then at his guest.

"Well thank you Mr. Peyton but no that painting is not for sale. My grandfather did that back in the old country, Czechoslovakia. The woman you see there is my Grandmamma, Rebecca Keurtz."

"Please do call me John. Remarkable painting. The colorings, the use of texture."

Charles Mihelic smiled remembering his happy childhood days with his grand mum.

"That painting is so real to me. See. Each time I look at it I am back there with Grandmamma."

"That is too bad."

"What?"

"Oh I am sorry. I meant, too bad that I cannot get you to sell the painting. It is truly exquisite."

"I see."

However, Charles Mihelic did not see. To him the painting had value because of the memories it brought to him.

Why would the Peytons want this painting? Just to hang on a wall in their fancy cottage. To Charles, value was only made with contact. He would never understand people like these Peytons.

Why had he agreed to this dinner?

"Well let's sit down all."

Mary thought to break the tension that seemed to have descended over the room. She led them each to a seat.

"I will go help mother with the food."

She hesitated to leave but felt that the sooner the food arrived, the better.

Nothing made people as relaxed as her momma's good cooking.

When she returned the room was quiet. Fiona had made several small talk comments but had not elicited more than short answers to each. The silence was stifling. Jennie entered with the first plate.

"Hot plate coming through."

A plate piled high with the freshest green beans with steam rising from them. They were mixed with some mushrooms. It was hard to resist them, but that was only the beginning. Mary entered with another bowl filled high with mashed potatoes. The potatoes looked so soft and fluffy it seemed as if they would melt in your mouth. By then, Jennie had returned with another platter. This contained the meat. It was a pork roast cooked to perfection. Mary brought in the fresh baked rolls and some creamy butter. Soon the food was passed around and everyone helped themselves to healthy portions.

The talk turned to the weather and how the crops were expected to turn out. Fiona relaxed.

Jennie and Mary are amazing. Yes as cooks but also in the way they can carry a conversation. Usually I do quite well myself thank you, but tonight, Janie, I probably should have stayed home.

After the food was passed out, Charles Mihelic called for quiet.

"Let us give thanks for this harvest to our Lord above."

All turned quiet.

"Lord, thank you for this food we eat. We thank you for giving us this land and for bringing us together here to share in this supper. Lord God be praised now and forever. Ah-men."

The talk resumed.

"I am sorry your Janie could not come tonight Fiona. We will have to give you something to take back with you."

"Oh, thank you Jennie. Yes. She is not feeling well. I do not know what is wrong. Tomorrow we leave to go back to Pittsburgh. I need to get her to the doctor."

"I will give you something. It is a drink I make called a hot toddy. It is good and cleans out the works."

Everyone laughed.

James said, "Janie sure could use her works cleaned."

Fiona reached over to James' mouth as if to quiet him.

"James! I apologize. He really does love his sister."

"As I do mine, now don't I Gracie."

Mary used her pet name for Grace that just sent quivers up her spine. Grace smiled at her sister and then stuck her tongue into one side of her mouth. Mary could not see it.

"Children are such a joy and at the same time such a challenge, don't you think so Mr. Peyton?"

Charles Mihelic turned to John Peyton who was enjoying the food more than focusing on the conversation.

"Yes. Of course. This food is delicious."

Had he stopped there the evening might have been salvaged but his next comments ended all prospect of a quiet end.

"You Hunkies sure do know how to cook!"

He beamed at this compliment not realizing the use of the derogatory term. Charles Mihelic rose to his feet. Mary looked over at her father.

Oh, papa, please, do not get angry. I am sure Mr. Peyton did not mean to use that word.

She knew it was too late.

Her father's face reddened. He looked out over the table to John Peyton.

"You Irish are all the same. Well this is Hunkie food you eat yes! But we do so much more, if only you let us. We are hard workers and we make good products. You think because you came over here one generation earlier that you have special rights, special know-how. I built this house. It may not be as big as your fancy house up there, but it is a good, solid house. You think you are better than us, Mr. High and Mighty. I think no. You are the same, flesh and blood. Bah, I waste my time here. It is no good. No good. I told you."

With that Charles Mihelic threw down his napkin and left the home.

"Oh dear. Oh dear."

Mrs. Mihelic was almost in tears at the turn in the dinner.

John Peyton was stunned.

What had happened? What was wrong?

He had offered a compliment. At least that was his intention. The food was delicious.

"It is all right Jennie. Really, it is fine." Fiona Peyton tried to intercede and set the meal on course once more.

James sat there almost dumbfounded. *How can this be? It was going so well.*

He looked over at Mary. She seemed to be looking up in the air like the answer was written there.

"Please let us eat. Charles will be back I am sure," Jennie Mihelic continued to try.

"I am so sorry. He is usually not like that. Really."

"No, it is I that should be sorry. I was not thinking and should have not used that term. Especially me since I have heard many slurs in my times and I know how it feels."

John Peyton had found his voice and realized the offense.

"Fiona, I believe it is time we left. I am sure we have all lost our appetites. Mrs. Mihelic, thank you for this wonderful meal. Please extend to your husband my deepest apologies."

Fiona looked sharply at her husband. She had hoped that he would get up and talk to Charles Mihelic. Explain to him. Nevertheless, she knew John Peyton would not do that. It was not in him. James looked at Mary.

No, What is he saying? It can't end now. Not now.

Mary saw James looking at her and mouthing something. *I will come back later. Meet me.*

Her face lit up. She mouthed, "Yes".

Jennie Mihelic tried once more.

"Oh please stay, really. Everything is fine. Charles will come back. You will see."

Even saying the words Jennie Mihelic knew the evening was ended.

"Thank you Jennie but I think John is right. We should leave now. Perhaps another time Maybe we can have you, Charles, and the children to our place up on the lake."

Fiona had put the final wraps on the evening. The coats were retrieved and the families moved to the door where the carriage awaited. Off in the distance Charles Mihelic stood, smoking his favorite pipe and staring off into the field.

"Good night Jennie. Again thank you so much for having us over. You have a true talent with your cooking."

Fiona Peyton smiled and hugged the still frowning Jennie Mihelic.

"Thank you Fiona. We must get together again, and soon."

John Peyton extended his arm to assist his wife into the carriage. James said his good-byes to Mrs. Mihelic and to Mary. Grace had remained inside, not wanting to be part of the sad ending to the night, and really quite hungry. She was one who would not let the happenings spoil her meal.

John Peyton did not talk on the ride home. The whole evening had turned to disaster.

It was not like I did not warn them. We just don't mix. I shouldn't have used that term, I know. But good grief we were guests in his home. How embarrassing. Well that is the last time we will see them. Strange people. Different. I need to have a talk with James too. He could be caught up in that young ladies beauty and not thinking clearly. Yes, we need to talk.

Fiona sat in the carriage wondering also. She had seen James several times look at Mary Mihelic, and she had returned the gazes.

This little issue is not going to stop them. They are in love. I must talk to John and get him to see that. We must work to get to know the Mihelics better. They really are nice people.

James Peyton could not wait to get his parents home.

The evening cannot end like this. Mary, please be waiting for me. Please.

At the clubhouse, John and Fiona bid their son goodnight and retired to the bedroom. They talked little of the sorry end to the evening and agreed that the morning would be a better time to talk. James had to take the horses and the carriage back to the barn and he would return as soon as possible, or so he said. At the barn he placed the horses in their stables, and then retrieved his favorite horse for riding. Once saddled up, he headed for South Fork and the planned secret rendezvous.

As he rode up closer to the Mihelic household, he worried that she had forgotten their plans. It was quite late and not a light was on in the house. He needn't have worried. Out of the door came Mary.

Gosh, she looks more beautiful at night.

"James, Oh I am so glad that you came. Go over to the barn. I will meet you there." James got off his horse and led him to the barn. Mary had already arrived and entered. She grabbed an oil lamp and lit it. The light showed across the barn.

"I-I"

"Oh James you are here. You came"

With that Mary rushed over to him and kissed him on the lips.
He stood there dumbstruck.

She kissed me. Really. Dang, I'm going to turn red. No I can't. It mustn't show. She kissed me. I must have something to say. What am I going to say?

"It was a disaster." *It was wonderful.*

"What?"

"The dinner." *The kiss.*

"Yes, it was."

She threw back her head and swished her hair from side to side then added, "a real catastrophe." She grabbed the clip in her hand and tied her long hair in a ponytail, flipping it up lastly into a tight bun.

"A mistake from the start." *It was magical from the start.*

"A colossal failure."

"My father was wrong." *You are beautiful.*

"Papa did not mean to get mad."

They looked at each other and laughed.

"I guess it could have gone worse. I feared your father would have reached across the table and throttle my dad. He scares me."

"Papa? Papa is not mean. It is, just that he works so hard. And he, he doesn't like it when people clump all of us together as if we all came from Hungary. Papa is Austrian, and momma is Czechoslovakian, not a "hunkie" amongst us." They both laughed at the simple irony.

"You still like me?" *I love you.*

"Of course you silly bean."

They kissed softly and gently laughed at the way the evening had turned out.

I'm not nervous. She makes me feel so at ease, so happy.

Reluctantly, James said that he had to go. Mary frowned.

"I promise you I will see you whenever I am here. We will meet secretly down by the spillway. You know the place."

"Yes."

"Whenever I arrive in South Fork I will leave a message at the train station for you. Check there every so often and then we can meet."

"I do not know if I can wait James Peyton. You have taken my heart don't you know?"

They kissed once more and then Mary pulled away.

"Go, you silly goose. Your parents may be waiting for you and then we will be in a real pickle."

James pulled away slowly and then in one smooth motion was upon his horse. He lowered his head to get out the barn and then quietly rode away. Mary blew out the lamp and walked back to the quiet house.

I love you James Peyton. You make me want to sing and to dance. I want to kiss you again and again.

CHAPTER 7

▼

JANIE

It was a month later before the Peytons returned to the lake. Janie's condition had worsened and the doctor mentioned that the country air might do her better. School had let out so it made the visit rather timely. James was excited but decided against leaving Mary a note. *I don't want to get her hopes up. I need to help Mother with Janie.*

The carriage pulled up to the clubhouse and stopped. The horses snorted and pranced seeming to enjoy the brisk mountain air. James jumped down from the back and slowly maneuvered the cot containing his sister. John Peyton arrived and took the other end. They moved carefully up the stairs and into the clubhouse.

"Slow now James. I don't want Janie to be hurt."

"Gosh father, I am going slow as I can. She gets heavy after awhile."

Even though she was weak and tired, Janie could not resist the chance to needle her brother. In a raspy voice she said, "Poor weak James."

Fiona stayed behind in the carriage. She was too nervous to watch the procession up the stairs. When James reappeared flying down the steps two at a time, she started to get out of the carriage.

"Wait! Mother! I'll help you."

James rushed up and held out his hand for his mother. She looked so much frailer now a days, he thought. She smiled wanly and started to enter the clubhouse.

With the door open she turned sharply back to look at James.

"James, why don't you go down and see Mary Mihelic? There is no need to stay cooped up in this clubhouse while we are here."

James looked at his mother and was conflicted. He really had hoped to see Mary while there. Still, Janie was awful sick and his mother needed him.

"No, Mother, I'll stay here for now. I want to help."

"Fine dear, I appreciate that. Can you bring up some warm soup from the kitchen? I think Janie could use something after that long trip."

"Sure mother. Are you going to be all right?"

"Yes James, I am all right. Now hurry."

She turned and ascended the stairs. Fiona stopped at the landing and rested. *Funny, these stairs didn't use to bother me. I guess Janie's illness is wearing me down too. Why is this happening?*

For the next several days Janie seemed to respond to the fresh air and the sounds of the surrounding forest. She even sat on the porch one day watching James play catch with Robert. Fiona also seemed to be re-invigorated by the peace of the lakeside. She decided James needed some time away from the worry of the past months. She called out to him.

"James. Come here."

James tossed the ball lightly to Robert and went up to his mother rocking on the porch.

"Yes Mother, what do you need?"

Patting him on his head and looking into his blue eyes, she recalled him as a little boy.

Now here you are James, growing up and becoming a young man. I must let you go.

"You remember Jennie Mihelic, Mary's mom?"

"Yes mother."

"I need you to go to her. See if she can give me some of that special broth she makes. I think it would do Janie some good don't you?"

"Are you sure you and Janie will be all right? I know father has been in meetings since we got here."

Smiling, Fiona said. "James, James. I have Robert here if I need anything. Please go. And bring Mary back. It has been too long since we have seen her."

"All right. I'm off but I will return shortly."

He jumped from the porch causing his mother to wonder at the continued exuberance of youth. He quickly told Robert of his mission and Robert's duty to watch over Janie and his mother. After that he ran off to find his horse for the ride down to South Fork.

Mary saw him riding from a distance and ran out to greet him.

"James! What are you doing here? I thought you were in Pittsburgh?"

"I was but Janie was feeling sick and we brought her here for some fresh air. It's working Mary. She is so much better. Mother is too."

"That's great James. But you should have let me know earlier. I could have come up there and helped out."

James hadn't thought to ask her to come. Both he and Mary wondered why?

"I came to see if your mother would have some soup for us to give Janie. She likes it so and well, it might help her get better faster."

"Yes. Come on in. I'll tell momma."

It took awhile for the soup to get warm. James told Mary and Jennie Mihelic the story of Janie's illness and remarkable comeback since being here at the lake. Mrs. Mihelic nodded but remained serious listening to the story. Standing, she patted James on the knee and went to the kitchen to get the hot broth. She placed it in a warm pot and then covered the pot with a tin lid. She then strapped it down with twine to hold it in place. "Now you children take this up there. I will send more in a few days if needed. Hurry now."

But James and Mary didn't hurry. It had been so long since they had talked. They stopped at the spillway and talked of the future and of their dreams. They kissed, softly at first and then with more urgency. Mary pushed away.

"James, now you heard my mother. Let's get this soup to Janie before it gets cold."

"Janie can wait. I can't."

Laughing he chased after her. She leaped onto her horse further amazing him. *How she does that, in a dress and all?*

He picked up the blanket and the broth and mounted his horse. By that time, Mary had climbed the rise and was racing across the breast of the dam. James said out loud.

"So it's a race you want Mary Mihelic. Well it is a race you will get."

Spurring his horse on, he quickly climbed the ridge and rushed across the dam.

Mary turned back laughing at his pursuit. Then she turned to the task of making her horse go faster. James' horse was racing full out now and closing the gap with each stride. They whisked up and past the clubhouse still galloping at a swift pace. James passed Mary at the last minute.

Laughing and winded they tied the horses up. James kissed Mary on the cheek. She gave him a mad look but soon burst out laughing again.

"I let you win Mr. Peyton. I knew if I didn't you would sulk all day."

"Ha! I beat you fair and square Miss Mary."

"James! Where in the hell have you been?"

James turned around to see his father standing in the doorway.

"Mother sent me down to the Mihelic's to get some broth...for Janie."

"While you and her were off gallivanting, Janie took a turn for the worse. Your mother and I had to carry her up the stairs."

"I'm sorry father. What happened to Robert?"

"Robert? What in God's name does Robert have to do with this? You were responsible. But no, you have to go off and play…with her".

With the last statement he pointed at Mary. Her face went white.

James grabbed the blanket containing the pan with the broth off the horse and ran towards his father. He tripped and the lid slipped from the pan as it fell onto the porch, smashing at his father's feet and spraying the hot broth onto the pants of his suit.

"Dammit James! Now look what you have done. Get upstairs will you and take care of your mother. I will have to clean up now."

Mary decided it was better if she went now.

"I can get some more broth and return later Mr. Peyton."

"Huh? No thank you. I think we have had quite enough from you here."

John Peyton said this while still wiping his pants.

"Father, I will say good-bye to Mary and get right upstairs. Is that all right?"

John Peyton had already turned to the door to go into the club-house. He wheeled around and glared at his son.

"Do what you will, but be quick. Your mother needs you now."

The door slammed shut.

"James, I am so sorry. I thought all was going well."

"I did too Mary, I did too."

Mary tried to suppress her anger at Mr. Peyton's words but she couldn't hold back any longer. The memories of past slights welled up in her until she could no longer hold it in.

"I hate your father James, I hate him!"

"What? What do you mean?"

"Nothing James." *Why did I let that slip out? Now is not the time.*

"My father's naturally upset with Janie being sick and all. What's gotten into you Mary?"

Mary looked at James. He was so hurt now. He didn't look at her but continued to wipe up the spilled broth. Under his breath and more to himself he said, "Maybe father was right after all."

Mary couldn't believe what she was hearing. A tear ran down her cheek.

"James," She called out. She wanted to explain further, to tell him why she hated his father, but James didn't wait. He turned and rushed into the clubhouse leaving her standing there. She mounted her horse and slowly rode off towards the breast of the dam and to home. *Maybe papa was right.*

James entered the bedroom quietly. His eyes went from Janie to his mother. Fiona looked up from the bed. She said, "James, oh thank God you are here. Janie is real sick. We need to get her home to Pittsburgh. Can you find your father? Now?"

"Yes mother."

He took another glance at his sister. Only hours earlier she had been sitting up on the porch and full of color. Now she was wheezing and pale as a ghost. He rushed out of the room and headed down the hall to the back steps, which was a faster way to the kitchen.

He almost ran headlong into his father who was talking to Henry Frick.

"Father, mother says we have to go now, back to Pittsburgh."

"Dammit son! I am conducting business. I will be with you shortly."

Henry Frick placed his hand on John Peyton's arm and spoke clearly.

"You go John. Take care of your family. Our business can wait. I'll be back in Pittsburgh early next week. Let's talk then."

"Are you sure Henry? I can stay behind if necessary."

"Yes John. Go now."

The trip back to Pittsburgh was quiet except for Janie's hacking cough and wheezing breathing. Once back there, a new parade of doctors was brought in. More pills, more treatment but no change occurred. Janie Peyton died three days after their return.

Fiona Peyton was devastated. She didn't cry, at least not in front of anyone. She just walked around as if in a trance. James did cry. *If only I hadn't left her. I could have done something, anything?* Would Janie still be alive? It was nonsense but he would not be consoled. John Peyton kept a stoic appearance but you could see the hurt in his eyes.

James thought to write Mary. But each time he started a letter he stopped. *How do I tell her about Janie? We spoke so harshly the last time at the lake. My gosh, I left her there standing at the door. But she had said mean things about my father. Are we through? What if I write and she doesn't respond? Perhaps it is better that this ends now.*

CHAPTER 8

▼

A WILD CARRIAGE RIDE

The time seemed to pass slowly after Janie's death. The Peyton's remained in seclusion and in mourning. Fiona Peyton in particular did not go outside their home in Pittsburgh. John Peyton buried himself in his work but took little solace there as his thoughts kept returning to the daughter he had lost. James was not much better, blaming himself for leaving Janie and his mother when he should have been there to help. He even went so far as to believe Janie would still be living had he been there.

John Peyton was working late in the office when he heard a knock at his door.

"Who is it blast it all? Can't a man get any work done around here?" He arose from his chair, scraping it against the wood floor and answered the door. Henry Clay Frick was standing there. "Oh Henry. I am so sorry. I thought, I mean…"

"Never mind John, I understand." Henry walked into the office. He looked around seeming to search for the right words. "Look John, my family and I are heading up to the lake this Friday. I know we have much to plan and I was hoping that you and your family would join us there. What do you say?"

"I-I don't know what to say Henry. I mean normally I would be glad to go but with Janie gone and all, well, the lake just brings back a lot of bad memories now."

"I understand John, but I really need you there this week. Please arrange your schedule. Thank you." He patted John Peyton's shoulder and walked out of the office still seeming deep in thought.

When John Peyton arrived home that night he debated what to say. He even thought of going to the lake alone and just telling the family it was a business trip. That would be worse, he thought. Not just the lying but being at the lake alone would be awful. *Janie, why did you have to die?*

"Fiona." Having made up his mind, John Peyton called out to his wife who was downstairs sitting in the living room staring straight ahead. She did not respond to his call. Sighing, he left the bedroom and went downstairs to the living room. He walked in there and Fiona instead of turning towards him turned instead towards a table with pictures of happier times for the Peyton family. He walked over to his wife and set his hand on her shoulder.

"Fiona, I have been asked by Henry to make a trip to the lake. I need you and James to come with me." At first it appeared as if she did not hear him, then she responded. "Fine John. When do we leave?"

"Tomorrow. I'll go find James." John Peyton rushed from the living room. *I just don't know what to say to Fiona. How to bring her, all of us, out of this sadness?*

James was outside pitching a ball against the house. The constant bang-bang of the ball first hitting the house and then bouncing on the ground seemed to drown out the thoughts that kept pounding in his head. "Ah there you are. James we are going to the lake tomorrow. I have business and it will do both your mother and you good."

"Why father? Why can't you go and mother and I remain here? I don't want ever to go to the lake again."

John Peyton's face reddened. He struggled to remain calm. "Son I realize it will be hard this first time, but my business interests require me there. I am treasurer of our club and we must plan for the summer activities plus Henry and I need to get with Andrew on a new steel initiative." James Peyton looked at his father. "All right father. Let me go help mother prepare our bags."

John Peyton stood outside awhile longer. *Was this trip a good idea after all? Couldn't Frick and his business been better conducted there, in Pittsburgh? We just need more time.*

The train trip was quiet. John Peyton offered to stop off at Johnstown for some shopping but both Fiona and James declined. In days past, both would have leaped at the offer. When the train pulled into the South Fork station, its wheels slowing to a stop seemed to take forever. Fortunately, Colonel Unger had seen to it that a carriage was placed there to take them on the trip up to the clubhouse.

The day itself was dreary as rain fell in a steady drizzle. The carriage almost got stuck in some mud as it climbed the hill to cross the dam's breast. John Peyton looked out on the face of the dam and saw some leaks springing up through the mud. *Crap! More leaks! It seems each year we get new ones. Our budget is so tight now but I had better have someone see if we can get to those patches earlier this year. Maybe we can get some good rocks to clog up the holes for now. Until we get the Annex completed, we won't be able to afford a real cleanup.*

As the clubhouse came into view, Fiona squeezed John's hand tightly. James was facing his parents in the carriage and looking back towards the lake. He looked into their faces now looking to see any blame they might feel towards him.

John Peyton jumped out of the carriage first. He stretched and looked up at the clubhouse, wondering if Henry Frick was there yet. James was next out. Seeing the mud he turned back to the carriage as his mother stepped down.

"Mother, take it easy now. Let me help you." James Peyton eased his mother down from the carriage.

"Thank you son. You are such a dear. I do not know what I would have done without you these past weeks."

"James, get the luggage and let's get in and get settled."

"All right. I just want to make sure mother is settled first."

"Huh? Yes. Of course."

James led his mother up the stairs of the Clubhouse. She leaned on him even more heavily.

"Now James go and help your father with that luggage or else he will try to bring it all in at one time." Shaking her head, she went into the quiet room of the clubhouse. James jumped the three steps of the clubhouse porch and ran to his father who was indeed trying to carry the luggage in one trip.

"Here Father, let me help you."

"Thanks son. I could have made it but it would have been hard."

"Yes father."

"What has gotten into you boy? You seem preoccupied lately?"

"I don't know father. I just can't seem to understand why Janie had to die? It seems so wrong."

"I know son but we have to go on. We need to. Perhaps this time at the lake will help us all."

"Perhaps father. It is good to be away from all that smog and soot and all."

"Hey now, you be careful about that smog and soot. That, son, is progress, steel progress. The country is growing and steel will lead the way. Now let's get these things in!"

Fiona Peyton walked inside the Clubhouse. She was startled to see someone else there. A man was standing by the fireplace gazing in at the burnt wood lying there. She debated going back out to her husband when the man turned to face her. It was Henry Clay Frick. His gaze, always so intense, seemed to pierce Fiona even more this day. She had hoped to be alone for a while. Now she had to face someone with her grief.

"Good day Mrs. Peyton."

"Hello Mr. Frick."

He seemed oddly awkward before her, and it surprised her, for Henry Clay Frick was not one to be ill at ease in most situations. The silence between the two was deafening.

"I am sorry to hear of your loss Fiona."

The words came out in a rush. He made a move as if to hug her but then turned and headed for the door. He burst out onto the porch and walked past James and John down to the lake's edge. There he stared out over the lake once again lost in his thoughts.

Fiona stood there in the middle of the main room in the Clubhouse wondering at Henry Clay Frick's words and manners.

He was always so distant, so aloof. Today I sensed something different. Perhaps I have been too quick to judge this man. Perhaps.

Fiona Peyton sat down on one of the stuffed chairs that surrounded the cozy room.

How many happy times have we had here? Yet it seems so empty now. Janie was always so full of energy. She and James would be rushing about by now yelling and fighting but not really. Janie, oh dear Janie, I miss you so. A little fever the doctor said nothing to worry about. Now you are gone. Gone for all times. Will life ever return to me? Do I even deserve it? I must be strong, strong for my family, for James. James, my son, I cannot lose him now. He is all I have. He is so good too. I must let him have some time off to enjoy while he is here too. As much as I enjoy his company, I feel that he may want to see someone else while we are here.

Adelaide Frick, Henry's wife entered the room quietly. She walked up to Fiona who was startled at being caught deep in thought. She wiped the tears from her eyes. Adelaide Frick paused to permit Fiona to gain her composure, and then said, "Fiona, I am so sorry."

Fiona took a deep breath, and then replied, "Thank you Adelaide. I didn't know if this trip was going to be good for us. But now I am sure it will. This lake always has a calming affect on us."

"Henry and I feel the same way. Our daughter, Martha, is sick. We thought some time here at the lake would be good for her."

Fiona Peyton leaped to her feet and hugged Adelaide. It stunned the normally reserved woman, and she backed away. Fiona, her voice choking, grabbed Adelaide's hands in her own, and her voice breaking, she said, "You take care of Martha. Treasure your time with her. You just never know when something will happen."

Fiona started to cry. Adelaide Frick comforted her, now clutching Fiona's hands tightly.

"There my dear, it is going to be fine. Janie is at peace now."

Even as she said this, she whispered a silent prayer that her own Martha's illness would pass. The two women spent the rest of the afternoon reminiscing over their children, the sadness of Janie's death, and Martha's lingering distress. Being able to share their pain and sorrow helped both women, who became close friends that day.

Later that evening, the Peytons gathered in the sitting room. Fiona Peyton sat on the rocker staring out the window. Her talk with Adelaide had given her strength. She decided it was time to help her family now. James Peyton was sitting on the floor reading a book. His thoughts remained conflicted. John Peyton paced the room nervously; wondering what the morrow would bring. He turned to his son.

"James, how about we do some hunting tomorrow? I got a feeling we could get some deer out there and have a good roast? What do you think?" Normally James would have jumped at the chance to go hunting with his father. They always had so much fun. His father had taught him how to stalk the deer, staying downwind so that the deer would not catch the hunter's scent. Looking for telltale signs that a deer had been there and even how long ago. Even more, James liked to trek through the woods just walking and enjoying the sights, sounds, and smells. Nothing like it. However, this time he had no desire to hunt. He had to take care of his mother. He also found himself thinking of Mary. Was it the lake that brought her back to his mind, he wondered? They had to talk. Their last meeting had been when Janie was so sick. Their parting had been intense. Would she even want to see him?

With all these thoughts swirling in his mind James replied, "I don't know father, I think we might just stay around here this time."

"What? Is this James the 'hunter extraordinaire' I am hearing? It will be fun. No more talk now. Tomorrow at dawn we shall track the mighty deer."

"James, go with your father. I will be all right here. I have some knitting and besides I want some quiet time which I shan't be able to get if you two men are lurking around here."

"Alright Mother. We will go hunting. Goodnight mother. Goodnight father."

"Goodnight son."

James bent over and kissed his mother goodnight. He left the sitting room and returned to his bedroom.

"Fiona, I don't know what has gotten into that boy? I am concerned that he is taking Janie's death harder than I had thought. He loves hunting. In the past he would have been jumping at the chance to go out into the woods."

"I know John but things are different now. I suspect he is concerned about me. What with Janie..." Fiona Peyton's voice caught on her daughter's name, but she continued, "Janie being gone, I don't think he feels good leaving me alone."

"You are right as always dear Fiona. Maybe we should not leave you alone. I mean, don't think that I haven't thought..."

John would have continued but Fiona had touched her hand to his lips.

"No John, I know you are worried about us all too. We all must find a way to go on. We can't ever forget our little Janie but we must get on with our lives. I will be fine here. Really. Adelaide Frick and I had a nice time talking today. I am beginning to see her and Henry in a new light."

"Well that is good news. I knew once you got to know them you would see that they are good people."

"Yes they are. Now, you and James go off tomorrow and have some fun."

"Fine, then we shall. I do love you Fiona."

John Peyton leaned down and kissed his wife on the forehead.

"I think I am going to bed now too. Morning comes pretty early. Are you coming my darling?"

"No John. I want to stay up for awhile. I will come along shortly."

"Alright, but do not be too long honey. It still gets a little cold down here. I will poke the fire a bit before I leave."

"Thank you John. Good night."

He walked over to the large fireplace with the intricate patterns woven in its face. He poked the logs lying there until the fire rose up once more crackling loudly and lighting up the room. Placing the poker back in the holder, he walked towards the stairs pausing briefly to look at his wife staring out onto the lake.

"Good night Fiona."

Mary Mihelic was so concerned. She had seen James and his family arrive at the train station, and then leave on the carriage ride to the lake. She had thought of just rushing up to him and telling him she was sorry. But she didn't think that would be proper. *James, is it really over? Did it ever begin?*

The next morning Mary made a decision. *I am going up there, to the lake. I will take some flowers for Mrs. Peyton. I have to know about James. If he doesn't care, then, well then I'll know.* The sun spread its rays out across the lake flickering the water with its trail of hope and joy. Mary had risen earlier to do her chores so that she could get up to the lake, up to James. Still it was mid-morning when she had completed the last feedings.

Those chickens I swear one of these times they are going to knock me down. You would think we didn't ever feed them. If they were patient the whole task would not take that long. Maybe today they sensed that I am in a hurry. Nah. They are just stupid hungry chickens. Now I must clean up and get on up to that lake. I am coming James, ready or not.

James had not even risen yet. Fiona had taken a walk about the lake earlier. She liked to get out there like this, alone, and at peace. She remembered times when she had walked there with Janie. Janie would talk incessantly and continuously interrupt her reveries. Fiona thought of how she had always been so frustrated at Janie then.

Oh, what I would not do dear Janie to have you here with me one more time.

This day was especially spectacular however following the rains of yesterday and Fiona let the suns gentle rays cleanse her soul.

Today is special. I wonder why I feel that way.

She noted a carriage heading for the dam and waved as the Frick's headed back to South Fork. They had told her they were going down to Johnstown for supplies and offered her to come along with them. It would have been nice but she was really looking forward to some peace and quiet. *Still, I am glad that Henry asked John to come here. Hmm, I wonder if he had that planned.* A smile crept over her face. *Yes, Mr. Frick, I am beginning to have a new appreciation of you.*

Fiona returned to the clubhouse and started to prepare breakfast. *Some nice bacon to start the day and some hotcakes too.* She remembered how much Janie had liked hotcakes. Each morning she would set up such a racket until she had her hotcakes. Now John Peyton, he liked his eggs and grits. However, for the children, only hotcakes wo ld do. She started the coffee and got out the plates as John and James came down the stairs.

John was first down. He said, "I smell something delicious. What can it be? Not my favorite grits and eggs?" James was next having leaped down the final three steps to the floor.

"Father, you and your grits and eggs. Me, give me them smooth hotcakes that mother makes so scrumptious."

"Now you two men sit yourselves down. You are about to be served."

"Yummy!"

James Peyton sat down to a large stack of five hotcakes, four strips of bacon and a side of grits.

"There is something about being out in the country like this that really sets a fellow's appetite going."

"Come Fiona, sit down and let's enjoy your wonderful feast."

Smiling at the wonderful table spread before them, the three Peytons sat down to the hearty breakfast. It was good they had come here.

A knock at the front door startled them from their breakfast.

"Now who in blazes can that be? I wonder if it is the Fricks. They might have forgotten something."

"John, I don't believe the Fricks would knock, would they?"

"You're right Fiona. Well then, maybe it is Elias Unger."

Elias was the new president of the club and lived nearby in a farm. He watched over the place during the winter and made sure that trespassers did not stay long nor rob the empty cottages that had arisen there through the years.

"You men sit there. I will see who is at the door."

Fiona swished her skirt and went to answer the door.

Mary stood at the door wondering whether she should knock again or depart.

I don't believe I did this. I am so stupid. They are up here for peace and some privacy. And here I come to interrupt them. I should leave now. Oh, there she is.

"Mary. What a surprise! Come on in. Please."

"Oh, I do not want to interrupt you Mrs. Peyton. I saw you arrive by train and felt I needed to stop by and offer my sympathies. I brought these flowers for you. I-I"

Fiona started to tear up, and then she wiped her eyes with a handkerchief and said, "Thank you Mary. I'm sorry, Janie loved to bring me flowers. That is so sweet. I do appreciate them. Now let me go find a vase to put them in."

She turned to walk away then noticed Mary was not following her. She turned, looking curiously, said, "Mary, don't you want to come in?"

Mary thought about how much she wanted to see James, to really know what he felt. But now so close, she changed her mind. Also, she did not relish another encounter with Mr. Peyton. She said, "I really must go Mrs. Peyton. I have chores waiting to be done down at the farm."

"Wait just one minute please Mary. I know James would want to see you. James!"

Fiona cried out to the kitchen. Mary wondered whether she should run when there he was standing right in front of her.

"Mary! You're here. I mean, hello."

His smile beamed from ear to ear.

Fiona took that as a cue to leave and went back into the clubhouse to find a vase.

"We have so much to talk about Mary. Gosh, I'm so glad you came."

"James. I didn't mean to interrupt your time here. I-I"

For the second time that day, Mary found herself left in mid-sentence.

"Mary, don't go anywhere. Please. Well, unless you wish to follow me into the kitchen. I want to ask mother and father's permission to escort you back."

Before she could respond he had rushed into the kitchen nook area.

"Mother, father, can I take Mary home in the carriage? She walked all this way. It's the least I can do."

John Peyton frowning, said, "Son I thought we were going hunting today? I was really looking forward to our trip."

"Father, we can hunt tomorrow. Please, Mary and I need to talk."

Fiona jumped in before John Peyton could continue.

"Go James, take the carriage and enjoy the day. Please be back for supper at five. And be safe children."

James smiled broadly and dashed from the room saying, "Thanks! I will. Don't worry mother. Father, tomorrow we will hunt like old times."

He grabbed his coat from the rack, latched Mary's arm and they rushed out the door.

"Do you believe that? That girl is certainly brazen. I mean coming up here like that, and acting like she wanted to see us."

"John, she is a sweet girl. And the flowers are so nice." She continued to place flowers in the vase and didn't turn to her husband but added, "They make a nice couple don't you think?"

"No, I don't think so. What kind of talk is that Fiona? I have plans for that boy and they don't include being with some girl from South Fork. I guarantee you that."

Fiona sighed.

"John-John, what am I to do with you? Let them be."

"Well, fine, at least for now. However, James and I need to have a father-son talk here soon enough. He is growing into a man and I want him to start thinking of the responsibilities that go along with becoming a man."

"There is time enough for that talk John. For now, let him be happy and enjoy life."

"Fiona, you are just too soft on him. But that is part of why I love you. Come here my darling."

They kissed passionately. It had been months since they had held each other tightly like this, holding onto each other as if no one else existed in the whole world. Fiona took John's hand and said, "I think it is time we made up the bed, don't you think?"

"Yes." John answered huskily.

"Hey, you don't think James is kissing that girl do you? I mean he had better not be. I mean…"

"John, shush"

With a smile that always excited him, Fiona Peyton led the way up the stairs to make up the bed. His memories of James and of the girl from South Fork were soon forgotten.

James and Mary walked behind the clubhouse and got the carriage. They rode off in direction of the dam. Both were deep in thoughts, James wanting to talk, Mary wondering how to start the conversation. When they crossed the breast of the dam, Mary stopped.

"James, just look out there. Look at that sun and the clouds. The whole valley is fresh with God's glory. Oh, it is meant to be this way, I know."

"Yes. Today is wonderful. Anytime I am with you is wonderful Mary."

Mary placed her hand on James knee lightly.

"James, I am really sorry about Janie. I don't know how I would exist without Grace. Although sometimes she does drive me crazy."

"It does leave a big hole in everything. Mother has been so down. It hurts. She has been a little better since we arrived here but I am beginning to think that nothing will ever be the same."

Mary looked directly at James. For some reason this did not bother him.

"We all change James. We grow, we survive, we move on."

She slid her hand off his knee. James urged the horses forward and they moved back into the woods surrounding the lake.

James guided the horse through a clearing looking for a place to turn around for the trip back. He stopped. "Why Mary, why did Janie have to die?"

"I don't know James. I guess it was God's will."

"God? I don't know if there is a God Mary. How could he let that happen to Janie?"

Mary's expression changed to one of shock. Her hand went to her mouth.

"James Peyton, what are you saying? Of course there is a God. He is watching over us all right now." He looked at Mary sharply, not denying her directly but not acceding to her on this point. Then a smile crossed his lips.

Mary looked into his face and seeing the smile could contain herself no longer. She blurted out, "I really like you James Peyton, I do. I think I may even be falling in love with you."

His eyes lit up at this surprise announcement.

"I love you too. I've wanted to tell you for so long."

She turned serious once more. She wanted to discuss James' father with him again but decided not to bring that up, not now. *Now, I just want to enjoy this moment, this day.*

Still, she wanted to be sure of his affection. Coyly, she asked, "And are you just toying with me Mr. Peyton? Just trying to fool me and make me one of your conquests?"

James' mouth opened wide. He couldn't believe what she was saying. He shook his head negatively and firmly.

"Mary, I love you! I really love you. I haven't said that to anyone before and never will again."

Taking her hand in his, James smiled and said, "Mary Mihelic, I will love you forever and ever, until death us do part."

Mary's face darkened and James was stunned. She said, "Don't say that James, even in jest. No more talk of death, please. And please don't promise me something that perhaps can never be."

James wondered at Mary's statements. *I tell her I love her and she frowns. I will never leave her, ever.*

As if reading his mind Mary continued, "We should just enjoy the time we have together, now, right now."

We are from different worlds James. Even if we care for each other, our parents, our family will not permit it to be. Oh James, I will always love you.

A tear dropped from Mary's eye. James reaches over and brushes it away. They kiss softly and long. James heart pumped madly. They break apart reluctantly both flushed and excited. James finally lets out a long breath and says, "We have talked so much I fear we have possibly gone too far."

"Oh dear," Mary said but she smiles for she knows her way around the woods and figures that James was only being flippant. He was, but for different reasons.

"Hey-yah!"

He whipped the horse and the carriage took off like a cannon ball.

Mary was knocked back on the carriage seat. When she recovered she only smiled and laughed. Both shared the excitement of the speed and the wind.

Faster they raced and faster the wheels spun. James spurred the horse on and the horse responded to the whips and the yells. Faster over the hills and through the woods, the branches hitting the carriage every so often but not slowing it down. Past the Unger farm, how fast were they going did not seem to matter. They only wanted to go faster, to feel more excitement.

James turned and smiled at Mary just as they hit large hump in the road. The carriage became airborne. They seemed suspended in air and the whole world seemed to stop for that brief moment. They sailed on high above the ground. Mary placed her hand high on James' thigh to brace herself for the inevitable landing. Then boom! With loud thumps the wheels hit the ground. James and Mary hit the soft seats hard pushing them down to where the seats touched the wood. James looked at Mary fearing that perhaps he had gone too far. If she was scared, she sure did not show it. She threw her head back and laughed a joyous laugh.

"Wow! That was really exciting," she exclaimed.

This girl is truly special.

She left her hand where she had placed it on his thigh. James slowed the horse down to a walk. They found themselves by the spillway that flowed water away from the dam. Mary slid her hand from James' thigh. He helped Mary down from the carriage and held her hand as they walked through the woods to some rocks near the spillway.

They watched the water pour out and down the spillway. They talked about the carriage ride and the flight through the air, laughing often. James took a blanket he had brought from the carriage and spread it out on the ground. He sat down and motioned for Mary to join him. Mary did so, spreading her dress out as she let herself down.

She looked at James and raised her hand to his face touching him there softly. James reached out and pulled her close to him feeling her breasts against his chest. His heart was pounding now. The heat was welling up inside of him. He kissed her. This time was not like before. This time he was possessed by a sense of urgency and need. He could hardly breathe. He kissed her face, her neck her ear. She responded with her body. Moving in closer and her hand moving through his hair. He moved back to her waiting lips and they met passion with passion. He placed his one hand on her face allowing his elbow to touch, to feel her breast.

Oh, so soft, so giving. I must have you Mary, now, here, forever.

They continued to kiss, their desire growing with each minute.

He let his hand off her face and slowly moved it down to her neck. She had moved her own hand down to the nape of his neck and was softly massaging it there. He moved his hand to cover her breast and felt her body stiffen. She pulled back breaking the embrace.

"I am so sorry James but I can't. I really can't."

"Why Mary? You know that I love you?"

"I think you do. And I think that you think that you do. Oh James just hold me."

James was confused but took Mary into his arms. He held her there but felt the warmth in him grow once more. He moved back and went to kiss her again. She put her fingers to his lips.

"Not now James please. Not now. It isn't right. Then I shall never know."

"Know what Mary? What? I love you. You love me. We shall be together always. What is there to know?"

"James I do love you. Don't you see? If we do something now, then we shall never know whether it is true love or just passion."

"I guess I see. No, I don't doggonit. If you love me and I love you, doesn't that make it right?"

"Let's give it time James. Right now, I want you so bad I could just scream. But let's wait. It's not right."

The passion and the moment had passed. James was bothered that he had pressed so hard for her to commit. It was different for girls he knew, or at least he thought he knew.

There is time however. We have our whole lives together. Always and forever.

James stood up and lifted Mary to her feet. He brushed off the dirt from his clothes and then said, "Well let's be heading back. I have to get you home and get back to the clubhouse before dark. Both our mothers will be worried."

Mary was stunned at the quick change in James' manner. She said, "James, you aren't mad, are you?"

"No, Mary, I love you and I do understand, I guess. It was wrong for me to press you so. I just got so excited, is all."

"So did I you silly bean. So did I." Mary reached over and kissed him gently on the cheek. He smiled wanly.

"You had better watch it me lady else you get me going again."

She returned his smile with that look she always gave. It told him that she just might let him kiss her. It also said, and yes, I might bop you one right on your lips too.

He dropped her off at her home and after a chaste kiss he rode off with the carriage arriving back at the clubhouse around nightfall. Sleep did not come easy for James that night. His mind tossed between Janie, God and Mary.

CHAPTER 9

▼

DIFFERENCES

Mary Mihelic was happy when she got off the carriage. Her thoughts were of James and their time together. *I do love him so. I know he loves me. When will we see each other again dearest?* As she went to open the door to her home it gave way and she came face to face with her father.

"Mary, where have you been?" Even as he asked the question, his eyes went off to the distance and to the departing James Peyton.

"You haven't been out with that Pittsburgh boy again, have you? It is not good, not good I tell you."

"Papa, you don't know James. He is good."

"Good. Ha! Boys like that, they come here for one thing and one thing only. Mary stay away from him. He will only bring trouble to you."

"Oh Papa!"

Mary rushed into her bedroom in the back of the house. Charles Mihelic looked frustrated and shook his head.

Crying into her pillow, Mary reflected on her father's words.

I am so mixed up. Is Papa right? Is James just using me, taking advantage of my feelings for him?

Mary looked up, and caught her reflection in the full-length mirror standing across the room. She stood up to get a better view. She wiped the tears from her eyes. She looked at herself in the mirror and even turned around to look at her own back.

I am pretty. I can see that. No, I am not boastful either! Other boys have told me that! Is that all that attracts James, my beauty? Is that all he wants, a possession, a trophy? I'm so confused. Does he just believe he needs to be with me just because I saved his stupid life? Or does he love me like I love him? Does he care really care, for me? Why is it so difficult? Why can't we just be in love? A knock on the door interrupted Mary's reflections. She wiped the tears from her eyes and straightened up her dress.

"Come in."

"Mary, are you all right?" It was her mother, and Mary breathed a sigh of relief.

"Yes momma, I am fine. I just don't know what is happening to me. It was always so easy for me before, now life seems so complex, so messy."

"I know child. I know. Love can do that to you." Mary was startled at her mother using that phrase.

Did she know something? I haven't told a soul.

"How did you know? I mean…"

"Mary, mothers just know darling. It wasn't too hard to see the symptoms. I think I saw something even back at the dinner with the Peytons. Now, fathers, it takes them some time, some time to adjust to the new order. To him, to Charles, you are still his favorite, his kochanka. He does not want to accept that someone may come into your life and share your heart."

"Momma that would never happen. I mean…"

"I know what you mean Mary, don't worry. I will have a talk with your father. He needs to notice that you are growing up now. You're not a little girl any longer."

"Momma, I'm so confused. I love James, but does he love me? What if Papa is right? What if James is just out to have fun, if you know what I mean?"

Her face reddened at this revelation to her mother. Her mother patted her leg.

"That confusion and the feelings you have are all part of falling in love dear, dear Mary. As to James, you must trust your heart. If he fails you, that is his problem, his loss. However, if you fail to love him, to trust him, even with your very life, then you will lose. For a love only half-given is a love already lost."

"I wish it were easy momma, like you and papa. You just love each other totally. I want that kind of love with James."

"Trust my dear, and go forward without fear. Now get some sleep. I will talk to Papa." Jennie Mihelic kissed her daughter on the cheek and left the room.

The door to the porch squeaked nosily as Jennie Mihelic came out. Charles Mihelic who was sitting on the front porch swing made a mental note to get it fixed, eventually. He puffed on his pipe contentedly.

"Charles Mihelic, I don't know what I am going to do with you!"

"What's the matter woman? I almost jumped out of my skin the way you came through that door."

"You know darn well what's the matter. Mary is in love with that Peyton boy. You hurt her with your words."

"Jennie, I don't mean to hurt Mary. You, Grace, her. You are my gifts from God. Hurt? I want to protect Mary so that she isn't hurt. That boy is no good. The whole family is no good!"

"Charles Mihelic, you know you have no good reason for what you just said! You have seen the boy. He's always nice, respectful of Mary, and of us."

"Ah, there is no talking to you woman. Jumpin jehosaphat! You can't see the nose on your face. They are rich people. We ain't. It's two worlds and a wide gulf, wider than that foolish lake up there separates

us. He wants only one thing from Mary and by all the saints in heaven
I won't let him hurt her that way."

Jennie shook her head.

Charles Mihelic was not going to give way easily on this subject.

She sighed and lowered her voice to a whisper.

"You have no choice now Charles. We both don't. It is Mary's
choice now. We must be there for her and to help her whatever happens."

It was Charles' turn to shake his head.

"Jennie, I can't do it. I can't just stand by and watch that boy take
advantage of my little girl. I just can't."

Jennie Mihelic sat down on the swing beside Charles and laid her
head on his shoulder.

"I understand Charles. But you must. She does love James Peyton
now. That you can't change. You shouldn't interfere."

"Momma, you always know best. I will try. I will try."

The rocking swing creaked on the porch, as both Mihelics became
lost in their own memories of the children, and of their life together.
Charles Mihelic's pipe smoke billowed up in swirls to the sky. The
night was quiet except for the chirping of the crickets and the creaking
swing.

A slight fog had come over Johnstown as two men had left one of
the local taverns and were moving towards their homes. One of the
men is slender with a beard the other is more rotund and shorter. The
slender one turns to his friend and says, "Cyrus, great God almighty,
when are we going to take care of that dam? It's a nuisance and should
be repaired. These last two springs were frightening. The water got so
damn high last spring I was sure that outmoded horse manure covered
pile of shit would give away."

Cyrus Elder looked sternly at his friend John Fulton who had just
spoken.

"But it didn't now did it John? I mean it held up as it has always.
Don't you ever feel like someone calling "wolf"? I wish, for God's sake,

that Dan hadn't given me that membership to the club. I barely use it. Still, the people are nice, friendly and don't mean Johnstown no harm."

"Them Pittsburghers! Ha! They think that a little mud and rocks will cover up the problems of the leaks and seepage. Not only that, they lowered the breast of that dam so that carriages could pass. La-te-dah! They will find out, mark my words Cyrus, they will find out. That dam is going to break and then all hell will let loose."

Cyrus Elder looked at the ground. There was no convincing John Fulton tonight. He was firm in his belief that the dam was not built well, or maintained. Wearily, Cyrus said, "Goodnight John. I will try again and meet with Colonel Unger to see if I can make him see what you are saying."

John Fulton patted his friend on the back.

"Thanks Cyrus, I knew you would help. It wouldn't cost them that much to fix up the dam either. Well, maybe a little more than just sloppin' more mud and rocks, which to date has been their shit ass solution to the problem. Serve them rich bastards right if that dam did break. Who do they think they are anyhow, putting the fine people of Johnstown in grave danger? If you need me to come along just ask."

Cyrus walked into his house holding his head. No matter how much rubbing he did, he couldn't shake off this headache. He nodded hello to his wife, said he wasn't feeling well and went off to bed. His daughter Nannie looked in on him later. Seeing him sleeping she didn't bother him but later asked her mother if her father were sick.

"Nannie, your father experiences many pressures these days. We must support him and help him during this time of trials."

"Yes, mother. I just hate to see him so worried. It isn't like father. I miss his laughter."

Cyrus Elder didn't sleep however.

I talk to John Fulton and I see his logic. I talk to Elias Unger and to John Peyton and I see their logic. Both can't be right, now can they? It does seem that we make too much of the fear of the dam breaking. Damn you

Dan Morrell, why did you have to go off and die like that? I just wish there were a simple answer. Why must it be so damn difficult? Ow. I wish this headache would go away.

Nannie went off to bed, stopping briefly in her father's bedroom to kiss him goodnight. Cyrus pretended to be asleep. After she departed, he thought to himself.

Headache's gone. The miracle of children. Perhaps I do worry too much. That dam is safe.

John Fulton walked into his home weary and down. *Cyrus Elder is a kind gentleman, but he doesn't have the fight in him to make the Pittsburghers listen.*

I wish that I could give them a piece of my mind. I would let them know. Damn vagabonds anyways. Milking our land for their high falutin parties and dances. And what of my fellow friends? Used to be we were all scared of that horseshit pile up on the mountain. Now they laugh at talk of the dam bursting. Every time I come around, they yell "dam's breakin', dam's breakin'". Well I tell you, without repairs that dam will break and then it will be too late. I told them in 81, and I say now in '88. That dam is unsafe by God!

The Fenn household had at last quieted down. John Fenn was a tinner in the town and made a good living with this trade. He and his wife had six children and it took quite sometime to get them all ready for bed. Especially now that Anna Fenn was pregnant with their seventh.

Mrs. Fenn crawled into bed beside her husband, John. It was getting harder to move around now that she was in her sixth month. While she loved all her children, her body was tired.

"John, are you awake? Honey?"

John mumbled and then felt his wife's arm on his shaking him gently. He guessed that he had better talk or he would never get to sleep.

"What is it Anna? I am awake now. Wide awake."

"I've been thinking John, we need to stop making babies. My poor body just can't take it much more."

"All right with me. Seven is enough," he turned hoping to end the conversation there.

His wife shook him hard. "John, I'm not done yet. How do we do that, without breaking God's will?"

"I don't know. Hell, I guess we just don't sleep together."

"Now, you stop that talk, John. I will have no more of it. And no more swearing too!"

"You asked me how and I said how. Good grief woman, what do you want?"

"You are no help John Fenn, no help at all."

John Fenn would have left it at that but then he heard his wife sniffling. He couldn't stand to hear her cry.

She is a good woman and has beared up with a lot of suffering with their ever-growing family.

"Anna, don't cry honey. You know how that hurts me. We'll be fine. Can we help it if you are such a fertile field and we like to cuddle so much? Huh? Can we now?"

Her sniffles stopped at the attention.

"Yes. We must find a way John. I love all of our children and will truly love this one too, but seven is enough."

"Good. Now come here and kiss your big honey bear."

They kissed. John turned over and was back to sleep within seconds. For Anna Fenn it took much longer. The growing baby within her made sleeping at anytime a challenge and she could not keep from thinking about her growing family.

I do love them so. John too. It will be all right, I know. Nevertheless, seven is enough for the love of God. Please don't be sending us another blessing.

"Victor. Victor Heiser! Get in here boy. Time to eat."

Victor jumped down from the hayloft and ran to his home. Time to eat. *I am hungrier than a horse, no a bear.* He growled like a bear and laughed.

I bet I could eat a whole pig right now, no a deer. Yea. A big one too.

"What's for dinner ma?"

"Macaroni and cheese."

"Ugh! No meat, no nothing?"

"It's Friday and you can't eat meat on Friday's."

"Stupid rule! I mean I don't see that on the commandments. No sir."

"Victor, now stop that. Eat the dinner and be grateful for it. It's good food."

Good yuck! What I would do right now for a big juicy blood-red steak. Um umm. Work hard all day and then all I get is this. Bleh.

Victor looked up to see his mother with tears in her eyes. *Criminy, what have I done now.*

"Ma, this is really good. Ya know, you don't think it's going to be good and then it is. Yummy."

His mother smiled. She knew he was fibbing, but it made her happy to know that he cared about her feelings. The rest of the dinner was uneventful and soon Victor prepared for bed.

"Goodnight ma, pa."

"Goodnight Victor. Sleep well."

A few blocks away, the Huffmans prepared for bed also. Ben Huffman walked into the bedroom that his two sons shared.

They look so innocent there, sleeping. During the day, these two can whip up more trouble than anybody. But now, here, calm and peaceful darned if they don't look like two angels. He leaned over and patted each one on the head. *Yes, someday you boys will take over my business. Will and Harry, I've worked hard to build this business up and to establish a reputation for timeliness. I know that youns will do the same for we are all from that same stock, Huffmans.* He walked out of their bedroom smiling. Life was good.

Old man Morley stepped into his back yard and looked at the tattered cord where his dog had once been tied.

You stinkin' old no-account dog you. I'm a'going to have to get rid of you. You keep getting into the neighbors' yards and running into mischief.

I keep getting' hollered at for all the trouble you cause, you dumb mutt. Ain't worth a lick neither.

Just then, the dog returned wagging his tail and almost smiling, if a dog can smile. Morley fixed the dog with a stern look.

"Where you been this time? Messin' up, yea I can tell. Well I'm goin' to have to get rid of you, ya know that?"

The dog rushed up to Mr. Morley knocking him over. He licked his face all over with his tail wagging a mile a minute.

"Stop it. Stop it ya blame fool dog."

The more Mr. Morley yelled the more the dog licked.

"Alright, now. Let's git on in. Looks like it might rain. Come on. I got some of them fixin's you like. Yea. Some nice red meat. Come on."

The dog knew by the tone of his voice that it was good news. Not often did he get into the house. His master must really like him.

Back up far in the mountains, the crickets are chirping and the clubhouse is quiet.

John Peyton is on the porch savoring a fine cigar when he hears voices.

"Ah James, that's pure bullshit and you know it. You shouldn't tie yourself down to one lady now. We are young and there are many delights to explore."

Robert and James approach the porch and recognize John Peyton standing there.

"Good evening sir," Robert nods. James is surprised to see his father and worried at what he might have overheard. He yawns and says, "Hi Father. Good night Robert, I am going to bed."

"Right James, see you tomorrow." Robert snaps his fingers and then points to the lake. It is a familiar sign of his that always brought a smile to James' face.

"We can go sailing and perhaps catch some fish."

He winks indicating an inside joke to his friend as to the particular "fish" that he is talking about catching.

James steals a glance at his father then says, "I can't Robert. Mary and I are going riding tomorrow. I'm sorry." Not waiting for more discussion James rushes off into the clubhouse and up the stairs.

Robert turns to walk off to his parent's cottage down the boardwalk. John Peyton calls after him. "Robert, hold up there."

"What is it Mr. Peyton, sir?"

John Peyton takes a long draw on his cigar. Smiling he says, "Come here Robert. I think we need to talk."

Mary Mihelic sits on her bed tired and ready to sleep but her mind still in turmoil.

James, I love you so. We shall be happy, that I know. When you kiss me, I almost cannot stand it. I feel so warm all over. What about our parents? They must know. They must accept that we are destined for each other. Please dear God help us with this problem.

Mary was now ready for sleep. She yawned and proceeded to dress for bed. Just as she finished, she heard a sharp knock at the door. Mary went to the door and opened it.

"Papa?"

"Mary. I've been doin' some thinking."

There was a long silence. Mary was dreading another lecture on the evils of being rich. Nevertheless she was more worried because she had never seen her father so stressed over talking. She had to smile.

Not papa, if he had something to say, well most times he would just say it.

Charles Mihelic ran his hand over his chin slowly as if collecting his thoughts.

"I've been thinking and well maybe I am wrong about, well about that Peyton boy. He seems good enough I guess."

"Oh Papa! Papa. You can't believe how happy that makes me feel."

She leaped off the bed and hugged her father and then kissed him on the cheek.

"Now now. Be still, I said I guess. We'll have to wait and see. You be careful just the same."

"Papa, I will, oh don't worry. I'm your daughter after all. But oh papa he is so good, you'll see."

"I guess. Goodnight my kochanka. Pleasant dreams."

He took hold of her shoulders and kissed her cheek, then retreated from the room. Mary climbed under the covers and pulled them up close.

Now I know it will all be well. Oh thank you God for making me happy. Mary Peyton. Mary Mihelic Peyton. Ahem, Mrs. Mary Peyton. Together for now and forever. I can't wait to see you my dear darling James.

Her mind drifted back to Mr. Peyton and his opposition to James and her being together. *I just won't think of that now. Besides, he will change too. How can he not, knowing how James and I love each other?*

CHAPTER 10

▼

THE INVITATIONS

Mary and James were inseparable over the next several days. They went sailing on the lake, talked of the future and reminisced of their earlier meetings. They kissed often finding it harder to keep their passions in check.

One day after sailing they walked across the breast of the dam and headed for Elias Unger's house to borrow a carriage for a picnic down by the spillway. James kissed her as they crossed the bridge over the spillway.

"James! This is not the time for that."

"I don't care. Mary Mihelic, I love you!"

She had to laugh at his sweet statement. Still smiling she said, "And I bet you tell all the girls that Mr. Peyton."

"No. I don't. Only you."

She laughed again then said, "That was a good answer Mr. Peyton. I believe that I may let you live for awhile longer as my eternal slave."

James laughed at her bringing up their old joke and then tried to grab her but she was off and running.

"Hey! What are you doing?" he yelled and then bolted after her.

"I'm running away from you, you silly bean. And you can't catch me."

Laughing she raced up the hill to the Unger's farm. James was gaining on her but she held her own even while holding her dress up to free her legs to run. He caught her just before the barn. They both fell when he crashed into her and they went rolling back down the hill's gentle slope. Her dress flopped up revealing a white petticoat underneath. She struggled to gain her balance while also pushing down the reluctant dress.

"James, someone may be watching you silly goose." Even as she said this, they rolled further down the hill.

"I don't care who sees us Miss Mary Mihelic. I want the world to know that you are mine and I am yours."

Mary finally stopped rolling and sat on the ground with her knees up under her body. James stood up, dusted himself off and yelled while pointing down to the still sitting Mary.

"World here is Mary, Mary Mihelic, and I love her!"

"James! Now stop that. You're quite embarrassing."

Still, Mary found herself smiling at the words and at the bravado of James.

"Now shush. Give me a hand here and help me up."

He grabbed her hand and brought her to her feet gently. He was about to steal another kiss when she blocked him and gave him a stare that said stop. The she relented, smiled and said, "Let's get to that carriage and our picnic before the day is gone. Come slave, bring me my carriage."

Mary pointed off in the direction of the barn and looked at James with the haughty mannerisms of someone born to wealth. She held out her hand for him to take.

James bowed deeply and ceremoniously.

"But of course me lady, right away. But first."

James put his arms around Mary, looked into her soft eyes and kissed her lips. He wondered if Mary could feel what he felt when their lips touched. It was like lightning charging from her to him. Her body was so soft and seemed to meet his as if they were one.

Mary pulled away. "Let's get to that carriage. We should not be out here kissing. I am sure Colonel Unger or his wife will see us. Come."

James reluctantly followed Mary. *There is always time.* He got out the fine carriage and hitched up the large horse to pull it.

The trip to the spillway was quick. They parked the horse and walked over to the gentle rocks and rolling water. James helped Mary as they leaped across some rocks to a shady spot on the other side. Mary spread out a blanket and they sat down. The afternoon passed all too quickly. James kissed Mary. She kissed him back. They embraced tightly, and the world seemed to pass away.

Suddenly, Mary pulled back. Breathlessly, she said, "I think we had better go James. I have to get home before dark." James inhaled slowly and willed his heart to stop thumping so wildly. Then he smiled, "Mary, I almost forgot. Will you come to the Regatta and the dance with me?"

Mary paused for a brief second as James' words sunk in. *The Regatta, how often she had thought of that event. Now she would get to see it from the other side of the lake.* Her thoughts turned back to the time when Mr. Peyton had chased her and her family away. Mary frowned. James taken aback said, "Mary, what is wrong? I thought you would want to come. It is a great event." Mary hugged James.

"Oh James, of course I will come. We'll have a wonderful time, I'm sure."

Laughing once more, they packed up and hurried to the carriage. Try as she might Mary could not shake a foreboding about the coming event.

The next morning Mary walked with a light step across the dam's breast. She and James had made plans for another picnic today. The sun was shining across the lake flickering its beams across the still water. Mary stopped to gaze at the lake and wonder at its beauty. She then spun around embracing herself.

I'm in love. I wasn't sure before, but now I am. Nothing will stop us. Oh James, I can't wait to be your wife.

Mary stopped quickly and looked around. Blushing that someone might have seen her, she rushed on across the dam and headed towards the clubhouse.

Reaching the clubhouse she found she was still uncomfortable with the people and this place. Where was James? He always eased her feelings of concern. She climbed the stairs to the porch.

The door to the clubhouse entrance swung open and a surprised Mary stepped back. Fiona Peyton, also surprised, stopped abruptly.

"Goodness Mary, I am so sorry. I almost knocked you down."

"It's alright Mrs. Peyton, I wasn't looking where I was going. Lost in my thoughts I guess. Is James around?"

"Oh Mary, He left with his father to go hunting. I'm so sorry."

Mary looked stunned. *Did James forget?*

Fiona's face brightened. "Mary, perhaps it is best they are gone. Please let's sit down on the glider here."

Fiona pointed to the green glider resting on the clubhouse porch. Mary moved to the glider slowly but was wishing she could just leave. The place definitely made her nervous.

Both ladies sat down. The glider squeaks as they rock slowly. Fiona Peyton smiled at the young girl sitting next to her. The low chirps of the crickets in the background mix in with the glider's creaking gears to make a gentle symphony. Fiona breaks the silence as she turns to Mary and says, "I need your help. I have been named chairwoman of the upcoming Regatta Dance. James told me he had invited you to go. Could you help me out in the planning and decorating? You have such good ideas and it would give you a chance to meet some of the other people around here." *And it would give me a chance to get to know you better too!*

Mary was shocked. She had been worried about James' feelings and here was his mother asking her to help out. Mary tried not to let the surprise show on her face. "I would be happy to Mrs. Peyton."

Fiona Peyton jumped up from the glider and patted Mary's knee.

"Well that's settled. Good. Let's go in and see what we can get done quickly while the men are in the woods."

They moved into the clubhouse, walking through the billiard room and into the main meeting room. "Now here is where the dancing will be," Fiona said. "Over there in that corner, we can place the band." She placed her hand on her chin thinking of the organization needed to make this event the best ever.

Mary followed Fiona around, seeing where the tables would be set for the dinner. The kitchen was in the back, through a narrow hallway. They talked of the decorations and Mary noted how streamers would look dazzling off the high ceilings.

The morning passed quickly. Mary had hoped that James would return, but got so caught up in the decorations that she soon forgot about their plans. Mrs. Peyton was so nice and so open to her ideas and thoughts. About two o'clock, Fiona asked Mary whether they should take a trip to Johnstown to see if they could pick up some of the supplies. Mary said, "I'll go Mrs. Peyton. That way you can work here and get the grounds people set up."

Fiona smiled, "Why thank you Mary. That is kind of you. Let's get that list together."

They talked and got a list together of things to buy. "Here's some money to handle the costs. This dance will be the best one yet, with us involved." Fiona left out a hearty laugh. It had been a long time since she had even smiled.

Mary prepared to go. "I'll bring these up tomorrow Mrs. Peyton, when I come to see James." Fiona nodded her head, "That will be fine my dear. Thank you so much for a lovely day!"

Mary smiled and said, "You're welcome Mrs. Peyton! But really, it's I that should be thankful. I feel so much better about this place than I had." Fiona looked at Mary with surprise. *How could anyone feel nervous at this place? It is so homey.*

With that, Mary made sure she had the list and started to walk towards the dam when Fiona Peyton called out to her. "Wait Mary. Didn't you bring a carriage?"

Mary looked sheepish and said, "No. We only have one carriage and Papa and Momma were visiting friends today."

"Well, we can't have you walking down to South Fork, goodness the day will be gone by the time you get to Johnstown. Here, let's go to the barn out back and get you a carriage."

Mary followed Fiona to the barn and they found a stable boy there to get a carriage.

After the horse was attached to the carriage, the stable boy inquired, "Ma'am, you sure you want her to have this carriage?" Fiona's stern look told the boy all he needed to know, although Mary had taken note of the slight. She grabbed the reins and took off, thanking Mrs. Peyton once more for the nice day.

The trip to Johnstown was pleasant and the shopping exciting. She made sure to bargain hard for prices and felt that she had saved Mrs. Peyton and the club some considerable amount of money. She couldn't wait for the next day when she could deliver the goods to Mrs. Peyton and see James.

As she rode up the path towards home a rider emerged from the opposite direction. At first Mary thought it was James. But as the rider neared, she saw it was James' friend Robert. She thought of turning off onto the road to down town South Fork and avoid a meeting with Robert but then decided to go on. *I am no longer going to shy away from these people. If James and I are to be together, I will need to meet with his friends.*

She had decided to wave to Robert and continue past him when he pulled in front of the carriage and blocked her way. He hopped down from his horse and walked up to Mary.

"Good evening Mary," he said tipping his hat to her.

"Good evening Robert," she replied, "Could you please move your horse so that I may continue home. It is getting quite late."

"Yes, yes it is, isn't it? Did you see James today?" He asked.

"No, I was busy and I guess so was he, with his father."

"Oh, so that's what he told you," Robert said with a smirk.

"No, James didn't say that at all," Mary quickly replied. Then with a note of superiority, she added, "His mother did."

"Dear dear me," Robert said shaking his head negatively.

"It does appear that I shall have to enlighten this sad child."

Mary was growing more annoyed at Robert and this conversation. She jumped down from the carriage intending to move Robert's horse from her path. He grabbed her arm. She cried out, instantly recalling the last time he had grabbed her.

Robert noticed her pain and said, "Wait, just a minute Mary, please."

She looked at her arm where his hand still held her. He dropped it to his side but offered no apology. She rolled her eyes but did not move.

"Look, I probably shouldn't be the one to tell you this, being James' friend and all. But he is using you."

Mary snapped back, "Using me! How dare you!"

"Wait, listen," Robert continued. "He isn't what you think. I know many is the girl he has stolen from me."

It was Mary's turn to shake her head negatively. "Come on Robert, and I am supposed to believe you?"

"No, but it is true he didn't leave you a note or any other message today did he?"

She paused remembering her surprise when James was not at the clubhouse earlier today.

Robert continued, "He's been going with Hope Wilson now for over a year. He told me he was going to have fun with the, as he calls you, 'the little South Fork girl' for this summer."

"I don't believe you Robert. James isn't that way."

"Fine, don't. Suit yourself. But don't tell me about James. He is so smooth. You would not be the first little lady to fall for his charms."

At this Robert laughed. He continued. "James never got over that lake deal. I guess he felt he had to make up for it by seducing you."

Mary growing increasingly tired of this conversation said, "That is absurd Robert, now please may I go."

"Sure. But since you don't believe me, I guess I shall have to offer proof."

Robert paused to make sure he had Mary's attention. She had stopped at the carriage with her back to Robert. Over her shoulder, she asked, "Proof? Please Robert, just go."

Robert moved to his horse but held fast there. She turned to face him once more. He smiled seeing her interest, "Yes proof. Go to the breast of the dam around nine am tomorrow. You can hide in that copse of trees close by. James and Hope will be taking a morning ride about then. You can confront him right there if you wish."

Robert mounted his horse and looked into Mary's eyes. He saw some concern and some doubt. It quickly vanished. She moved her hand to her hip and said, "I know James and I know what he and I have together." Mary stuck out her chin as she said this, looking straight at Robert with haughty disdain.

He shrugged and tipped his hat. "Sure, sure, nine am, be there and see for yourself."

"I have no intention," Mary started to say, but Robert rode off clipping his horse with his heels to speed away before she could finish.

I don't know why I even listened to him. I hate him. James would not lie to me. We can't have kissed and talked like we have. No, I refuse to believe it! It's all lies.

CHAPTER II

▼

DOUBT CASTS ITS SHADOW

That night Mary didn't sleep easily. She kept going over Robert's words of evil and James' words of love. *It isn't possible. Yet James seemed nervous when I would be at the clubhouse. No, he invited me to the Regatta! Papa said I should watch myself. Was he right? Was I just a game? No! And I am not going up to the lake tomorrow. I don't have to spy on him. That's it.*

Grace was up before Mary and sitting at the table when Mary came into the kitchen. "Good morning sleepy head." She crowed and after seeing her mother was not looking stuck her tongue out at her older sister. Mary gave her a stern look. Grace smiled and decided to dig a little deeper. Impersonating a high society nasal twang, she said, "Oh Mary." Drawing out the 'Mary', she continued, "When you marry that rich boy up at the lake, will you let me live with you in Pittsburgh?" She placed her index finger to her cheek as she said this last sentence. Mary turned red and said; "Don't you bother me you little insect. I won't live in Pittsburgh and I am not even sure I will marry "that boy".

Grace should have left it alone but continued to needle her older sister. "Mary loves James Peyton! And he doesn't love her!"

Mary reached over and slapped her sister hard on the face. Grace was surprised, as her sister had never raised a hand to her. At first she just sat there stunned, then crying she ran to her room. Jennie Mihelic was also shocked. She turned to Mary and said, "What has gotten into you child? You don't ever hit your sister like that! Mary, what is the matter?" Mary was angry and nothing could change her at this time. She ran to the kitchen door and out down the back steps with her mother calling after her.

Jennie Mihelic stood on the porch and watched as Mary Mihelic headed off in the direction of the lake. *What got into her? She will definitely be punished for that little episode. If being with James Peyton is going to change my daughter, well then, it will stop. Perhaps Charles was right. Oh dear.*

Mary stomped off in the general direction of the lake figuring to cool off before heading back to apologize to her sister and her mother. She was still mad as she neared the breast of the dam. *Stupid Grace! What does she know anyway? I hate her. I hate everyone!* She looked up to see a carriage coming across the breast of the dam. *Could it be James…and Hope? Well, I don't care. I am just going to stand here and wave as they go bye.* But she didn't. She hid in the small copse of trees off the main path and awaited the carriage's passing.

She didn't have long to wait. A carriage came by moving slowly due to the steep incline at that point. Mary saw right into the carriage. There was James and next to him sitting very close was a lady that she presumed was Hope Wilson! She is beautiful. As the carriage neared it came to a stop. She strained to hear the voices but was too far and they talked in low voices. Like lovers she found herself thinking.

I have to go. I can ask James later. I am sure he will have a good reason…

She stopped suddenly as she saw Hope lean over and kiss James on the lips. Mary started towards the clearing then stopped again waiting for the embrace to end. She could stand it no more. Mary turned on her heels and left quietly through the trees and shrubs to near the spill-way. *This is where we first embraced.* Mary sat there and cried for hours.

James dropped Hope off at the train station in South Fork and headed back towards the clubhouse. He stopped at Mary's place hoping to see her and wondered at the strange reception. Mrs. Mihelic, usually so open and friendly was cold and distant.

"I don't know where Mary is Mr. Peyton and she is in trouble with me in any case."

He pondered waiting there for Mary to return or of inquiring of Mrs. Mihelic what the issue was with Mary. Judging from Mrs. Mihelic's tone of voice, he figured it was best to move on. "Thank you Mrs. Mihelic. Please tell Mary that I stopped bye and will see her tomorrow." Jennie Mihelic nodded her head and turned to go back into the house. James waited there on the steps for a minute then decided to go. He got back in the carriage for the ride up to the clubhouse. *Sometimes I don't understand these people. Mary and I need to talk.*

Just as he cleared the home setting and turned towards the lake, Mary returned, still in a daze at the way the events had transpired. Jennie Mihelic saw her through the window and came out to confront her. "Mary! Where have you been child? I almost sent your papa out to find you." Mary looked up at her mother; her tear stained face showing more than words how she was feeling. "Mother, I am sorry I hit Grace and ran off. I'm sorry. Really sorry."

She ran up to her mother and embraced her. Her mother held her close and patted her hair. "There there Mary. I know you are sorry. But you must apologize to Grace and you must be punished. You will do Grace's chores for a week, that should give you some time to think about respect for your family." Jennie Mihelic expected some sort of complaint from Mary but heard none. Instead Mary said, "All right momma. I will do as you say." She pulled away from her mother and not looking at her but rather at the kitchen door, she climbed the steps stumbling slightly. Jennie Mihelic called after her, "Your boyfriend,

James Peyton stopped by to see you." Mary paused, not turning around but answered her mother with a question, "He did?" Then she continued into the house.

Was James coming to tell me more lies, or maybe to explain? Oh my goodness, I completely forgot Mrs. Peyton's goods. Well Mr. James Peyton, maybe we will see what you have to say. Does it really matter? We are so different. I see that now.

Mary walked to the back of the house to where Grace's bedroom was. The door was shut. Mary knocked and Grace responded, "Who is it?"

"Mary."

"Mary who?" Grace replied.

"All right, I deserve that Grace," Mary spoke through the closed door. She continued, "Look, I'm sorry I hit you. I've been having a lot of problems lately."

The door opened, but Grace retreated immediately back to her bed.

"That hurt Mary. You never hit me before, ever."

"And I never will again Grace. Mamma says I have to do your chores for a week, but I would have offered anyways. Friends?" Mary extended her hand to her sister who eyed it warily. Then with a leap she jumped up into Mary's arms, startling her. Grace said, "I love you Mary. You are the best big sister ever!" Mary smiled, and replied, "And you Grace, you're the best little sister anyone could ask for."

Grace released her tight grip on her sister. "Mary, let's play house like we used to, remember? We were going to be rich and have servants waiting on us and all."

Mary nodded at the memory. *Children's dreams, that's all it was.* Turning back to her sister, she said, "I can't Grace, not now. I have to go up to the lake, to see Mrs. Peyton." Grace started to throw out a tease but thought the better of it. She said, "All right, but maybe later, when you return?"

"Yes Grace, maybe later, when I return."

Mary got the goods from the icehouse where she had placed the perishables. The cold air made her shiver. She thought back to the incident in the winter by the lake. *Why can't we just be in love? Why do the rich people think us so different? Are we?* She shook herself back to the reality and finished her packing the carriage. With a sigh, she looked up to the lake and began the journey. *Well at least I will have time to think for it is a nice ride to the clubhouse.*

As she neared her destination, she crept slower and slower. Finally, the horse looked around at her thinking she wanted to stop. "Giddyap! This is ridiculous. What happens happens." With that, she whipped the horse and shortly reached the large and for her foreboding clubhouse.

Mary tied up the horse and grabbed two hands of the goods and started up the porch's side steps. A lady came around the side and appeared lost in thought. Seeing Mary she smiled and said, "Are you the new cook? I certainly hope so. The food around here lately has been so dreadful." Mary gritted her teeth. "No, I am not the new 'cook', or the old cook for that matter. I am here to see James Peyton."

"Oh dear me, I am so sorry my dear. I just saw you carrying that food and well I thought…"

"It's quite all right. I understand. Now if you will excuse me."

"Oh wait. I saw James Peyton earlier. He was with Robert. They went out on the lake, sailing I believe. Probably getting ready for the Regatta. Oh how I love the Regatta." The woman stopped and thought back on past Regatta's. Mary looked out to the lake hoping to see James. She saw a sailboat off in some distance and moving away. *Is Hope in there also? Perhaps it is best I don't see him right now.* To the lady she said, "Thank you. Can you tell me where I might find Mrs. Peyton?"

"My yes. She is in the sitting room just inside that door there."

Mary breathed in, thanked the lady for her help and moved to the door where the woman had pointed.

Opening the door, Mary spotted Fiona immediately. She was speaking to another lady in an animated conversation. Mary strained to hear but could not so she walked up to Fiona whose back was to her. Fiona Peyton swung around as she approached and smiled widely. "Mary, Mary Mihelic. Hello. I can see you have the goods we ordered. Let's get to planning. Oh Mary, this is…" Fiona turned back to see her friend had departed up the stairs. "Never mind, she is not important, now let's get those decorations and food off of your carriage. Wait here while I go get someone from the kitchen help."

"There's no need to do that. I can get it down. Please wait here."

Fiona looked at Mary with surprise. *Men should do these things. I shall have to work more with Miss Mary. But there is time. Always time.*

Mary returned with two large loads of goods, streamers, horns and candies. "Only one more load," she called out as she went back to the carriage. Fiona nervously twisted her handkerchief. When Mary returned she let out a sigh of relief. "Now, come here Mary. What do you think about this?" She showed a drawing of the room with the streamers hanging from the top; the tables all decorated in resplendent blues, reds and whites. Mary looked at the drawing and at the room. A long silence ensued. Mary finally spoke up. "Mrs. Peyton, I am sorry but I must beg off. I can't help you anymore this year."

Fiona Peyton looked up from the drawing. "Why Mary? We've just begun. If you like something different with the decorations…" She would have continued but Mary was shaking her head in the negative and waving her hands to interrupt. "No. No, the decorations look beautiful. I am sure it will be quite beautiful. It's just…it's just that my sister, she is sick right now and Mamma and Papa are so busy…"

Fiona stopped her. "Please say no more. I recall my dear Janie's time. Oh, I hope it isn't like that."

"No, it isn't, not at all. She is just under the weather but with all that's going on, I must take care of her."

Fiona Peyton placed her arm around Mary Mihelic. "And so you must. We can do this again next year, but I do hope we shall be seeing more of you around here."

Mary stiffened for a small second but then relaxed. "I'm not sure Mrs. Peyton. Do you have some paper, I need to write James a note?"

Fiona Peyton tore off a sheet from the drawing pad she had used for the planning of the room. "Here you can use this. I'll go get an envelope from the study. But why don't you just wait a bit. I'm sure James will be back shortly."

"No, thank you Mrs. Peyton. I would but I must get back, you know, to Grace."

"Of course, please sit here, while I find that envelope." Fiona Peyton rushed off to find the envelope and Mary sat down to write. She watched as Fiona moved off. *Oh, I shall have to go to confession now, for lying to her. But it is better this way. Until I know what is up with James, and us, it is better for me not to be here. She is so nice, but enough.*

By the time Fiona returned Mary had completed the short note. She stuffed it in the envelope and handed it to Mrs. Peyton. "Here. Will you make sure this gets to James?"

"I will. Here, take this bracelet for Grace. It's nothing much, Janie used to wear it. Please."

Mary looked at the bracelet feeling once more guilty for having to lie. "I'll make sure she gets it Mrs. Peyton, thank you."

Mary Mihelic wanted to tell Mrs. Peyton more. *Maybe I should just ask her. She would tell me, I am sure. I can talk to her. See what she thinks. Yes, that's it.*

"Mrs. Peyton…" Boom. The door from the billiard room had opened and in entered John Peyton. He looked at Mary Mihelic and said, "What are you doing here?"

Fiona's face lit up with surprise once more. "John! Please. Mary is my guest. She was helping me with the planning, for the Regatta. Alas, Grace, her sister is sick, so now she can't help me. Mary, you were saying?"

"Nothing Mrs. Peyton. It was nothing. I had better be going. Thank you for letting me help." Fiona Peyton smiled once more and walked Mary to the door.

"Don't you worry Mary, it will all turn out all right. It will."

She hugged Mary and watched as the young girl walked down the boardwalk away from the clubhouse. Fiona looked out on the lake but could not see James' boat anywhere. *That boy had better get home soon. It will be dark and I am sure he wants to read this note.*

Fiona Peyton now turned to her husband John. "John Peyton. You mustn't be so rude in the future. After all, that young lady could well end up being your daughter-in-law."

John's face turned red. "I wouldn't be so sure about that my dear. I see it as a passing fancy, nothing more. She is quite a beauty I must say."

"She is much more than that John. You really should get to know her, and her family better."

John looked out to the lake, then turned back to face Fiona. "Perhaps, perhaps. Well, why I came in here is to tell you we must go back to Pittsburgh early tomorrow. Henry Frick and I are meeting with Andrew on an expansion of the plants. It'll be tight but if we catch that first train I can make it."

"John. How am I to get this planning done? We have only one week to go."

"I don't know for God's sake. Let someone else handle it. I'm not sure if we can even make it back for the Regatta."

Fiona looked at her husband. She knew that the strain of business was telling on him. He loved the Regatta as much as she did.

"All right John. I can get someone to finish up the planning. I'll go pack."

John Peyton kissed his wife on the cheek. "Thank you Fiona. I love you."

"I love you too John." Her dress swished ever so lightly as she walked up the stairs to the second floor.

James Peyton arrived back at the clubhouse late. He and Robert had sailed almost the entire lake. Practicing for the upcoming Regatta race but also enjoying the summer breeze and sailing over the clear calm surface of Lake Conemaugh. He paused outside his parents' room and thought about knocking and going in. *Nah, they're probably asleep and I need to get some shuteye myself.*

He entered his room and an envelope on the floor caught his attention. Next to it was another small note from his mother. He read the note from his mother first.

James, Mary left this note for you when she was here today. I asked her to wait but she declined. Love, Mother.

James smelled the envelope from Mary. Her scent remained on it. *How fragrant. I wish I hadn't missed her.* He read the contents and his smile quickly turned to a frown.

> Dearest James,
>
> I write to you because I fear that we shall no longer be able to see each other. So much has changed, is different. We are different. I will not be able to go to the Regatta with you. I hope you understand.
> Please meet me tomorrow at 9am, at our place by the spillway if you desire to know more. I'll be waiting. If you don't come, I will understand.
>
> Mary

What does she mean? If I don't come? Wild horses couldn't stop me. What happened to change her? Did I do something wrong? Has she found another? Nonsense.

James couldn't sleep that evening, his mind swirled with thoughts, words he might say, and words she might say. He awoke to a large pounding noise on his door. *My gosh, what time is it? It's still dark out?*

John Peyton entered the room.

"James, get packed. Where were you last night for God's sake? We're going back to Pittsburgh now. Hurry." His father turned to leave the room. James called after him, "Wait father. I can't go, not now. I have to talk to Mary. It's really important."

"Well I'm sorry son, but that'll have to wait until the next time we are back here. Please hurry now." He rushed from the room leaving a perplexed James sitting upright in his bed.

He leapt up and got dressed hastily but he didn't start to pack. He rushed over to his parents' room and entered as the door was ajar. His mother sat there on a chair looking out at the moon shining on the lake. "What is it James?" She inquired as he entered. "Mother," He replied, "Father has to go back to Pittsburgh but I've got to see Mary. It's important I do. That's what her note said. I was to meet her down by the spillway. Fiona pondered her son's words then replied in measured tones. "James, it's important for us to go with your father at this time. You can leave Mary a note of your own with Robert. I am sure he will deliver it for you." Her calming tone didn't settle down James. By now he was beside himself. "I'll go now and you can pick me up there."

"Are we ready to leave?" His father had returned to the room and started to pick up the bags. "James, did you get packed? Hurry now. We are leaving as soon as you are ready. Be quick!" James eyes darted from his father to his mother and then to the lake outside. He bolted towards the door. His father reached out and grabbed him by the collar as if expecting such a move. "Hold on there. I said be quick, not suicidal. Here help me with these bags. We can come back for your things after we get these on the carriage."

"I...I'm not going. I'm going to the spillway. I'm meeting Mary there."

"What? Get your backside over here young man. Where have you learned this disrespect, from that country girl? Now grab those bags and follow me." James stood stock still for a moment, then reached down, grabbed the bags and started to load the carriage. He moved swiftly and packed in an even more rush. He then wrote a quick note of apology to Mary promising his love and to return as soon as possible.

James ran back downstairs and found Robert in the billiard room shooting pool.

"Well James, care to take me up on a game of 9-ball? I dare say I could use a challenge."

James looked at the pool table and once more considered a rush out the door. Instead he extended the sealed note in his hand to Robert. "Here, will you please get this to Mary later this morning, no later than 9am. My father has been called back to Pittsburgh and we must go now. I can't even stop to see her."

Robert eyed his friend and the proffered note. He smiled. "Sure James. Have a good trip back. You are coming back for the Regatta now, aren't you? I mean we do have a record to defend."

At the mention of the Regatta James heart sank further. He had not asked his parents but given the circumstances, a return trip within a week was highly unlikely. "I don't think so Robert. You'll have to defend without me this year."

"Ah, I see. Well, you can count on me dear friend. I will cover you as always. This note will reach its proper destination."

"Thank you Robert. You're the best!"

"James, come on. We're late. We'll miss the train." His father called out to him as he crawled into the carriage. James rushed out of the clubhouse and leapt up and into the carriage. As the carriage crossed the dam and headed into South Fork he debated a jump and a run to Mary. *I could make it that I know. But my father would miss his train and I would jeopardize all that Mary and I have. Robert will leave my note for her. Oh Mary, please wait for me.*

Robert peered at the note to Mary. He tapped it on his open palm leaning on the fireplace. Robert looked into the fireplace and saw wood there waiting for the first frost. He smiled. *You know, for summer it is quite cold in here.* Quickly he built a small fire and watched as the sparks flew. He picked up the letter from the desk and patted it once more on his palm. Robert pitched it into the flames and watched it burn. *James, someday you will appreciate all that I have done for you. I mean that set up with Hope, my girl friend after all, was a delight. Although I must say the dear girl did appear a little too eager for her role.*

Robert stared into the flickering flames for a while longer and then he used the poker to slowly spread out the wood and bring the fire to a close. *Yes James, the letter has reached its proper destination. Good-bye Miss Mihelic and good riddance.*

Mary was up early that morning but was out at the barn as the Peyton carriage rumbled by. *I've got to get going. I don't want to keep James waiting. We have to talk. If we are going to be together, to really be together, I need to know how he feels. I need to know that we can work together and overcome these…these differences.*

The chores finished Mary started to walk back to the home to tell her mother she was going off for a walk. She stopped. *I can't. I've got to go now. They'll never miss me, not for this short bit of time.* She took one last look at her house and ran towards the path to the spillway. *I'm coming James.*

The skies, which had started the morning cloudy, now grew darker and more ominous. Mary felt light droplets on her face. *Why didn't I bring an umbrella? Where is James?*

The water poured down the spillway, the rain, which had started as a light summer sprinkle had turned into a deluge. Mary sat there waiting. Hearing footsteps approaching Mary turned anxiously towards them. Grace, her sister appeared from the small grove of trees.

"Grace, what are you doing here?" Her sister yelled out, "Mary! I found you. I told momma and papa that I knew where you were. They told me to stay at home, but then went off towards town to find you. I knew you would be here. I knew it!"

Mary smiled at her little sister and placed her arm around her. "Yes Grace, you knew. Now go home. I will be there shortly."

Grace looked at her sister and her face turned down. She didn't look up but addressed her sister saying, "Mary it is past noon and it's raining. Please come home now."

Mary patted her sister on the knee. "I'm waiting for James. He'll be here any minute."

Grace looked at her sister again. The rain had ruined the pretty hat that Grace knew had been Mary's favorite. Mary's hair was soaked through and limps hanging in strings off of her shoulders. Her dress was also soaked through and little resembled the soft green brocade it had been. Mary's shoes were covered in mud.

Grace huddled closer and brought Mary under the umbrella. "I know. I will go up to the clubhouse and get James. I'll bring him down here Mary. I'm sure something important has held him up." Her eyes brightened at a possible solution. Mary turned sharply on her sister. "Don't you dare! No. Go home."

But Grace didn't go home. She sat closer to her sister saying nothing more. She held the umbrella up high even as her hand ached. The rain continued to pour on them both. Minutes passed, then an hour. Mary looked over at her sister who was still holding up the umbrella, her head resting on her chest almost as if asleep.

Mary leaned over to her sister and kissed her cheek. "Let's go home goofy Grace. It's time." She put her arm around the smaller girl and they walked back to the path that would lead them home. Mary sighed and then said half to herself "Dreams die hard, I guess."

Jennie Mihelic stood on the porch but when she saw her two daughters approaching she rushed off towards them ignoring the downpour. "Mary where have you been. Papa and I were so worried. Oh dear, you are so wet. Quick, into the house with you both."

Charles Mihelic had heard his wife step off of the porch and came out of the small home just as the trio was coming up the steps. He didn't say a thing, opening the door for them to enter. He followed them in and went to get the blankets that would surely be needed. It was going to be a long night.

The next morning, in Pittsburgh James had made up his mind. *I'm going back to South Fork. I can meet Mary and talk and still make it back before anyone will notice I'm gone.* He told his parents he was off to the library for school. He kissed his mother good-bye, which she thought strange given he was just going to the library. John Peyton nodded his head and was pleased that his son was taking more interest in learning.

James had raided his savings and collected just enough for the roundtrip fare to South Fork. *I know that I shouldn't have lied to mother and father but I had to. I can't write letters and I can't wait until we are together again. Mary and I need to talk. Something is very wrong.*

The trip to the small village seemed to take forever. When the train arrived slowly chugging to a stop James stood at the door poised to jump down once the conductor opened the doors.

The walk from the station to the Mihelic home was less than a mile. James soon found himself walking through the small gate at the front and up to the freshly painted porch.

The door creaked and Mrs. Mihelic appeared. "Hello James," she said, "I am surprised to see you here." James Peyton stopped on the bottom step of the porch and looked up at Mary's mother. "Good day Mrs. Mihelic. I'm here to see Mary. Is she around?"

"I'm sorry Mr. Peyton, James, but Mary is very sick. I'm afraid she can't have visitors."

"Sick? How sick? Is she dying? Is the doctor here?" His rush of questions brought a smile to Jennie Mihelic. "No, no. She is just down with a cold. Please, come here and sit with me on the swing. Why is it so urgent you speak to Mary?"

They sat down on the swing and faced each other. James felt comfortable with Mrs. Mihelic and soon told her the story of the note and of his missing the planned meeting with Mary. Jennie Mihelic listened carefully and pieced together more of the story from what she knew of Mary's recent behavior. James finished up the story in a rush and said, "Now you see that I must talk with Mary. I must let her know how I feel."

Jennie Mihelic paused and rocked the swing a bit with her foot. She smiled a little smile and then patted her hands on her lap rustling the material. "James, sometimes we can rush things too much. Push too hard and a fragile gift can be broken. Love you see must sometimes be given a chance to breathe."

"I don't understand Mrs. Mihelic. How is Mary to know what I feel? If I don't tell her, she'll find another."

"And if you do tell her, then what? You chance everything and risk everything that she will understand what you say, how you say it. No James, go home now. Let love breathe and move in its time, then when the time is right, it is right."

James looked at the older woman thoughtfully. He said, "How will I know, I mean, how will I know when it's time, time to tell Mary what I feel?"

Jennie Mihelic smiled once more and rose from the swing. "You'll know James, you will know. Or Mary will know. For sure God will know. But for now, go back to your home. Your parents will be getting worried."

"All right Mrs. Mihelic. Are you sure this will work?"

"Yes James. I am sure."

Jennie Mihelic watched as the young man trudged off back to the train station. *He is a good man. Patience is a difficult virtue to learn.* Her face shone with a bright light and her eyes crinkled. Jennie Mihelic opened the creaking door and went into the house to tend her sick children.

CHAPTER 12

▼

THE DANCE

A year had passed since the incident at the spillway. Mary and James hadn't seen or spoken to each other in that time. The year was 1888, in the late summer.

A carriage pulled up to the small house in South Fork. The driver got down first and assisted the lady inside down. Shortly a knock was heard at the door from inside the house. Jennie Mihelic moved to the door and greeted her visitors. After a brief discussion, Jennie called out to the back of the house.

"Mary, someone here to see you. Please come out here now."

She walked out of the bedroom and was surprised to see Mrs. Peyton there in the doorway.

"Hello Mrs. Peyton. It's nice to see you again. Is everything all right?"

"Hello Mary, how are you today? Yes, everything is quite fine except maybe for the weather. The rains have been so hard lately and the roads so muddy. I had thought to mail my request to you but when today showed up so sunny and such, well I just decided I would take a nice carriage ride and talk to you and your mother."

"Please come in and sit down."

Jennie Mihelic offered the fluffy sofa, which always seemed to invite sitters with its soft puffy cushions. Then she moved off to the kitchen before Mrs. Peyton could protest.

"Momma is like that Mrs. Peyton. She feels if you aren't eating you must be hungry. I hope that you don't mind?"

"I don't mind. I find it very thoughtful. Please sit down here beside me Mary. I talked to your mother about my modest proposal and now would like to discuss it with you."

Mary sat down on the sofa wondering what could Mrs. Peyton want?

Fiona Peyton smoothed out her dress and collected her thoughts before speaking. This was a habit she had which had aided her many times in the past.

"Mary, as you know the Regatta and dance are coming up again. Now I realize that you and James aren't a couple anymore..."

Fiona watched to see if Mary had any reaction. She was saddened to see none. She continued, "We worked so well together last year. I could really use some help."

Mary began to respond negatively when she heard Fiona Peyton add, "The chef in the kitchen just quit and the whole celebration is in chaos."

"I'll do it!" Mary piped in.

"Oh thank you Mary. We can meet tomorrow and go over the decorations for the Clubhouse."

"No, Mrs. Peyton. I mean I'll coordinate the kitchen for you. I'll take care of that work."

Fiona Peyton looked back.

"Oh no, my dear Mary. I wouldn't have you do that work. That's for..."

She stopped before saying "hired hands".

"...other people. You are much more useful with me on the planning side."

"Thank you for the offer, Mrs. Peyton. But I must insist. If I'm to help you with this…dance, then I will work in the kitchen."

Fiona wanted to offer some resistance but she saw the young lady in front of her was not going to change her mind. "All right then Mary. Please come by the Clubhouse tomorrow and I'll give you a list of things to get at the store."

Mary, showing her first signs of emotion looked wide-eyed at Fiona Peyton. "I can't. I-I mean, wouldn't it be better if you just gave me the budgeted dollars and I worked up a surprise. It would be good, I promise you."

Fiona Peyton laughed. "Oh goodness Mary, I would never worry about you. I just thought…well never mind what I thought." She reached in her purse and took out the requisite dollars for the food. Patting Mary on the leg, she said, "Now, Mary, you are in charge of the kitchen. I'll miss you on the other side, but perhaps this'll work out well."

Just then, Jennie Mihelic entered with some fresh baked cookies and offered them to Mrs. Peyton.

"Try these peanut butter cookies, they're fresh from the stove."

"Thank you. Um, delicious. Yes, maybe this new approach will work. Of course I must also pay you this time. And don't you protest."

Mary smiled. *I won't protest. I'm just a worker.*

"Thank you again Mrs. Peyton. I won't let you down. Now if you'll excuse me, I must leave." Mary got up and walked back to her room.

Jennie Mihelic's face creased with worry. Fiona Peyton's concern matched hers. *Mary seems so different than last year. First, she is so pale. She doesn't seem to have that vibrant spirit anymore. I do hope this will not be too much for her.*

Jennie Mihelic said, "I'm so sorry Mrs. Peyton. Mary hasn't been feeling well."

"That's all right Mrs. Mihelic…Jennie. If she has any troubles with the work, please let me know. I hope that she isn't pushing too hard since we are friends."

Fiona Peyton rose from the couch and moved to the door. Jennie Mihelic followed. The two ladies stood at the door and said good-byes. They hugged and silently acknowledged each other's concerns.

Up at the lake, John Peyton sat in a boat with his son, James and James' friend Robert. John Peyton, proud of his work in getting the lake stocked with bass this spring, nevertheless remarked on the fishing with acknowledgement to the club's president, Elias. "I have never known fishing such as we have here at Lake Conemaugh. I fear Elias is even outdoing Ben Ruff in keeping the fish in the Lake. That new screen at the spillway is working wonders."

James added, "We won't have to worry about what to eat for two weeks."

They laughed at this impossibility, since they were only here for one week. Besides, the week was already half over. They would end up throwing many of the fish back into the lake. The challenge was not in eating the fish but in the chase and the catch. Mr. Peyton had always had a sense of when and where the fish would bite. The summer days pass all too soon with the relaxation of good fishing.

As they sat there fishing, John Peyton stopped and looked at his son. He sighed and remarked, "James, your mother asked me to go with you to town tomorrow to get some new clothes for the dance this Saturday."

"Father, I don't think I'm going to the dance this year. It's boring and besides it's mostly for the younger ones."

"What are you saying James?" Robert accentuated the 'you' drawing it out slowly. He dropped his reel down and turned to his best friend, saying, "This dance is grand. Girls are everywhere and dressed up pretty as a picture. I for one can't wait. We'll have a fantastic time!"

"Listen to Robert, James," said John Peyton, "besides, your mother is in charge of the preparations and working hard to make the dance a big success."

"Father, Robert, I understand. It's just, I don't know, I'm just not interested this year."

John Peyton shook his head in frustration. He said, "Well you're going son, and that's that."

Mr. Peyton turned to Robert who had turned back to fishing to avoid an awkward discussion on the upcoming dance.

"Robert, perhaps you would like to join James and I on our trip to Johnstown. You know it is amazing how this town keeps up with fashion. I can find clothes here that have not even made it to Pittsburgh yet. And the storekeepers are so pleasant."

James decided against continuing to protest. *What's the use? I'll go to the dumb dance.*

John Peyton patted each boy on the shoulder.

"Well boys, I believe it's time to call it a day. What say we make that clothing trip to Johnstown tomorrow, early, and then maybe we can catch some evening fishing?"

Both boys nodded agreement although James remained uncertain whether he wanted to return. For some strange reason the lake didn't have the fascination that it used to.

They dropped the small fish back into the Lake to grow a bit larger until next year. Still there were more than enough large bass in their bucket for taking back to the Clubhouse.

The Friday shopping trip was actually fun. James and Robert laughed at some of the new suits being touted. A "Little Lord Fauntleroy" fashion statement had them both glad that they were beyond that age. Both picked quiet brown suits with small white stripes. James joked that they would be twins at the dance.

Saturday passed swiftly by. The sailboat races were exciting as always. James had not participated this year. His father found that strange but did not comment. Robert won his race and walked up to the Peyton family laughing.

"Hey, what did you think of that, James my man? Of course, you didn't enter because you knew that I would defeat you as always. Still I would have preferred a little competition."

The laugh rolled out of Robert easily. James smiled and replied, "Robert, had I entered you would have only saw the back of my head as I would have beaten you once more."

Both friends laughed and hugged one another, more like brothers than friends. Robert pushed James the gentle push of a friend, then said, "Hey, let's get ready for the Regatta, then the ladies. Wooha!"

The friends rushed off to set up their boat for the parade across the lake. Lanterns were fixed to the sailing mast and decorations were added to set each boat apart.

"Let the parade begin!" shouted Elias Unger. The boats made their gentle slow trek around the marked course, lanterns swaying in the breeze reflected off the surface. Mary watched from the clubhouse porch with some of the help. *How strange it is to be here, seeing this from this side of the lake. And yet, still not really a part of it at all. What silly dreams it all was!*

After the Regatta had finished, and the sailboats glided into the shore with their lanterns glowing brightly, fireworks lit up the sky. Mary watched James and Robert's boat come into shore. Robert was out first, waving his arms around and shouting something which Mary could not hear as she was too far away. James was second out of the boat. Mary was about to turn away when she saw him reach back and help another from the boat. *Hope Wilson, of course. Why was I so stupid?*

Mary sighed and went back into the kitchen. Work was needed. *No time now for silly dreams.*

After returning to the kitchen, Mary Mihelic was a one-person dynamo. For her young age, she had a natural ability and knack for organization and leadership. The other staff listened to her and followed her directions. She appeared to be everywhere at once, checking on the main course dinner, looking at the salads to make sure each had just the right amount of color. *For food to be good, it must assail all of the senses.*

In the grand hall, Fiona Peyton was concentrating on being the hostess, leading the people into the room and getting everything arranged. Still, she found an occasion to walk back into the kitchen to observe how all were coming along there.

Young lady, you are truly amazing. I only wish that you and my son had stayed together.

She left without a word to Mary. No words were necessary. She returned to the main room. The trophies from the sailing races held that day were being awarded. Fiona remembered all of James' trophies and achievements. She also recalled the heartbreaks of dear Janie. *How she had wanted to win and be like her big brother.* The recollection brought back the memories of Janie's sickness and eventual death. She fought them off, wiped a tear from her cheek and then busied herself with the guests.

The dinner came off without a hitch. Well from all appearances, it came off without a hitch. Inside the kitchen, it was organized chaos. Mary was aching in every bone of her body. She prayed that everything was going well outside. *I'll show them, all of them.*

Andrew Carnegie pulled Fiona aside as desert was being served.

"Fiona my dear, you have really outdone yourself here. This food is exquisite. I have been to some of the best restaurants in Europe and I dare say this meal was equal to them all."

"You are quite welcome Andrew, but I can't take the credit for the meal. Mary Mihelic of South Fork deserves most of the praise for it."

"Well then, I shall have to meet this Mary Mihelic later to give her my compliments in person. Nevertheless, let me also tell you something, my dear Fiona. I do not make any steel myself. I hire the best people and give them freedom to do their jobs. Yet, I get the credit. You, my dear, deserve credit. This is the most splendid end of summer celebration ever. John Peyton is one lucky man."

Fiona blushed and smiled. She curtsied to the steel magnate.

"Thank you Andrew. You are too kind. I will bring Mary by later so that you can meet her."

"Yes. I would like that."

The dinner complete, the tables were cleared and moved to the side. The local band set up their instruments and prepared to play. Mary Mihelic continued rushing about in the kitchen. Now that the meal was completed, she was organizing the cleanup crew. *A job hurried is a job not done that's what papa says.*

As if on queue, the music began. Robert rushed up to James. "James can you believe all these ladies? So many, and only one of me. You must help me James. I fear there are not enough dances for me to get around to each lovely rose."

"Thanks Robert, but I think I'll pass."

"Are you still hung up on that girl, what's her name, Mary? Granted she is a lovely creature, but James, she isn't here, and my man, you and I are."

Robert had a twinkle in his eyes but his smile appeared more a smirk. James shook his head in the negative and replied, "Go ahead Robert, I shall pass thank you."

The music swelled up into a waltz and Robert walked off saying, "your loss dear fellow. You have no idea what you are missing. Be patient my sweets, Robert is coming."

He walked up to one lovely lady and proffered his hand. She smiled and accepted. Robert was a good dancer and moved across the dance floor with ease.

"Per chance you saw me in the race today? I led from the very beginning."

"Yes. Your race was truly thrilling. You are quite the sailor. Perhaps one day you can take me out on a sailboat ride."

"It would be my honor."

"Perhaps I could bring one of my friends along, for James?"

"Yes. Yes of course. Good to get him out and about. I do declare lately he has become awfully boring."

The dance was finished and Robert turned to go back to James, who was standing off in a corner sipping on a drink of punch. *Wait until I tell him about this. He'll forget that little hunkie girl quicker than ever.*

John Peyton also had observed his son. He frowned, and sought out his wife.

"Fiona, what is wrong with James? He isn't dancing with anyone."

"John, I do believe that he has eyes only for one."

John Peyton looked at his wife and glared.

"No. Never. It'll ruin everything."

"John," Fiona had wanted to tell him more of Mary but he rushed off to speak with Henry Clay Frick who was holding forth with several club members near the bar.

Mary debated going home. *I know I should wait for Mrs. Peyton but I'm tired now and the sooner I leave this wretched place, the better I will feel. Perhaps I should look out and I could wave her over to the kitchen? I don't want to rush her.*

Mary peered out from the kitchen door. It was hard to see anything from that location, however, as the kitchen door was in a recessed hallway from the main room. She cautiously moved forward towards the dance floor, her eyes scanning the guests, looking for Fiona Peyton. Her gaze stopped suddenly. There, in the corner was James. He was with Robert. They were both laughing at something. *Probably some girl they have tricked, like me! Oh James, why did you do that, why?*

She then looked at the ladies standing around the dance floor.

They are all so elegant. I could never afford clothes like that. What must I have been thinking? These girls are all so refined, so polished. I just can't compare to them. She looked down at her dress. *I mean, my dress is nice; momma made it, but their dresses, all that lace and silk.* Besides after this time in the kitchen the dress and I are a mess. She looked into the mirror on the wall. Her hair, which had been styled so nicely earlier in a wide bun, now was loose and strands hung down on her face. Her face had some flour smudges on it. She shook her head. *Well, it's not like anyone will be seeing me.*

While these thoughts ran through her mind, she looked over to see James one last time. He was standing with Robert still.

"James you cannot pass this up, I am telling you. She is ready and willing. Come. We can take a midnight ride out on the lake." James admired his friend's persistence but shook his head once more. He replied, "No. I have other plans for tonight. Now go off and tend to your harem master Robert." Robert shrugged as if to say 'you poor boy', then he pointed to the girl he had danced with across the floor.

"That I shall master James. That I shall. By the way, there she is, over there."

Robert pointed off towards the opposite side of the dance floor close to the entrance to the kitchen hallway. James turned in that direction. He noticed the girl standing there. *Robert was right she was a beauty.*

Just then, his eyes felt something, someone looking at him. He half turned and looked directly into Mary's eyes. Mary found herself pleading, hoping that he had not seen her.

Oh no! I think he saw me. I look a mess. Her eyes dropped and she stared at the floor. *Please don't come over here. Please just let me go home. This is awful. Just awful.*

She looked up to see James walking purposely across the dance floor. The music was starting up another waltz. Hope Wilson had also spotted James. Actually, she could not keep her eyes off him. She let out a smooth sigh and pouted her lips.

He is coming this way. Finally he has noticed me.

Mary felt trapped. Tears welled in her eyes. *What do I do? Why are my legs so weak? I must leave. He's going to ask Hope Wilson. That will be my final humiliation.*

James moved past Hope, who had a look of bewilderment on her face as he walked past her. Hope then turned to see him addressing a pretty girl who was one of the help staff.

"Mary, may I have this dance, please?"

Mary raised her face to meet his and wiped tears from her eyes. *Say 'no'. No. No!*

"Yes." *Wait! I mean 'no'. I mean I'm not ready.*

James had already taken her hand and turned to lead her onto the dance floor.

"Mary, you are the most beautiful lady here. I don't know why or how you are here, but by God, I am not going to miss this opportunity to dance with you."

They began to dance and Mary remained tense. *I mustn't fall for this. I must tell him. I can't. Oh how I have dreamed of this moment.* Tears welled in Mary's eyes again. *I don't care what happens or why. I am just going to treasure this dance.* She grabbed James' hand tighter and let him lead her across the dance floor to the music filling the ballroom. They danced as one person with such grace that many around stopped to look at the handsome couple.

James looked at her lovingly. "Mary, please tell me why you left me, I need to know." Mary looked back at him a bit startled, then said, "What about Hope? Robert?"

James stared back with an equally puzzled look. "Hope? Hope Wilson? Heck, she's Robert's friend. I hardly know her. Why do you ask?" Mary's mind began making the connections. *How foolish I have been! Lies, all lies, but not James. James, my love.*

The music continued and James awaited an answer. Mary smiled, then said, "Hold me closer James, there will be time for talk later." James brought her in closer to him and both swirled around the floor to the soft music playing.

The dance ended too soon. Mary excused herself to freshen up. James made her promise to return soon. She smiled, no longer afraid. Together they would face the world and all its challenges.

As she cleaned up she debated telling James the story as she had pieced it together. *It had to have been set up by Robert. But why?* She decided not to tell James what she had surmised. *James would probably want to flog Robert and I don't want anything to ruin this magical night. Nothing.*

When she returned they danced again and again. During a break, Mrs. Peyton introduced her to Andrew Carnegie. "I do believe that I

have lost a cook and that you Fiona may be gaining a daughter-in-law."
Mary blushed at the reference and was greatly relieved to see Mrs. Peyton smiling.

Alas, all things had to end and the band played one last song to close
out the evening. James told Mary to get ready. That he would take her
home.

John Peyton walked up to the two as they made their plans to leave.
"Hello Mary, nice to see you again after so long a time."

He turned to his son. "James I am afraid I'll need you to help us out
here tonight. We are going need your help to move some furniture into
one of the new cottages for one of our club members. Of course I shall
see that Mary gets home safely."

"Father, Can't it wait? I want to see Mary home."

His father smiled, turned to Mary and said, "Mary, you must be
tired having worked most of the day in the kitchen." She caught the
hidden meaning in James' father's words. She knew that she and James
would need to discuss Mr. Peyton and Robert, but that was for later.
Nothing was going to ruin this night, nothing. She replied to James,
"Your father is right James. We shall have time tomorrow to get
together. Now go. I shall get home safely. Don't worry. I can walk."

John Peyton puffed out his chest and quickly responded, "No way
young lady, you are not going to walk home. My goodness, after that
feast tonight I fear you are going to get many offers to become a regular
cook around here. I will get someone to take you home." Mary did not
miss the second obvious slight but smiled anyway.

"Thank you Mr. Peyton. Goodnight James."

Mary walked out with Mr. Peyton but turned around to take one
last look at James. She found him looking at her. Both smiled. *Nothing
will stop us ever again.* When she turned back around she was surprised
to see that John Peyton had already arranged a carriage, which was
waiting on the road beside the clubhouse. He held the door open when
she arrived.

"Goodnight Mary. I hope you had a good time." Mary ascended the step and got into the carriage. She turned around to address Mr. Peyton through the carriage window. "Mr. Peyton, I understand that you don't like me, or my family for that matter. I do hope that will change. However, no matter what happens, James and I are going to stay together."

John Peyton's face could not be read. It was stern and his lips pursed. He stepped back, and then he spoke directly to Mary.

"Mary, I surely don't understand what you are saying? I have nothing against you or your family. As long as we are getting things straight however, let me assure you, that I only want the best for James."

"Goodnight Mr. Peyton." Mary closed the curtain on the window shutting off any further reply he might have made. *I am not going to let you ruin this wonderful night. Tomorrow, James and I can talk and work out these issues. I must tell him. I wish James had driven me home.* Then she laughed. *Perhaps it is best that he didn't. I am not sure if I could have trusted myself with him.*

Her passions were still aroused when she went to sleep that night. *So much to remember. James and I dancing. Together. That is the way it will always be.* Thoughts of Mr. Peyton continued to interrupt her dreams but she shoved them aside. *There is time enough for worry. Tonight I reserve for you James, my love, my everlasting love.*

The next morning Mary could barely contain herself. She wanted to rush right up to the lake and kiss James. However, her chores came first. She rushed through them and then went into the small home to clean up. Her mother was there. "Great lord, what has gotten into you child?"

"Nothing Mother. I just want to go up to the lake today, if that's all right with you and Papa?"

Her mother replied, "Of course Mary. Just be back for dinner. Perhaps Grace would like to go too?"

Mary frowned. "I don't think she would momma. She's still not done with her chores."

The door opened and in popped Grace smiling widely. "I'm done with my chores! Momma is it all right for me to go up to the lake today?" She then looked at her sister and grinned even broader.

"Good. Both of you girls go off now and enjoy the lake. I'll tell papa where you have gone. Now be off."

As soon as they were out of the house Mary turned on her sister.

"What are you thinking? Please, for once in your life, be a good sister. I have to talk to James about a lot of things."

Grace looked at her sister. Mary braced for the comeback and denials. She was surprised when Grace finally spoke. "All right Mary. I'll stay here. Good luck." Mary almost cried. She kissed her sister on the cheek and rushed off to the lake. Grace waved but Mary never turned back hurrying up the path leading to the breast of the dam.

Mary slowed down at the top as she started across the dam. She was tired and winded from the run up the path and the excitement of being in love. Still walking at a good clip she looked across the dam and saw a carriage approaching from the other side. She slowed even further as she recognized the carriage as the one used by the Peytons.

Around the center of the dam, she and the carriage met. Both slowing to a stop, James popped his head out of the carriage waving wildly at Mary. He jumped down and rushed up to meet her. She wanted to kiss him right there but knew it would not be proper. Fiona also got out of the carriage but stood off at a distance.

"Mary, I'm so sorry. Father has gotten called back to Pittsburgh again and we have to leave a day early."

Mary looked at him with eyes glistening with tears. "James, we've hardly had time to talk. Is it always to be this way? I have so much to tell you."

James didn't lose his smile nor appear at all concerned. He pulled Mary into his arms and held her tight. "James, your parents will see us," Mary whispered into his ear. He laughed and pulled back from the hug. "Good! I just want to make sure that you know that I love you and nothing, distance or absence will ever change that."

"When will I see you again?" Mary asked.

"Soon, I'm sure Mary. We get here about three weeks during the winter. And we can write each other until we meet again."

"Yes, I guess that will be good. We do both have school. But oh James, I just have so much to tell you." James looked at her and replied, "So do I Mary, have so much to tell you. We must make up for the lost time. I love you Mary Mihelic."

"And I love you James Peyton."

Mary was about to say more, but Mr. Peyton called from the carriage. "James. Fiona. Let's rush. We are going to miss the train!" Fiona waved to Mary then called out to James to hurry back to the carriage. "Just one minute mother, please. Write Mary! And I will write you. Tell me everything, I can't wait until we are together again."

With that he swung up and into the carriage in one easy motion. His mother waved once more and climbed in behind her son. The carriage passed Mary and she watched as it descended the path towards South Fork and the train station. She then walked down by the spillway and sat there for an hour thinking of the events of the day and the missed opportunity. *Why must we be apart? Is this the way it is to be always?*

When she went home she wrote James a note. She had decided not to write about her feelings about Robert and James' father. That subject would wait until they met again. During the winter they exchanged several notes. All the notes espoused love and dreams for the future. None treaded the subjects of the dance or of their families. Despite James' assurances when they met at the top of the dam, they did not meet again all winter. In fact, it was not until near Memorial Day when Mary received the letter saying James and his family was coming to share in the holiday. *This will be the best Memorial Day ever!*

▼

CHAPTER 13

MEMORIAL DAY 1889

Rev. Beale waved his arms at John Fulton who was walking down Main Street in the opposite direction. The date was Wednesday May 29, 1889, the day before Memorial Day. The sky was overcast and threatening rain.

"John, I'm so glad I caught you," Rev. Beale said as he came to a stop. He caught his breath and then continued. "I heard you were heading out of town and not going to be here for the Memorial Day festivities."

"Yes. Business never takes a holiday I'm afraid. I should be back by next Tuesday. Judging by those clouds I don't know if there is going to be much celebrating."

"Well, in any case, you will be missed. Mind you; make sure you get to church while you are gone. Business only for six days, the seventh remains the Lord's."

"Of course Reverend, of course. I believe Cyrus is due back Friday from Chicago. I had hoped to catch him before I left. I have some issues that we really need to discuss."

"Yes. I look forward to Cyrus' and your return. Good day John."

"Good day Reverend. Here comes Ben Huffman to take me down to the train station. Good ole Ben, always reliable. Sorry I must miss the festivities. I'm sure we will have many great Memorial Days to celebrate. Bye."

John Fulton waved at his friend and hopped up and into the carriage. Reverend Beale waved back as the raindrops started to come down. Reverend Beale looked up to the clouds as if to ask his master why so much rain had to fall on this town. The carriage moved off towards the station and the awaiting train.

The rain continued most of the day increasing in strength. Its patter on the Mihelic roof was like an orchestra's drums playing that constant beat. Charles and Jennie Mihelic sat on the sofa watching the rain beat on the window. Jennie Mihelic frowned.

"This May has been so rainy. I don't remember a time like it before?"

"Momma you must be getting old then, for in '87 it was worse. I thought we were going to lose everything then."

"Well, tomorrow is Memorial Day and I must get to the graveyard and do my annual planting. Dear me. We also had so many great plans for meeting our kin downtown. Do you really think this rain will continue Charles?"

"Could." Charles Mihelic was not exactly a talkative fellow. Never felt at home with the English language but was just as taciturn in his native Austrian tongue.

Mary entered the room and overheard the conversation. She was combing her hair as she entered the room. She said, "It just can't rain tomorrow. James is coming to meet us downtown. We have so many plans." Her mother looked at her and frowning said, "Well then Mary, we will just do a lot of praying tonight and see. Lord knows we have had our share of rain already."

Grace who had been coloring on the floor looked up and said.

"I for one hope it rains and rains." Grace had a way of being obstinate and contrary. Her sister gave her a look of daggers. Mary turned her back on Grace and smiled at her parents.

"Goodnight Momma. Goodnight Papa."

"Mary say goodnight to Grace also. Grace it is time for your bed too."

"Ah momma, I don't want to. Why do I have to go when Mary goes?"

Charles Mihelic was quick with the rebuke. "Be still child and listen to your mother!"

"Goodnight Goofy Gracie." Mary smiled and left the room chased by her sister.

Charles Mihelic spoke almost to himself saying, "Children, they are both blessings and burdens". Even as he said this Charles Mihelic smiled for he loved Mary and Grace very much.

"What say we go to bed also momma? We have a lot of praying to do if we are to convince God to stop this rain."

"Charles do not joke like that. It is not good you know." They both laughed and arm in arm they went off to rest and to pray.

The next morning Mary awoke, and listened even before opening her eyes.

No rain. It had stopped! When she did open her eyes, she noticed bright and gleaming sun coming in the bedroom window.

`She rushed out the door not trusting that it would be the same in the parlor room. She caught site of her papa on the porch smoking his pipe.

"Papa, can you believe it? It is so beautiful. Everything is green and the flowers look so fresh." She then danced around to the delight of her father.

"Now get inside. Wake your sister too. When your Momma comes back from the graves we need to be ready to go to town."

Mary kissed her father on the cheek and ran back into the house.

James will come now. We will be together.

Johnstown was all a bustle with activity Because of the rains the stores and hotels on Main Street had not had time to put up the buntings and streamers for the parade. Memorial Day was always a big day for the town and the stores looked forward to many sales as people from around the county came to sample their goods. James Quinn was working to do last minute clean up in his shop when Max McAchren walked in with a vexed look on his face. James Quinn took note of his customer and sighed.

Max McAchren was Scottish both in blood and in temperament. James Quinn knew Max well. Max had helped James Quinn with some shelf stocking awhile back. However, neither were they close friends nor was Max one of the Quinn's favorite customers. Max looked around quickly, grabbed a couple of blankets. He strode up to James Quinn and spoke hastily, "the missus sent me on this errand now. I dinna want to come. These blankets, you're charging too much. I'll give ya $1.50 and not a penny more for these."

"Max, you can see the price, they are $1.55. I have to make a living you know."

"Fine living too, I see. No. You can make your money from those other fools. $1.50 is what they're worth and $1.50 is what I pay." His Scottish brogue was usually a joy to hear but not in terms of business. James Quinn shook his head.

"Fine Max, give me $1.50. I hope that is all today."

"Yes. I told ya, I would not be here except for the missus. Surprise guests come in from Bedford just for today. More mouths to feed. Good day Mr. Quinn."

"Good day Max. Come again soon," James Quinn waved to the quick departing McAchren. *Now to close up the store and get to that parade.*

Diagonally across the street at the Hulbert Hotel, a young Maggie Irwin was looking out on the festivities. She had come to Johnstown from Pittsburgh and hoped to make some money by being a waitress at the Hulbert hotel. It was hard work but the money was good.

Well, looks like I won't be using my new umbrella on this fine day. I do wish I could be out and about. Everyone looks so happy. I'm sure the parade will be grand. However, today I must work and waitress to the fine people in the Hotel. That's all right because soon I'll pay off my coat at the Quinn's store. This winter Maggie Irwin is going to look so fashionable with a new coat and clothes.

"Maggie, get over here girl. We have guests needing service."

"Be right there mum. Right there." She rushed off to serve the breakfast guests.

Gertrude Quinn was beside herself. She was James Quinn's daughter and patience was not her strong suit.

"I want to go out now. Can't we go? I want to see the parade."

Libby Hipp answered her young charge, "Be still my precious one. We will go. Your father and mother are getting ready."

Libby Hipp was Gertrude's Nursemaid and constant companion. James Quinn had rushed back from the store to get ready for the parade and the following festivities. His sister-in-law, Abbey Geis had come from Kansas for a rest and a visit with her family. The Quinn household was in chaos on that day with all rushing about.

"Rosina, where is my tie? I cannot find it."

"It is funny that my husband who owns a dry goods store can never find anything especially his tie." Rosina Quinn remarked to Abbey and rushed off to find the missing tie. Abbey was thinking that the idea of getting some rest by coming to Johnstown might have been a foolish idea. Abbey remarked back to Rosina, "Let him find his own tie once. From then on, you'll have no problems with him."

"Be still Abbey. You mustn't talk so."

"Maybe it would have been better if I had stayed in Kansas?"

Abbey Geis smiled at her sister while saying this. She hated Kansas and loved being back with Rosina, her sister. Rosina continued the search for the missing tie. Abbey helped to round up the children even while mumbling under her breath about men.

James Quinn rushed into the room looking vexed. He looked around and noted, "Do we have everyone; children, Vincent, Helen, Lalia, Rosemary? Libby, do you have Gertrude? Abbey, you have Marie and of course Richard. Rosina will bring down Tom. Rosina, are you coming?"

Abbey Geis snapped back, "James, be patient. Rosina will be here. She had to find your tie if you remember."

Abbey Geis was one of the few to talk to James Quinn in that manner. He didn't often tolerate back talk. He was not known as a mean person, just forceful. He and Abbey had many disagreements but shared a mutual respect for each other. At last, the full Quinn family was set and marched out the door and up the street. They would make an impressive site in any case being a large family and so behaved. Since it was the Quinn family, there was even more exchanging of helloes and smiles. The Quinn's were one of the leading families in Johnstown.

The Mihelic's arrived downtown in time for the parade. The parade up Main Street was both exciting and colorful. The bands played the Sousa March music and some Civil War favorites. The men were smartly dressed in red and blue uniforms. They played the music with a fervor brought out by the amassed crowd. The crowd cheered as they passed. The streets were lined with people from all walks of life. Johnstown on this day did resemble the great melting pot of the United States. Mary looked out over the crowd to see if James was around.

It will be impossible for him to see me. I am so far back and can hardly even see the bands.

Mary feels someone bump into her. She turns to see Miss Laura Hamilton. The Hamiltons and Mihelics were friends although not close. Mary and Laura had played together when young but had drifted apart, as they grew older. Mary said, "Hi Laura. Excuse me I am so sorry. I am looking for my boyfriend."

Laura Hamilton laughed, "Why, so am I? That is, I am looking for "my" boyfriend. He was supposed to be here. I bet he is off playing pool. Well soon, that will change. We are to be married this coming Tuesday." Laura Hamilton showed Mary Mihelic her ring.

"That's beautiful! I'm so happy for you. Best wishes. It must be exciting."

"Yes, oh there he is, across the street, handsome isn't he? I must go, nice talking to you."

Laura Hamilton disappeared back into the crowd to find some way to cross the busy street now filled with the marching band. Mary Mihelic turned and continued her search through the growing crowd. A frown etched her face. She heard a voice from behind. "Excuse me miss, but is this spot taken?"

Her heart skipped a beat. She turned to see James Peyton standing there with the large grin on his face.

"James! You made it. How did you find me?"

"I just looked for the prettiest girl here and spotted you at once."

"Isn't it just wonderful, James? This day is so exciting. I was so worried. I didn't know if you would come. Are your parents here?"

"Now which question do you want me to answer first my sweet one. Yes this day is spectacular. My parents are here and up at the club. I thought that they might come down today but they declined. Old fogies huh?"

"Now James, don't say that. We still need to talk."

"Yes, speaking of talking, let's go. I have the carriage parked over there by the park."

"Do you? I should check in with my parents before we go. I'll let them know that I will meet them at home later. Now where are they?"

James looked around with Mary. He spotted Grace and said, "There's your sister Grace. Let her know and let's hurry. It is too noisy here to think let alone talk."

Mary rushed to Grace who was watching a juggler flipping several sticks into the air.

"Grace, have you seen momma and papa?" Mary inquired?

"Yea, they're right over there." Grace said, pointing off to the crowd and the bands marching by. Mary looked to where Grace was pointing but could not locate her parents. She turned back to Grace and said, "Well, can you tell them I went with James and I'll meet you all back at the house?"

"Why? Why should I? You go tell them."

Mary hesitated for a minute. She worried that her parents might not let James and her leave if they knew.

"Fine, my sweet sister, but here is a nickel if you'll tell them that I have gone."

Grace looked at the nickel and thought of an ice-cream cone at the local drugstore.

"All right." She grabbed the nickel and returned to watching the juggler who now was up to five sticks in the air at one time.

Mary grabbed James' arm and they rushed through the park and the crowds to the carriage.

They found the carriage where James had placed it. Laughing, James helped Mary up and off they went, up into the mountains and away from the town. It took awhile because the climb was steep. James and Mary didn't mind the slow trip. They were enjoying the ride together as much as the anticipated destination.

In what seemed to be too soon, they had reached the point where they would have to leave the carriage and walk. James helped Mary down from the carriage and retrieved the basket from the back. The road continued up to the breast of the dam where it split in two directions. The first, to the left, went back over the spillway. The second, to the right, went across the breast of the dam.

Although James and Mary referred to this area as their secret special spot, many picnickers, including James' family, came there to enjoy the setting. The spillway waters trickled by on one side while through the trees you could view the dam itself on the other. Today James noticed the spillway was running faster than usual but it just added to the beauty of the area and of the day. Mary laid out a blanket that she had brought from her home.

"James, let's promise each other that we shall always come back here and picnic even when we are old and gray. Please promise."

"Mary, I'm not sure when we are old and gray that we shall be able to get back here! It's not for the faint of heart."

With that they both laughed. Laughing with Mary Mihelic was fun, thought James. She appreciated all of his simple attempts at humor and her touch was electric to his skin.

It is time. I must tell her now. Mary looked at James and for a brief second frowned. *It's time. I must tell him now.*

She quickly replaced the frown with a smile. "Come on James, let's eat. That walk has me famished." James nodded his head. Yes, it would be better to eat first he thought. *Then I can ask her. Sure. That'll work.* Mary placed out the food and plates in neat areas on the blanket. *First we'll eat, and then we'll talk.*

James ate quickly, and asked for seconds. He said, "Yummy, Miss Mary Mihelic, you have outdone yourself this time. This chicken is delicious. I dare say that I have never tasted better, except maybe that time our families had dinner together." Mary frowned both at the reference to the awkward and total debacle of a dinner that they had planned to bring the families together and to the subject of his father. *Interesting that both are connected.*

"You frown my dear one, why?"

"I don't know James. It just seems like we come from different backgrounds. Do you think we shall ever get them together again?"

James paused, then smiled. "Well I would think that we must. For we shall never part." Mary however continued to frown. This time she didn't pick up on his witty remark. Instead she looked away to the spillway with the water running down and said, "James, how I do wish it could be true. But I know it shall never come to pass."

James could not be contained. "Oh Mary, you are much too serious. Someone once told me, 'Love must have a chance to breathe'. Let's give our families time and see how it all turns out." He looked at her with a twinkle in his eye and said, "I thought you loved me?" Mary looked back at James. Her eyes glistened with tears. She said, "I do love you James, oh so much."

She leaned over and kissed him gently on the lips. He placed his arms on her shoulders and they moved as one to the ground. He moved his hand to her face and caressed it softly. Mary broke the embrace reluctantly and turned away with a tear finally breaking free and running down her cheek.

"What is it, my darling? I know. We promised that we would not do anything until we married, but I can't help myself. You do these things to me."

"No, James. I would like to become one with you. I would like to grab you now and press my body to you and just love you until you could not stand it anymore."

"Well, I am willing, but you had better be ready to stay a long time cause I could never tire of you."

"Be serious now."

Mary tried to have a stern look on her face but James would not let it happen. He looked at her with the craziest, silliest face mocking her request. Mary would have knocked him over if he had not already rolled away laughing. Soon they were wrestling with each other and trying to pin each other to the ground. James thought once more, Mary Mihelic is not your ordinary girl. *No sir, she really is special.* Not many girls would wrestle let alone, prove tough doing it. Ultimately, James was able to pin her arms down with his knees. She squirmed underneath him but could not break free.

"I've got you now Mary Mihelic and you must surrender."

"Never!" She shouted and she struggled some more until breathing heavily she stopped. However, no words of surrender passed her lips. James looked at her there beneath him with grass in her hair and her eyes sparkling in the day's light. Her mouth with that look she had, both asking to be kissed while implying that she might just whack him one if he tried. It was time. He took a deep breath and then said the line he had rehearsed for all week.

"Mary Mihelic, will you marry me?"

He moved slowly off her and knelt beside her as she sat up and brushed her hair aside. It was her turn to be caught off guard at the turn of events. He asked once more.

"Mary, I love you and will forever love you. Will you make me the happiest man on this earth and marry me?"

Mary stood up, turned away from the still kneeling James Peyton and walked a little ways towards the spillway. This time the tears came flowing down and she could not stop them.

James rose to his feet and looked towards Mary. After what surely seemed an eternity Mary turned to face James. He saw her face stained with the tears and felt the urge to rush to her but held back. She breathed in and wiped her face with her sleeve.

"Yes, James. I will marry you."

She said the words simply and calmly, but then the true emotions poured forth from her. She rushed him, and started to hug him and kiss him wildly.

"I love you. I do and we shall be happy. I will be a good wife. I know that I will. I don't care what our parents think. I will make you happy. Oh James!"

James stopped, looked in her eyes and then kissed her again, this time with real passion. Soon Mary pushed back once more and sat down. She wiped her face once more and then said, "We must talk James. I have things that we must discuss."

Could we not do that later?

He saw that Mary had once more got that serious look on her face. He took a deep breath and lay down beside her.

"What is it Mary, what is it that concerns you so much on what should be our happiest moment...at least for now?" James smiled broadly and awaited Mary's reply.

"James, it's...it's your father," She started to say.

"Oh. Of course, we will both have to inform the parents. And then I will ask your father for your hand. I didn't mean to imply…"

She placed her hand on his lips. "No James, I mean your father. He doesn't like me. He won't let us marry."

James sat bolt upright and turned to Mary. For a moment he sat quiet, and then he laughed. "Mary, you don't know my father. He has his ways that I know. But you'll see. And so will he. Me, I worry more about your 'papa'. He's so big and well at that dinner, he wasn't too excited about us Peytons if I recall."

Mary thought about what James had just said. *Perhaps James is right. He has the same worries about my father that I have about his father. After all, I didn't actually see Mr. Peyton conniving with Robert. I can tell him about his friend's betrayal later. No need for that discussion now.*

She waved her hand at James and said, "Don't worry about Papa. He'll be fine." Even as she said this, clouds of doubt entered her mind. James seeing her concern decided to close this part of the conversation. He said, "I'll tell my father and mother tomorrow, Friday. You can lay the groundwork with your folks at the same time. Then we can get together back here Saturday morning to tell each other how it went. After that, we will both go to your home so that I can ask your father formally for your hand in marriage."

James noticed that Mary still had a furrowed brow. He lay down again beside her and placed his hand under her chin pulling her face towards him. Then he said, "I vow to you, Mary, that nothing, not my parents, not anything, will keep us apart. I know that we are meant to be." He kissed her lightly, and then continued, "Our parents have to agree. We will make them see. They have to have noticed, especially after the dance. We'll be happy too. Forever." *Forever.*

The day, which had started so clear and bright, started to cloud over. The sky darkened. The thunder broke the silence. James and Mary were oblivious to all. The thunder just accentuated the growing need each felt. James pressed his body to Mary's. He looked into her eyes and saw the reflection of his own passion. Their lips melted together as the two hearts pounded. He caressed her face, her cheek. She pulled him closer matching his desire with her own. Then he moved his lips to her cheek and down to her long neck. She turned her head slightly away to give him more room. James then moved slightly back from Mary. His hand drifted slowly downward. Mary's breathing was labored and rough. She arched her back to provide James with more space. Inside she was burning at his touch. James was almost shaking. His hand kept moving downward feeling her breathing through the blouse. His hand came to rest on her breast. She hesitated and stiffened for a second but then sighed and let his hand remain there. He moaned and began to untie her bodice.

In his nervousness, he found he could not get it undone. She moved to his side and looking into his eyes with that bewitching look, she finished the untying herself. He moved his hand inside her blouse and touched her neck. Slowly he moved it down and over her soft full breast. Mary kissed him with renewed frenzy.

Without any warning, the rains began with a fury that was unexpected. With a shout, they moved apart. Mary hastily tied up her loose blouse and straightened her dress. Their passion was broken. James reached over and grabbed the picnic basket. Mary folded up the blanket. He took her hand and they moved back across the spillway carefully due to the wet rocks, but also with some degree of urgency. They made their way to the horse and awaiting carriage. There was little talk as they rode down to South Fork and the Mihelic home. They clung to each other and there was no need for words.

Back in town the rain surprised all too. The ladies rushed to put up umbrellas. All were reluctant to see an early end to the festivities. The rain was light at first and seemed to make the flowers and grass brighten even further as it touched them. Rev. Chapman looked out and across the park to the people rushing now to get home. "What a great day the Lord has made. We must welcome the rain as we welcome the sun. I think I will use that in my sermon Sunday. I do hope the rain ends by then." He walked back into the rectory to record his thoughts.

When James arrived home drenched, he had decided to tell his parents right away.

Why wait? The sooner the better. I will burst if I don't let them know.

Wet, he rushed into the clubhouse and up the stairs. The clubhouse was quiet as few guests were there since it was so early in the summer season. He knocked and entered his parents' room after a commanding "Come in" from his father.

One look at his father told him he should not say anything. He looked from him to his mother sitting in a rocking chair and calmly knitting something. It looked like a sweater. His father spoke first. "What in blazes is it James? Can't you see I am busy? And look at you; you are wet and dripping all over the place! Good grief! Go get cleaned up and then clean up this mess you made! Now!"

James' mother looked up from her knitting and then smiling told him, "James, do as your father says. You do look a fright dear. Whatever you have to tell us can wait until morning, I'm sure? I do hope this weather clears up tomorrow. Today began so nice."

James bid his parents good night and rushed off to get into some dry bedclothes. He could not contain his feelings.

Soon he and Mary would be engaged and then married. It was going to be grand, just grand.

James slept little that night even as the storm continued to pour down on the clubhouse and on Lake Conemaugh. He had plans to be made futures to be set in place.

Mary also had rushed into her home expecting to spill the news to her awaiting parents. Instead, she found Grace there waiting for her.

"Grace, what are you doing here? Where is momma? Papa?"

Grace looked at her sister with that look that little brothers and sisters often give when they know their sibling is in trouble. "You're in big trouble Mary. Momma and papa didn't expect you to go running off like that. We were having such a super time. You shouldn't have left. And just where have you been all this time? Kissing with James I'll bet."

Mary went to get a towel and started to dry herself off. All the while she was thinking whether to continue her conversation with her sister or to strangle her right then and there. Grace continued as if she did not care that her sister had not answered her early questions. "We had a simply scrumptious dinner and all of the relatives were there. Everyone was asking papa, "Where is Mary?" and he was getting so angry." Grace emphasized "Everyone" and "so" to make the point all the more strong. She continued, "I do believe he was about to explode when the rains started. My goodness I don't think I have ever seen papa so mad, except maybe for the dinner with the Peyton's. Then he was really mad." This time Grace emphasized the "ever" and the "really" which made her sister decide that strangling was too good. *Boiling in oil, yes that'll do it.*

Grace continued, "Well Mr. Bronkoski had to come back to South Fork to get his chickens in so papa asked me to go along and fetch you. When we got here, I saw that you were still gone and told Mr. Bronkoski. He said that was all right by him. It was late enough already, and we would wait until morning to go back into town. You are in big trouble Miss Mary, big trouble."

Mary felt a sense of relief even if she did still want to throttle her sister.

Her parents would have time to calm down overnight and she would have time to plan how she would address the subject with them in the morning. She also would have time to clean up and make an elegant entrance. One must be elegant when one is engaged.

A smile came to her face, which puzzled her sister Grace. *I have been giving her the best teasing ever and there she is smiling. Mary sure is acting awful strange lately.*

Grace decided her sister was boring anymore so she said "Good night" and went off to bed. Mary spent some time cleaning up the water that had come into the house. *Tomorrow will be just great. Mrs.*

James Peyton Mary Peyton. Mrs. Mary Peyton, wife of James Peyton. Yes, she thought. It will be grand, truly grand.

CHAPTER 14

▼

FRIDAY, MAY 31, 1889

The next morning the rains continued harder than ever. Mr. Bronkoski thought twice about the ride back to town. He had promised Charles that he would bring the girls back however. He could not go back on a promise. Josiah Bronkoski hooked up his horses and rode off to the Mihelic home. When he arrived they were waiting on the porch. He jumped down and opened the carriage door while saying, "I hope we can make it down to Johnstown. The roads are becoming treacherous. It looks like another one of them flash floods. But I promised your father and that is that."

"Don't worry Mr. Bronkoski, the roads will be fine. I don't want my parents to be worried so," Mary said. Her thoughts, however, were of the words she must tell her parents and how she must explain the love that she and James shared.

Mary stopped just before entering the carriage. *I must leave a note for James to tell him where I am.* She rushed into the house and dashed off a quick note to James telling where they would be if he should come down later that day. She pinned it to the door and raced to the waiting carriage. As she climbed in, Grace viewed her suspiciously.

"What took you so long Mary? Getting pretty?"

Mary gave Grace a stare that foretold her sister's demise if she continued. Mr. Bronkoski smiled to himself thinking of his own growing brood.

Children, they are such a blessed torture. I swear. "Come on you horses, get a move on. Git now."

Downtown the people geared for the coming floods. Each spring the rains would come and the two main rivers meeting in Johnstown would overflow their banks. The Stoney Creek and the Conemaugh joined at a point in Johnstown. The channel walls had been narrowed over the years to permit a greater amount of housing and business. The surrounding hills were pilfered for trees, which caused greater run-offs of water and increased the chance of flooding. Johnstowners were used to these happenings and would prepare accordingly.

May 31st started out in just that manner. The rains, which had begun yesterday, continued their constant rush. The waters already had flooded the streets making passage difficult. Cyrus Elder arrived on a train from a trip to Chicago. He was finding it difficult just to make it home a few blocks away. Rev. Chapman looked outside his home flanking the park to see his old friend standing in the waist deep water. He laughed to himself and went outside.

"Cyrus, have you any fishing tackle?"

"Well I was in a skiff and it upset and left me here, and I am waiting for a man who has gone after a horse, to take me out, and I thought I may as well put in my time fishing."

"Why don't you come in here for now and wait then?"

"No. Here he comes now. Thanks much Reverend. I believe I will be making my way home."

The man arrived with the horse but try as he might the rather hefty Cyrus Elder could not make it up onto the animal's back. Cyrus sent the man off for a carriage and shrugged to the Reverend still standing on the porch.

"Guess I ate too well in Chicago. Well more time for fishing."

The carriage arrived, and Cyrus Elder made his way up and into it. They started slowly down Main Street and toward his home on Walnut Street. His driver looked at the rising waters and leaned back to his passenger in the carriage, Cyrus Elder. "Sir, I don't think we can make it there, not with this rain. The horse is bolting back. Perhaps we should go over to your brother's place?"

"But I can see my family over there. There. See, they are waving to me."

The driver looked out to Walnut Street and indeed saw Cyrus' wife and daughter waving and yelling. Neither he nor Cyrus could make out what they were saying.

"Go back you fool. It is too deep," yelled his wife.

"Mother, do you think father is going to make it here?"

"I do not think so Nannie, although knowing your father it will not be for lack of trying."

Cyrus was determined to make it home. He needed to be with his family.

"Blast it all, can't you get that horse to go?"

"No sir. The water is too deep. This horse ain't goin' any further."

"All right. Let's head to my brother's."

He shrugged his shoulders once more, and waved to his family. He continued to watch them as the carriage made the wide turn and headed back up Main Street. It was around noon on May 31, 1889.

Jeremiah Smith lived close to the Stoney Creek. He was a Stonemason and had brought his family to Johnstown because the work was so good. His wife had been pushing him to move uptown and away from the river. Till now he had resisted. Today, looking outside his door, he felt that maybe his wife was right. The waters were rising higher, and had already entered his ground floor.

"Mother we ain't staying here today. I got a feelin' this house isn't going to make it through this one."

"Jeremiah, I don't want to go anywhere. This is our home. Let's stay here."

"I'm telling you woman, this house is going to go. Besides, I think you and the kids deserve some fine eating. Let's go across town, away from this water. I will take you to a fine dinner at the Hulbert Hotel. Now what do you think of that? A night in a fine hotel."

"I think you are crazy Jeremiah Smith, but I'll get the children. Florence! Frank! Come now. Jeremiah, please get the baby."

"All right now, the Smith adventure is about to begin."

The trudge across town took longer than expected. The rains had already caused flooding in the streets. Jeremiah frowned as he moved with the family.

Damn floods anyway. I would like to move away from this town but the work is so good. I promise, as God is my witness, this summer I am going to move up town. My family is growing and the work is good. Yep, no more Stoney Creek for me!

"Dad, are we there yet?" An expectant Frank asked his father.

"I think this is stupid, trudging through the rain. Why didn't we stay home?"

"Questions, questions boy, you're sure full of 'em. We're almost there. Hush your mouth now. We will be visiting with civilized folk."

Frank rolled his eyes. He knew better than to sass his father lest he get a whack.

The Hulbert Hotel was busy as several others also had the idea to get out of the floodwaters. Maggie Irwin greeted the Smith's at the door.

"Hello, and welcome to the Hulbert Hotel a haven for the drenched. If you are interested in registering for the night, please proceed to the desk. Otherwise the dining room is straight through those doors." Her smile was contagious and the Smith family entered the modern hotel. The "Smith" adventure had begun.

"Thank you ma'am. We will be registering for the night. Some rain out there."

"Yes. I do believe it's worse than last year's floods. Such an annoyance! Good for business I guess."

She had said it with a smile but Maggie dreaded the work that was coming. *Crowds all of them wanting food and good service and not giving too many tips.*

She left the Smith's to check on the dining room. It was already packed full with people. As she had expected, most people were doing more sitting then buying food. She started to make the rounds asking if there was anything anyone wanted.

The registering completed Jeremiah turned to his wife. "Mother, I'm going back to the house to get some more things. If we're going to have an adventure we could use some dry clothes don't you think? We rushed out so fast we forgot to pick them up."

"Yes," his wife laughed.

How he loved her laugh. She didn't laugh often lately. I know that last child took a lot out of her. I'll make it up to her. I swear.

"Don't you fret now if I'm gone a piece. With these rains and those streets it's going to be slow going."

"Be careful honey." *It had been awhile since she had called him "honey". Now he knew this was a good idea.*

Jeremiah got them settled into the room and then rushed off and back to the flooded house on Stoney Creek St. It was about 1PM.

James Quinn and his brother-in-law Andrew Foster were at their dry goods store stacking up the clothes and moving them to the second floor. They wanted to get them out of the way of the rising waters. It was a hard job but necessary.

"James, can you hand me that box over there? I need it for these clothes."

James Quinn got down off the ladder and retrieved the box that Andrew had requested. As he went over to hand box to him, the bell that announced customers dinged its familiar chime. James turned to look back to the door and inform the person that the store was closed today when he recognized a familiar face. It was Max McAchren the tight fisted Scotchman. Not a word was spoken and none was needed. James Quinn, by now, knew the Scotchman well. He would argue for hours over a penny spent, yet he would more often than not give a dollar worth of work for every penny saved. The work moved faster with the extra hands and the store was soon shut up. James turned to thank Max for the help but he was already gone.

James Quinn peered out the door at the continuing downpour. He turned to his brother-in-law. "What do you think of this water Andrew, getting pretty high?"

Andrew Foster looked outside and then responded, "Yes, but no more than usual. I believe we can ride it out."

"I don't know. I think I'm going to take my family to the hills."

"To the hills? You don't think the ole dam is going to break now, do you James?"

"No but I would rather be safe than here if it did."

"Gaw'on, too much trouble if you ask me. I'll sit it out."

"Well take care Andrew, I had best get home."

"See you tomorrow. I sure hope we don't lose two days to this mess."

"It sure doesn't seem close to stopping does it? Bye."

James rushed off to his home, his umbrella little assistance against the hard driving rain.

I don't care what people think. This flood seems different, ominous. We will go to the hills and be safe.

It was 2PM.

Rev. Beale was trying to get his Sunday sermon written but it was difficult this day. Rainy days always seemed to bring out the visitors. Seemed more problems occurred then, or at least it appeared so. Maybe people just wanted to get out of the rain and talk. Usually he enjoyed the company but today he had hoped to get the sermon finished and enjoy a leisurely Saturday.

Oh well its God's will that I tend to my sheep now. So that I must do.

He greeted the families as they entered the parlor. Being a parsonage there was room and seats for all. The discussion of the weather held forth and some talk of the end of the world was raised. Rev. Beale smiled.

This could be a good day after all.

It was 2:15PM.

Mary had worried that her father would be too angry over the sneaking away that she might not get to tell him the wonderful news. She needn't have worried. Her father and mother had been so glad to see her and Grace that the past day's events were forgotten.

Her mother came to the door as they arrived. She waved as Josiah turned the horses and began his return trip up the hill.

"Oh you're here, thank God. I was so worried. I didn't know what had happened. The rains keep coming down. We must remember to thank Josiah Bronkoski. I know he was feared of coming to town. I'll bake the family a cake. I do so hope he makes it back safe." Charles Mihelic came up behind his wife. He looked out to the continuing rain and to the departing carriage. "Yes, Jennie that would be good. Don't worry about Josiah. He wouldn't have come down if he couldn't have gotten back. Come girls, give your papa a hug."

Both girls hugged their father and he grunted.

"You're squeezing me to death." With that he picked them both up and spun them around. They laughed with glee. "Well we aren't gonna let a little rain spoil us"

His bold laughter filled the room.

"Charles watch the furniture. Goodness. We are guests here now. It was so nice of the Hamiltons to put us up for the night. Especially with the wedding so soon."

Mary saw this as the perfect opportunity and seized it as her dad dropped both girls to the ground. "Momma, papa, James and I, well, he asked me to marry him."

A lull came over the room. Even Grace did not speak. Mary smiled and looked at one face and then the next. Jennie Mihelic was first to speak.

"Mary, I am so happy for you. James is a good boy. This is truly a wonderful day."

Charles Mihelic just grunted. Grace, however, found her voice.

"You are getting married. Yippee! Do I get Mary's room now?"

Jennie fixed her daughter with a stare and she quietly sat down.

Mary looked at her father but as always he was inscrutable.

"Papa, you haven't said anything. Please tell me what you feel. I do so need you to say it is all right"

Charles Mihelic walked to the window as if to check out whether the rain was continuing. The room was quiet except for the constant pitter-patter of the rain on the roof. He continued with his back to his family and spoke softly. "You know how I feel child. Why Mary, why could you not find a good boy from Austria? Czechoslovakia? Why an Irishman?"

Mary's face clouded up and tears came to her eyes. She wanted to talk, to tell her father that James was different but she didn't get the chance. Her father turned from the window. He faced his family, his eyes teary. He spoke in the broken English tongue but his words were from the heart. "I love you kochanka, more than life itself. If you love this man, this James Peyton, then by God so do I. I will welcome him into our family." He stiffened and then added, "However, he had better treat you right. Or else!"

Mary rushed to her father, hugging him as the tears fell. "I love you papa."

"I love you my child. Now. Stop. Or it will be flooding in here." Grace's face lit up brightly. "I'm going to tell the Hamiltons! Now we are going to have a wedding too!"

Grace started to run off. Jennie Mihelic grabbed Grace before she could get out the parlor entrance. "Be still child. We must await James. He must first ask papa for Mary's hand before it is time to spread the news." Grace frowned and plopped into a big easy chair.

"Great fun. News you can't tell, a bedroom you can't have, and it's raining. What a dumb day."

Jennie Mihelic listened to the rain beating steadily on the roof above. She looked to Mary, "Mary, I do hope James will not try to get here today. It is awful out there."

"I hope not too Momma. He is to tell his parents today. I do hope he stays up on the hill."

Laura Hamilton entered the parlor interrupting the conversation.

"You're welcome to come to the second floor. Father thinks it's going to start flooding into the house. He feels we would all be safer up there."

"Thank you Laura. We will join you shortly."

It was 2:30PM.

At the Heiser house on Washington Street, concern had mounted over the course of the day. Floods had been bad in other years but they didn't often get up this far on Washington Street. George Heiser paced around and looked outside.

"Mathilde I am concerned that this flooding will frighten the horses. What if it gets too high and they drown?"

"George I don't think that's possible, do you? I mean even as bad as it got last year the water didn't rise near that high."

"Well I think I'm going to send Victor out anyway to loosen the horses. I would rather they run off than get caught in this mess." He placed his hand on the banister and called out to his son, "Victor!" Mathilde Heiser shushed her husband and then said, "I'll get him George. I'm going upstairs anyways."

It wasn't necessary. Victor had heard his father and bounded down the steps.

"Son, sometimes I wonder if you're going to kill yourself one day, leapin' and jumpin' the way you do. Look, them horses out there could be in trouble. I want you to go out there and free them up in case it gets worse."

"I'll go right now dad."

Victor surveyed the mess outside the Heiser house. The water was pretty deep. He decided it might be best to strip down a bit and not ruin his good pants. He slipped on some knickers and took off his shoes and socks.

"Here goes nothing." He called out to his mom and dad; "I'll be back shortly."

"Don't stay long son. Those horses might be a bit spooked by all this rain."

George Heiser looked out to his son dashing through the waters. *That is one good boy we have there. Always listens, always respectful. A good boy.*

"Watch your step Victor!" He called out to his son but Victor could not hear him over the rain. It was 3:45PM.

May 31, 1889, James Peyton arose early. He had prepared himself all night and had gotten little sleep. *That rain is really coming down. Mary, how did your tale go with your parents? I hope you have had better success than I have. Now I will succeed. I am ready.*

The continuing downpour disappointed him. He had hoped for a sunny day so that his father would be out of bed and getting ready for some fishing. Fishing always made his father happy and it would present the perfect opportunity to talk with him about the future. Besides, the fishing would be good just after a rain like this one. It was not to be. His mother was up and looking out at the rain with a furrowed brow. He thought of telling her right then since she would be able to help him figure a way to tell his father.

Father was not going to be easy, that's for sure. I'll bet Mother already knows. I can tell. Nobody keeps anything from her. Maybe she would help him tell father.

Nevertheless, he held off telling her. For some reason, his mother was deeply concerned and he forced himself to focus on that, at least for the time being. James moved towards his mother and inquired, "Mother, what's the matter?"

She turned to her son and smiled. "It's still raining. This weekend was supposed to be relaxing for your father. Last night he was up late with so many papers. He tries to do too much and really needed this rest. Maybe it's this awful weather. Now I fear we'll be trapped in the clubhouse this weekend, which can only add to his frustrations. You'll have to help him James. He loves you so."

"Mother, don't worry. It'll be all right. This weather is going to clear up and all will be well, you just wait."

"You're such a good boy James." She tousled his hair as she always had.

"You always know how to make something good out of something bad. You're growing so fast too. I look at you thinking you are my little James but now you are a man. Just look at you."

Her voice trailed off at the end. She was lost in thoughts of the past.

Such wonderful times. Would they ever return? Would joy be forever lost for the Peyton's? I do so hope that James is right, about the weather, and about us.

Fiona Peyton returned to the present and looked at her son once more.

"Now what was that you wanted to tell us last night that seemed so urgent?"

Now. Now is the perfect time. I can tell mother now.

"Fiona! Fiona! Come up here. I can't get this blasted pen to work. Please hurry, I have to get this done now."

Fiona looked at her son and shrugged her shoulders. Then she rushed off to assist her husband, leaving behind a bewildered James.

The only good news is that with the rains my parents are trapped in the clubhouse. They won't be returning to Pittsburgh. I have got to have some time to tell them. This rain can't continue forever. Maybe I had better practice my speech some more. A little more practice won't hurt.

CHAPTER 15

▼

CONFRONTATIONS

It was noon before his father and mother emerged from the bedroom. He had thought of going up and interrupting them. Then he recalled the debacle the previous night and decided to await their appearance in the main room. The wait was agonizing. The rain pounded on the roof of the clubhouse accentuating his anxiety.

James Peyton paced the floor. He tugged on the suspenders of his trousers, a nervous habit he had picked up. He was just eighteen, tall and gangly, just over six feet tall he appeared all legs. His light brown hair fluffed on his head looking as if he had just awoke from a sleep. His blue eyes were piercing and darted about the room as he walked. Clean shaven, like his father, which was rare for these times. His skin was soft and blemish free.

His mother was the first down the stairs. James Peyton watched her descent. Gracious and striking in her beauty, she lifted the broad skirt that she wore and the rustle of fine silk could be heard. She shared her son's smile. It lit up a room.

"Good afternoon James. Oh, that frightful rain! Will it ever stop?"

She took a glance out the window viewing the continuing downpour. "You can hardly see the lake it is coming down so hard."

James continued his pacing looking every so often to the stairs and the expected appearance of his father. "James, do sit down son. You seem a bundle of energy today. Such a shame this rain had to ruin our plans." Fiona Peyton sighed and sat down in one of the overstuffed chairs in the room. She spread out her dress and picked up some knitting she had been doing the night before.

James sat down in another chair but soon started squirming, patting his hands on the arms chairs. Then he bounded up and resumed his pacing, now pulling harder on his suspenders.

Upstairs a chair was heard sliding back on the hard floors. John Peyton was moving. He was a large man standing six feet four inches in a time when the average height was about five feet six inches. He shared his sons blue eyes but his hair was blonde and thinning. He was stocky, but not fat. His glance was intimidating and he knew how to use it in his business dealings.

He licked the envelope in front of him as his mind focused on the plans he had just finished. He spoke out loud but no one was in the room to hear him. "Good. Now it is complete. The hard work is over. James will be so excited. With this letter, I will set in motion his future. He will be a leader of industry, just like me."

He tapped the letter on the table, his mind going through the plan once more. Finally, satisfied, he snapped the letter on the table once more and turned to the stairs.

James looked up sharply when he heard the noise. The stairs creaked under the weight of John Peyton. Shortly he appeared in the room, smiling broadly. "James, how are you son?" John Peyton was anxious to tell of his plans for James and didn't wait for his son's response, but continued, "We have so much to discuss. This bloody rain is making life so dreary but not too dreary to discuss your future. I have been working on this plan all week. I still need to get some things settled, minor flourishes really, but now we can talk."

His father would have kept talking but James interrupted him.

"Mother, father, please sit down."

John Peyton looked at Fiona with a questioning shrug. She returned the look with one of her own. John Peyton walked over to where his wife was sitting and sat on the arm of the chair, placing his arm on his wife's shoulder. She leaned on the arm as they awaited their son's news.

James pulled a straight back chair up close to address them. He started to sit down but then realized he couldn't. He was too nervous. He moved the chair to the side and turned to his parents. A smile lit his face and even with the rain and dreariness, his boundless exuberance sparkled.

"I have something important to tell you, to share with you."

"Well go on, what is it son?" John Peyton could hardly contain himself. *James will be so excited by my news. Everything I have worked for him, for our family now bearing fruit.*

John Peyton was so lost in his thoughts he almost missed James next words.

"Mother. Father. I have asked Mary Mihelic to marry me and she has accepted."

"What?"

John Peyton rose from his seat in one fluid motion. His face was beet red.

"John." Fiona Peyton reached out to catch her husband, to restrain him. It was too late. He was right in James' face yelling.

"You what? Have you lost your mind? Are you thinking that you are going to throw away everything I have done for you? And for what? What I ask you? For some stupid little Hunkie girl who saved you from the lake?" His heart was racing. John Peyton looked at his son standing with head down in front of him. *I must stop myself. No I must stop James. He will throw his life away!*

"The little tramp probably thinks she can marry into wealth and live high off the hog. Well I won't have it. Do you understand James? That is final. Final!" *Once I tell him my plans, he will understand. I should not be so harsh on that girl. Nevertheless, James must understand. I am only looking out for him.*

John Peyton stared at his son. He looked for a sign of understanding. Then, he continued, pointing a finger at his son he said, "You are going away to study in England. For two years. Afterwards you will come back and find a nice refined young lady to marry. You are not even old enough to marry. You have no idea what love is. If this girl really loves you, she will wait."

John Peyton shook his head. It was his turn to pace. He didn't know what more to say, and there was an awkward silence. *This is not how I planned it.* Finally, he blurted out, "Now go to your room. This discussion is over."

James Peyton was stunned to silence. His face blank, he lifted his gaze to meet his father's. John Peyton stood there, hands on hips, weary from the shock but wanting to impose his will on his son. James' eyes were burning with their own fury. Thoughts raced through his mind. *What was happening? He had expected some resistance, yes, but his father was offering him no option, no way out.*

Rage found a home inside of him. His anger at his father grew.

His father was attacking the woman he loved. The sweetest, most gentle, most beautiful woman that he could ever hope to meet. The woman he had vowed to love forever. That he would love forever.

He breathed in deeply trying desperately to settle himself.

I must explain to them, make them understand.

"Father I do so want yours and mother's blessing on our union. However, with or without it, I do plan to marry Mary Mihelic, and she is nothing like you say. Nothing."

James had hoped to be calm and rational while defending his position but his voice rose at the end. Now there was no turning back, for either of them.

"You foolish boy! To let a woman dictate what you should say or do. Go to your room. As soon as this weather clears we'll go back to Pittsburgh and discuss this there in a much more dignified manner. I'm much too upset now to discuss it with you. You're too emotional to listen to reason. I want you to think of your behavior here today.

Now go!" John Peyton pointed with his fingers to the stairs but his eyes remained on James. James returned the stare.

"I will go Father, but not upstairs. I'm going to Mary, my love, and soon to be my wife whether you accept it or not!" The last words of defiance broke through any composure that John Peyton was trying to retain. He saw his plans, the future of his family at stake. "What? Dammit boy, you see here! I brought you into this world and by God I can take you out of it! Get your little ass upstairs now and be quick about it!"

The line had been drawn. James Peyton had never before disobeyed his parents. He had always been willing to listen. John Peyton wrestled with his own feelings. *He will back off now and tomorrow we can discuss this again. I will even listen to him then if he half makes sense. Love. I am offering him the world and all he speaks of is love.*

"Good-bye Father. Good-bye Mother."

James turned to leave. The finality of the words hung in the air. John Peyton reached out, seized his son by the sleeve, and whirled him around.

"You think you are really something, don't you boy? You think you can take care of that little lady without any money? Do you think she will even stay around if you don't have money? I doubt it! If you go out that door now, I don't ever want to see you again, ever! You will not get a cent of my money. You or anyone that woman brings forth as bastard children. DO YOU UNDERSTAND THAT?"

James Peyton lifted his father's hand off his sleeve, looked him directly in the eye. Tears flowed freely down his cheeks.

"Yes, Father, I do understand. Perfectly."

With that he turned on his heels and was out the door into the driving rain.

John Peyton stood there in stunned silence.

He left. He really left. All these years he had been the best son, loving, and obeying our every command. Now, why now? Why this?

He turned to ask Fiona what she thought of James' behavior. She was standing there staring at the open doorway. Her face was as white as a sheet. The knitting she had been working on lay at her feet.

"Fiona?"

"John. John," her voice, halting at first, but then finding surprising strength.

"John, go after him. Please don't let him go. Not like this. Not now. Please, oh God please."

"Fiona, it will be all right. I know I was a little harsh but so was he. He..."

He never finished the sentence. Fiona came up to him, a wild look in her eyes and still pale, so pale. She grabbed John Peyton by the shoulders, her grip tight.

"Go John, now! Please! Get him before he goes forever from us. Hurry!"

John Peyton was shaken for the second time that day.

My God, what have I done? I have been so stupid.

He said no more but quickly put on a heavy overcoat, his bowler and rushed out into the rain. Out into the rain. Out after his son.

When he stepped out of the Clubhouse, the pounding rain greeted him. He noticed that the lake was extremely high. The water was running over the boardwalk and in some places was up to the cottage doors. He wasted little time there watching the water, as he knew his son would head for the Unger farm to get a horse. Colonel Unger was the President of the South Fork Fishing and Hunting Club. His farm was near the breast of the dam and the road that led to South Fork.

I must reach him there.

He headed for the dam. When he arrived there, he was further shocked. The water was almost to the top of the dam. Laborers were running everywhere although few seemed to be doing much of anything but watching the water rise.

I have no time for this now. Jesus that water is high. Will the dam hold?

As he crossed the breast of the dam, he ran into Colonel Elias Unger who was supervising the efforts. "You men, get over there, and dig another spillway. Be quick about it now. John! What is it with you Peytons? First James, and now you. Good God man, get back to the clubhouse, this dam may give at any moment."

The rain whipped at the two men standing there. John held onto his hat trying to keep shaded from the downpour. Elias wasn't wearing a hat. The rain dripped down his face and his receding hair looked even sparser as he directed the efforts of those at the dam. John Peyton responded to his friend, "I am looking for my son Elias. I assume he went up to your stable up there."

John Peyton pointed to the barn higher up the hill. Colonel Unger nodded his head and said, "Yes. He asked if he could borrow a horse. He said someone had to warn the folks below. I tried to talk him out of it John but he flat out would not listen. I sent young Clarke down to South Fork earlier to get the message out."

"I understand Elias. Too much like me he is. Thanks."

John went to go. Elias Unger stopped him.

"John, it is dangerous. Get your son and get back to the clubhouse. This dam can't hold much longer."

He released his grip on John Peyton who nodded but continued up the hill in search of his son.

Let me get there in time. Don't let him have left yet. I can't let him go, not with the waters raging like that. Elias is right. The dam is going to give way. The thought sent a chill down his spine. *Dear God!*

He arrived at the stables just as James came out on a large powerful horse. The horse was reluctant to go in the pouring rain. It whinnied its protest. John Peyton rushed up to his son and grabbed the reins of the horse. The horse looked at this strange person and its eyes shown white with fear. It pulled back slightly but James held it steady.

What was his father doing here? Hadn't everything that needed to be said been said?

They had to speak loudly to carry over the rush of the rain and the roar of the water down the lone spillway at the dam. *So much force. So much pent-up power.*

"James. Stop. Don't go. It is foolish. Crazy. The water is too high. The dam may break. Don't go. Wait until later, tomorrow. Let's talk."

"We have talked enough Father. I have to go. Those people have to be warned. I must see after Mary."

"She's safe. Believe me. Her house is above the path even if the dam should break. Wait till morning and you will see."

"Let go father, I must go."

"Son, you will fail. Those town people should know by now with the amount of this rain. There is nothing you can do. You will get yourself killed. You will fail. My God son, you will die."

The rain seemed to answer John Peyton by falling even harder. John Peyton could hardly see his son directly in front of him. James pulled free of his father's grip and moved the horse slightly forward and away. Then he turned to his father still standing there wet and defeated. John Peyton's shoulders slumped. His eyes turned downward, but still he heard his son's words.

"At least I'll have tried Father. I will know that I did all that I could. God be with me!"

James gave the horse a slap on the side. He was off at a gallop.

CHAPTER 16

▼

THE DAM BREAKS

John Peyton watched him race off into the storm. The incessant downpour continued. A piercing scream came from the dam interrupting John Peyton's trance. Rushing back to the dam, he saw that the water was now flowing over the crest at the most crucial spot, the center. The men on the far side were still digging attempting to open another spillway. Some men were down below the dam trying to fill in the cracks and fissures that had opened in the dam where patches had been sloppily applied. They had to step back because the water shot down on them as if a fountain had burst. It was only a minor set back however, and as soon as they gauged the water flow, they resumed their work. *Brave men. Like my son. Brave and foolish.*

Elias Unger seemed to be everywhere at once. At one point rousing the men to work, at another surveying the damage to the dam's structure. Elias spotted John standing by the one overloaded spillway.

"John. John Peyton. Come here. I need your help."

He rushed up to his friend and shouted out.

"Elias. What can I do?"

Colonel Unger looked into the face of his friend, and fellow club member.

My God, what am I thinking? John looks like he has lost his mind. He will be of no use here. I had better get him to safety.

"Go home my friend. Go home. It is too late. Your wife will need you now."

"No. We must keep trying. There has to be a way. There has to!"

Where did those words come from? Am I crazy? Elias is right. We are too late. No. There must be a way. There has to be a way.

Colonel Unger did not have time for arguing. Besides, he could use another leader. He raised his voice once more above the roaring water and pounding rain.

"John, go over there and take charge of that group of men. If we can get that spillway going we just may be able to ease the pressure at the center."

John Peyton nodded his head. Placing his head down at the driving rain, he cautiously began to make his way across the breast of the dam.

The water is flowing too fast over the dam. If we don't relieve it soon this center will give way.

He looked up and over to the group of men digging out a new spill-way.

They will never finish in time. They're not making enough advancement. Those rocks must be delaying their progress. We have to get more water flowing out from this dam, and not over the center.

Wait!

He turned to look back at his friend and the one operating spillway.

Yes, of course! The bridge across the spillway. Why did I not think of this before? We placed grills up underneath the spillway bridge to prevent the fish from escaping the lake. Now they are clogged and holding back the water. The bridge must go.

"Elias! Elias!"

He shouted turning back to the side from which he had just left. Elias was focused on the work there and men trying to enlarge the spill-way.

"Elias, my God man, knock out the bridge! Knock out the bridge!"

The rain and the noise drowned out John Peyton's voice. While he yelled, he rushed back towards his friend. In a short while he had worked his way to one side of the bridge over the spillway.

There is no time.

He looked about and saw a worker using the sledgehammer to loosen the rocks in the spillway. John Peyton grabbed the sledgehammer from the startled worker.

"Give me that!"

With a mighty swing, he began to hit the bridge at its base.

Come on you lousy stinking bridge. Break! Give way.

Elias Unger heard the pounding and looked up.

Yes. The bridge. "You there, with the hammer. Come here. Smash the bridge. Knock it down. Hurry!"

"If I knock the bridge down there will be no way to get across sir."

"I bloody well know that! With the bridge gone we can get more water flowing. This bridge will be worthless if the dam gives way. Now you idiot! Now!" The large man bent to the task and swung the large hammer into the bridge. Smash. Pound. The bridge had been solidly built and the weather did not help the effort, but slowly it began to give way. John Peyton on the other side hurled himself into the work.

Come on. Come on. Break up you bastard. Bang. Bang. The rain poured down.

Time was slipping away. Then a large crack was heard. The bridge had moved.

It's going! A couple more swings. .

Elias Unger poured out words of encouragement.

"Go men. Go John. It's going to give! Its ready to go!"

Then with a loud roar it split apart and tumbled down the spillway. The water flow surged down the spillway, roaring down the newly found way to escape the confines of the lake.

John turned back to look at the center.

The water flow has slowed! But dammit it hasn't stopped. God, why? .

He looked over the side to see the damage to the face of the dam.

Oh, Jesus, have mercy!

The dam was sprouting leaks everywhere. The three men continued working below but could not even keep up with the pace of the new leaks.

We have to stop this water over the center now! Those men below cannot even make a dent in there until we stop this water flow!

He yelled out to Colonel Unger on the other side of the spillway where the bridge had been.

"Look, Elias, we're never going to get that second spillway dug. The area is too rocky and we haven't time. Let me get some men on that side and let's dig a ditch along the breast of the dam. We can get the water to roll along there and down the one spillway we have. We have got to slow the flow over the dam!"

"I agree! Go ahead. I will get a group of men going on this side."

He turned to the men who were now standing around watching the water pour down the spillway. There was no way they could move rocks now since the water was rushing down and over the spillway sides.

"You there! Place some boards across where the bridge used to be. Hurry! Be quick about it!"

Two men leaped into action and found the boards placed there for an emergency. They set them over the chasm of the spillway and created a shaky bridge to the main part of the dam.

"Good! Now, let's get over there and starting from the center, we are going to create a ditch and drive the water to this spillway. Two of you stay here and work from this side. You others come with me."

Colonel Unger walked across the newly formed bridge.

You had best hold up here now. If I fall, I am lost.

After he had crossed, he looked back to the men still standing there. "Come on now! What are you afraid of? Get moving! We don't have time to waste!"

John Peyton for his part raced to the other side. He fairly flew across the dam without concern for the water or the mud. Mid-way across the dam, the water moving under his feet caused him to stumble. Luckily, he regained his footing.

That was almost it Johnny boy. Can't go dropping over there now, can we?

He shivered for a second at the thought of shooting over the precipice and then more slowly moved forward. He wanted to yell to the men still digging on the other side but knew it would be fruitless.

Time. Please just a little more time. We can do it.

Arriving he gave similar instructions to his team of men.

"Let's go to it men!"

They dug and dug. The ground was loose from the rain and gave away directly which gave them renewed hope. One of the workers who had been trying to dig the new spillway for almost two hours thought, this is better than digging at those rocks over there.

God that was impossible! I can do this. Hell, we just may make it.

"Push. Dig. Move! Push. Dig. Move. Come on now!"

Still too much to go! Damn, I did not ever think how bloody wide this dam is. The men are tiring. They will never make it!

He rushed ahead of them and as close to the water rolling across the dam as he dared. He began to dig with his hands. Push. Dig. Move.

Come on you lousy dirt, get out of there. Move.

The other men noticing their recognized leader digging with such frenzy put themselves to the task. Dig. Push. Move.

They would make it. They had to.

John Peyton was a man incensed. His back ached. His hands were bruised and sore. His fingernails once neat and trim were now broken and filled with dirt and grime. His suit was no longer recognizable, covered as it were with mud, and drenched by the rain. Still he dug and dug. He felt a gentle hand on his back. He knew it must be Elias. Still he plunged on digging, digging. He felt water all around him. The water must have risen higher yet.

God, I have to move faster. Go away. Can't you see I am busy?

He heard a voice as if from far in the distance. It was Elias.

"John. John. It is too late."

Elias Unger was fairly screaming now. He was concerned for his friend. The water here was flowing over the dam freely now and it was only a matter of time before the dam gave way.

"John, come on. Get up. We must get to the side now before the dam takes us away also."

John permitted his friend to help him up. The water was well over their ankles now and spreading across the entire center portion of the dam.

It is over.

They walked to the side of the dam and turned back. John Peyton looked below. There, he saw the three workmen still working although the water now was pounding down on them. He yelled for them to leave, to move away. Whether they heard him and ignored him or whether they just had to keep on going, he would never know. For at that moment the dam broke.

He turned to watch it. It was eerie in the way it happened. Not at all like he had pictured or thought it would. Not like a big burst or geyser, but more like a large slow push. The earth just seemed to move forward at the center of the dam and the water rushed into the new and large opening roaring down into the unsuspecting valley below. The three men were swept away in one brief moment. Vanished.

"God be with them. God be with those poor people in Johnstown."

He stood there awkwardly for a brief time, and then he fell to his knees.

"Oh God, watch over us all. Please. Please watch over my son."

He looked up at the heavens and the still pouring deluge and then he added, "and his fiancée."

He knelt there and watched the water empty from the lake. The roar as the water raced down the valley was deafening. It did not take long before most of the lake was emptied. The grand lake once filled with sailboats and laughing vacationers, now looked like an enormous pit of mud. John Peyton continued to stare at the gaping hole in the dam.

Is it only a dream? Some god-awful nightmare from which I will awake? No. It had really happened. Soon Johnstown would be flooded, inundated with tons of water. My God, why so much rain? Why didn't we do those repairs? Nothing would have helped. Nothing.

Once more John felt his friend's hand touch him on the back.

"John. It is over. Go home now. Go home to Fiona. She will need you now."

A weary John Peyton stood up.

"Yes. I must go. Fiona needs me. She will want to know what has happened."

As he moved away from the dam, from his friend, John Peyton gave way to his feelings. *What do I say? How do I tell Fiona? My God, I have failed. Failed my son. Failed my wife. Failed all those people in Johnstown. Wait. The valley is quite long and the town is miles away. Surely by the time the water reaches there it will be nothing more than the usual flooding of that town. No more than the flood of '87 and no worse than ' 88 for sure. Yes. I can tell her that. James, why did you go son? I told you it was fruitless. Where are you now? Are you safe? What can I tell Fiona? I know. I will say that I told James to go down to see that his girlfriend was safe. I told him he should stay there until the weather clears. I am sure he will return tomorrow and all will be well. That is it. She will believe me. No, I must believe. Oh, God, please, please, watch over them all. Let me be right. Let it be.*

CHAPTER 17

▼

THE MADMAN RIDES

James drove the horse harder than he had ever driven one before. He kicked his heels into the horse's side even as the horse stretched out its nose, grabbing the bit in its mouth, and straining to get more speed. The down hill trek to South Fork added even more speed to the movement of horse and rider. Coupled with the slipperiness of the path from the continuing downpour, it was a miracle that they made it to the small house on the side of the hill.

James dismounted and rushed up onto the porch and up to the door. He raised his hand to knock but caught sight of the note left by Mary. He read it swiftly. His worse fears were confirmed. Mary was in Johnstown. He gave some quick thought to his few options. To travel the roads to Johnstown presented a round and somewhat longer route to the town. It was very possible that the roads were washed out anyway. If he could follow the rails down to town, he could save time. However, it might be both risky and troublesome for the horse.

I really have no option. That dam is not going to last. I have to follow the tracks. They are my only chance.

Once committed to the course of action, he mounted the horse once more and moved to follow the train tracks to the town, to Johnstown, to Mary.

God be with me.

As he rode to the tracks, he shouted out to the houses.

"The dam is broke. Head for the hills."

He knew that it had not broken yet, but he also knew it had to be soon. He saw little knowledge that Clarke's earlier warning had any effect on the people of South Fork. They had apparently heard that shout more often than he had realized.

The rain poured down as he made his way carefully on the horse. The pace was slow. He began to regret the decision to take this route. He spotted a railroad man walking up the tracks swinging a lantern as he moved. The man was surprised to see James.

"Good Glory man, what in hell are you doing here? Can't you see the rain?"

"There's no time for talk. The dam broke. Head for the hills. I am heading for town."

"Are you crazy?"

James shook his head in the negative but headed off for town.

"Crazy bastard. If the dam broke, the last place you go is to town. I'd better hustle up to those hills. If the tracks are broke up ahead, they can wait. If that dam really did break, well look out below."

The man continued to talk to him self as he headed, still in the general direction of South Fork, but angling to the hills rather than following the tracks cut into the hills.

James rode on. Soon he arrived at the small town of Mineral Point. It really was not much of a town, more like a village. A couple of streets flanked by small homes and an equally small railroad station. A creek ran by Mineral point. Usually the stream was tranquil and the waters barely a trickle. With the rains, the stream was now overflowing its banks and threatening the homes.

At this pace, I shall never make it to town in time. Mary, Mary!

Right then, he spotted a train sitting just up from the Mineral Point station.

I can get that train to make the trip there of course. It's the only way.

He pushed his loyal steed to make shorten the distance between him and the idle train. Suddenly, a loud deafening roar was heard off in the distance. The ground seemed to shake. The dam had broken.

"Come on horse we're running out of time!"

To the closed up houses, he shouted loudly trying to overcome the roar of the rain and the impending floodwaters.

"The dam has broke! Head for the hills!"

Then he heard the engine of the train gaining strength. The horn started to blow loud and strong.

Good God, he's leaving. I have to catch him. It is my only chance. My last chance!

With that he kicked the horse once more and raced closer and closer as the train backed out of the station and headed back to Johnstown.

"Come on boy, you can rest soon. Just catch that train. Come on!"

The train took time picking up speed and the horse and James were flying by now at top speed. The conductor, John Hess, could not see James, because James was approaching on the opposite side from where John sat, and the rain was falling in torrents. If he had seen him, it is doubtful he could have done anything, since the large train was already in motion and quickly picking up speed. James released his legs from the stirrups and leaned off the horse.

I have to jump now. I have to get on that cowcatcher. I don't think I can make it. Here goes!

In one fluid motion, James Peyton swung up and off the horse. He found himself feeling as if he were floating on the air in slow motion. The train continued to move away from him, which was fortunate. Otherwise, the impact from his abrupt landing would have been greater. Still the iron of the cowcatcher stung hard when James' body hit. He grabbed on, hanging on for dear life as the train reached the maximum speed under the conditions. He clung on, hoping soon to reach Johnstown, before the water did.

The train continued down to East Conemaugh, the small borough before Woodvale. John Hess had planned to go further and on into Johnstown but his way was blocked by the Pittsburgh Day Express. Stopped, he hurried to get to his family and to safety. He felt a tug on his arm and was shocked to see someone standing beside him.

"Where can I get a horse?"

"A horse? What do you want with a horse man? The dam's broke. Head for the hills!"

"I need a horse to get to Johnstown."

John Hess could not spare more time with this obvious crazy person. He pointed to a barn just over one hundred yards away. He did not know if there was a horse there. However, he did not want to stand there talking while everyone, including his family, were in danger. The strange young man hurried off and John Hess moved off in the opposite direction with great speed.

James found a horse in the barn and leaped on its back.

No time for saddles now. Sure hope this horse has some life in him.

Out of the barn he rode and turned for town. The rivers surrounding the town had already flooded and made the going a little more challenging then he had expected. However, James didn't hesitate. He drove the horse through the waters of East Conemaugh, down through the proud borough of Woodvale, and down into Johnstown. All the while screaming.

"The dam has broke. The dam has broke. Head for the hills."

Some noticed him and some even took the advice. However, all would later comment on the strange lad, the "Paul Revere" who had raced through the streets calling out to people of the coming flood.

One who heard the cry was Ben Hoffman, the hack driver. He was already on his second floor to wait out the floodwaters when he heard James' cry. Fearful he called out to his wife.

"Mary, I think we have some trouble coming here! Get the kids."

Ben Hoffman took off his shoes and socks, stuffing his socks into his pants pockets.

I think I am going to be taking a little bath now. So best be ready.

Mary grabbed the children, Bertha, Marion, Joseph, Frieda, and Florence and rushed to her husband's side.

"Ben what is it? Is there trouble?"

"Someone just shouted that the dam broke. I think we should head for the hills."

"Ben, now you know people are always saying that. It is an old tale every time we get this high water."

"Well maybe you are right dear, but there was something eerie in that cry I heard. Something down right scary if you ask me. Where are Harry and Will?"

"Harry and Will are out there in this rain with most other boys. I declare they seem to like the rain. The more it comes down, the more they like it."

"I guess you're right. We can all relax. I'm probably over-reacting."

James headed down Clinton Street and across Main, down to the house where Mary had said she would be at the corner of Vine and Bedford Streets. He continued yelling but had to admit he sounded like a damn fool.

Please let them listen. Take heed. Leave the city.

Three boys watched him splash past on his tired horse. Will Huffman looked up and yelled to his brother Harry and their friend Vincent Quinn.

"Look out!"

The knee-deep water splashed as James Peyton charged up Clinton Street. James had to swerve his horse quickly to avoid the three boys standing there in the knee-deep water. He barley missed them. One of them yelled out.

"Hey you crazy dunce! Now look at me. I am all wet!"

Will Huffman laughed at his slightly soggier friend Vincent Quinn.

"I told ya to watch out."

"I'm soaked to the bone."

"Ah, you were soaked before that happened. Just look at us. We are a mess. Course that crazy guy on the horse looks worse than we ever could. Hey, lets go for the hills. This flooding is becoming too messy anyway. Didn't I hear that guy say, "The dam's broke"?" Harry inquired, looking at his two friends.

"I got to go home guys. My mom said to be home by three. What time is it anyway?"

"About a quarter till four. Shoot Vincent, come on. We can get up on the rocks and have a good ole time." Will wrapped his arm around his friend's shoulder. He pointed ahead to where Harry was, already heading in the direction of the nearest hill.

"Nah, you guys go on ahead. My mom'll worry. I best scoot home. Beside I need to change into something drier than this."

"Vince my friend, I'll never understand you. You're the only person I know who worries about being neat in the rain. Take care ole pal. See ya later when this rain stops."

"Bye guys." Vincent hurried off down Main Street.

James Peyton reached his destination. Stopping in front, he whacked the horse on the back urging him away. He leaped the front stoop and entered the door without knocking.

"Mary! Mary! Are you here? Hello?"

No one was on the first floor as the rising waters had flooded that level and they had moved to the second floor.

Mary heard a voice yelling out, but could not make out the words.

James is that you? My darling, you have found me.

"James, we are up here, on the second floor. Hurry. Hurry my darling."

James vaulted the stairs two at a time to reach the top. He burst into the bedroom from where he had heard Mary cry out to him. His appearance shocked the families huddling there. James Peyton looked quite the mess. His hair was matted down but stuck out in several places. His face was splashed with mud from the town and from his trip. His eyes shown both with fear and yet with a certain fire. Jennie Mihelic reached out and covered him with a blanket. She handed him a white linen handkerchief to clean his face. He nodded his thanks and gathered his breath.

"The dam has broke. We have to get out of here. We must head for the hills."

Charles Mihelic studied the young man in front of him.

"Be calm son. Even if it has broken, it would take some kind of power to cause the town much damage. We are so far away from it and all."

"Begging your pardon sir, but you didn't see it, water, so much water. We must find the hills."

Charles made a quick decision to trust his future son-in-law.

"Then lets git."

Charles Mihelic didn't get to finish that sentence for the flood hit with its full force. The house was gone in an instant.

At about the same time, further downtown, the Quinn's were preparing to head for the hillside and safety. James Quinn had organized the family and told all to move with haste towards the hills.

"Where in blazes is Vincent? Does anyone know?" James Quinn was showing his frustration at his absent son. Rosina Quinn replied to her husband.

"He went out earlier with the Hoffman boys. I told him to be home by 3 PM."

"Well it is well past three now and he is not here. Write a quick message to him that we have gone to the hills to seek safety. Shoot. He should be here!"

James moved out with his family and to the hills. Alas, one last time Aunt Abbey would choose to disobey her brother-in-law. She held back as James and the others moved off towards the close by hills. Libby and Gertrude Quinn were standing behind her. Abbey Geis looked down at the muddy water flowing in the streets. She turned and spoke to Libby; "I'm not going out in that mess. This house is strong.

I'm sure no flood will crush it. No, we'll stay here. Besides Gertrude will get sick walking in all that water. Come on we will move upstairs."

"Are you sure, Mrs. Geis? I do think we should follow Mr. Quinn?" Libby asked, looking at the fast disappearing James Quinn.

"Well go if you want. I cannot stop you. But I am keeping Gertrude here with me and my child."

Libby looked out and saw the departing Quinn family sloshing through the rising waters.

Perhaps Mrs. Geis is right. Besides, I do not want to leave Gertrude here alone.

"I'll stay. Let's hurry upstairs then. The water is almost in the doors now."

"Come."

"I don't want to. I want to go with my daddy. I want to go with him."

Gertrude now was crying but it was too late. They had made their choice. They would stay.

CHAPTER 18

▼

THE FLOOD

The water released from the dam surges down the mountain. It follows the valley path winding its way ever downward, reaping death and havoc in its wake. A large rail viaduct holds it back briefly but the new dam can only hold it temporarily. The viaduct soon gives way crumbling under the pent up force. The stone from the bridge adds to the growing amount of debris as the waters continue on their deadly course.

The small village of Mineral Point is next in its way. The town is obliterated in seconds. Every house gone, crushed like toothpicks. It rushes on smashing through East Conemaugh and Franklin wrecking havoc in its path. The flood tore up the trains stopped there and continued on smashing the mill works all the while building up into an unstoppable force.

The water roars on into the level plain that contains the local steel company's model community of Woodvale. Every building there save a lone mill falls to the onslaught. The mill is left standing but remains only a shell. It stands out in sharp contrast to the now barren plain. The rushing water then gathers even more strength as the valley narrows at this point just prior to entering the town itself.

When the now raging waters finally hit the town reports describe it as "a wall not of water". To some, it appears as if the whole mountain has descended upon the town. The 'mountain' is over 40 feet high as it explodes into the town of Johnstown.

Victor Heiser had tended to the horses and was ready to go back when he heard the awful roar announcing the coming flood.

What in blazes is that? It sounds as if the whole world is being ripped apart.

Victor looks back to his home. His father is motioning to him frantically to go back into the barn and climb out to the roof. Victor doesn't hesitate. He runs into the barn and up to the roof as quick as he can. Once on the roof, he looks back over it towards his home.

There it is whatever "it" is.

Victor sees not water but a mass of trees, train cars, and parts of houses moving rapidly in his direction. In the blink of an eye, the wave hits his home and it and his parents are gone. The barn is hit next and in a second, it too is crushed. Victor Heiser clings on for dear life.

If somehow I can just get on top of this moving freight train, I will be all right. Just get and stay on top. Come on Victor old boy, you can do it.

He starts to climb moving from one piece of debris, trash, wreckage, to another. For a while it works. He works his way, ever upward.

Where in blazes is the top? My fingers and toes are getting numb. Oh-oh.

He slips trying to reach a tree jutting out. He finds himself falling in the open air.

Waving his arms about him, he finds nothing with which to grab hold.

This is it. I am going to die.

Victor calls out to no one in particular. "Help!"

Thump!

"What?"

Somewhat miraculously Victor Heiser had fallen onto the roof of a house.

Whew! I am still alive. My God, what will happen next?

He clings to the roof for support being carried forward by the massive wave. His hope for making it to the top now dashed.

Just down the street from the Heiser's John Fenn is rushing back from the store.

I have enough provisions for three days. That should be enough to get us through this mess. What is that noise? Oh my God.

John drops his groceries. His fate is inevitable as the wall of water bears down on him. He looks to his neighbors peering out of their house at the coming destruction. He cups his hands and yells out to them, "Say good-bye for me to my family." In the next instant he is swept away. John Fenn was within two houses distance from his home when the wave hit.

The evil wave continues on its deadly mission and smashes into the Fenn house hard. Inside, the terrified Fenn family brace themselves.

"Watch and hold on tight children. It will be all right. Hold tight!"

The house slowly creaks and crumbles under the awesome power of the raging wall of water.

All is chaos. Furniture and children are tossed about in the mixture of mud, water, and whatever else brought by the terrible wave. It is dark inside and much screaming is heard. Anna tries to hold her baby close to her but is buffeted back and forth. The baby slips from her grasp. She lunges out saying, "Oh no. Please no!"

She reaches out trying to get her baby back. The baby is lost from her sight sinking into the muck and the water.

A loud bloodcurdling scream cuts into her efforts to find her baby. Anna turns to see her son, George Washington, blood gushing from his face.

Bricks from my own home killed my son. Fell in on him. George!

He disappears beneath the water. Anna is close to hysteria. She has lost two of her children and there is no end in sight to this awful calamity. She tries to recover.

Must not panic. Dear God, must not panic. Bismarck, Anna, John. Must think of the others.

"Momma! Where are you?"

Bismarck cries out as he is sucked down into the waters.

It is so dark. Where are you, my precious Bismarck? Come to momma.

He is gone.

Anna Fenn calls out to her namesake child, her father's favorite, little Anna.

"Anna, darling make it over to momma. Hurry honey. Come. Come!"

Anna Fenn sees the terror in her daughter's eyes as her daughter moves towards her.

I can almost reach you. Just a little further. Now. Anna!

Anna's fear leaves her face replaced by a look of calm resignation. She disappears within seconds. Her mother cries out in anguish.

"God help us. Anna!"

Everywhere Anna Fenn looks, there is death. Her oldest John Fenn holds on the longest.

I must be brave. Momma is hurting so. I am so scared. So tired. I can't hold on anymore. Momma, I am sorry.

John Fenn looks at his mother. She is staring off into blank space.

He lets go of the coat rack he is holding for support and is at once swallowed up by the churning waters.

Anna Fenn is alone now. Pregnant and barely able to move, she floats along with her seven dead children in the remnants of her broken home.

This God, this is too much to bear.

Anna Fenn would survive.

Ben Hoffman and his family did not know what hit them. The force of the wave ripped the house into many pieces and carried them off in its wake. They would not survive. The Rev. Beale was more fortunate. The flood did not hit his parsonage directly. Even so, the force of the wave hitting the house pushed a hat rack against him.

"Come we must get upstairs. I fear the water will crush us here."

His family and some neighbors who had stopped by to visit moved up to the third floor. Just then the window smashed open and in flew a man.

"Who are you? Where are you from?" Beale fairly shouted.

"Woodvale." The man gasped. He had been carried on a roof for a mile and a quarter.

"Folks, let us gather and pray for deliverance for this is a fearful time."

In the midst of the room, Reverend Beale led them in prayer as outside the floodwaters raged through the city. Rev. Beale and his flock would survive.

Maggie Irwin looked out on the street with concern. The waters were rising every minute. More folks had come into the hotel since earlier in the day.

I do fear we will be filled to capacity today. The last thing I need is a bunch of hungry people and no food. I wish this rain would stop.

"Please people go up to the second floor. We cannot keep you here until the waters recede. You will be safer up there."

The wave hit the hotel head on. It crumbled. Many in the hotel that day, including Maggie Irwin and the Smith family drowned. Survivors from the Hulbert hotel would be few. Ironically, Jeremiah Smith, trapped back in the house at the Stoney Creek would survive, as would the house.

Vincent Quinn heard a roar as he approached his home. He didn't turn around but tried to outrun the onrushing waters, to make it home. He never made it, swept away in the frightening power of the deluge.

James Quinn and his family had reached the hillside. So he had thought. He turned around and found Gertrude, her Aunt Abbey, Abbey's son, and the maid Libby missing. He started to go back to get them, then looked up to see the mass of water coming towards them all. He turned and ran to the hills with the water coming ever closer.

Please, dear God watch over them. Watch over Vincent!

Back at the Quinn house, they had begun to regret their decision.

"Libby, this is the end of the world. We will all die together."

Abbey Geis cried out softly and fell to her knees praying.

"Jesus, Mary, and Joseph, have mercy on us, Oh God!"

Gertrude kept screaming, "Papa! Papa! Papa!" Libby held her close to herself while growing ever more terrified. The flood smashed into the house hard.

The plaster started to fall from the ceiling and the whole house seemed to give out a shudder. Water sprouted up through the floor at Abbey Geis' feet. Gertrude looked at the shocked faces. The floor broke apart. In the next instant her Aunt Abbey and Libby were gone. Gertrude found herself flailing in the water. Gertrude Quinn struggled to get out of the crushing water. She looked up and saw light through a hole in the roof. Struggling, she pulled herself up and through the hole. After squeezing through the small hole, she grabbed a mattress that was floating by. She climbed aboard the shaky craft and held on for dear life in the dangerous waters. Gertrude Quinn was too stunned to call out at first. Her attempts to remain on the mattress amid the rushing waters occupied her attention.

Mary Mihelic found herself deep in water, mud, and debris.

"Where am I?"

She opened her eyes but could not see anything. It was completely dark.

Of course, the flood hit us. I am in it. Where is everyone? Where is James?

She struggled to move but her clothes were caught on something and dragging her down. *Have to get out of these clothes now.*

She swiftly slipped off her clothes and stripped down to her under garments. Relieved of the drag she moved up swiftly through the turgid waters. Still, when she reached the surface she was gasping for air.

"Where is everyone? Oh God, where is everyone?"

Her head turned everywhere trying to see someone she knew. Her arm bumped something. It was a tree uprooted from the ground and bouncing through the waters.

"James? Momma? Papa? Grace? Where are you? Please?"

Victor Heiser saw Mary looking around in fear.

Poor girl, I fear they are lost. Lost as we all are.

He looked beyond Mary Mihelic and saw the Mussante family also floating on a raft of some sort. The Mussantes owned a little grocery store by Victor's home.

I find this oddly strange. I want to wave at them. What kind of lunacy is this that makes me think such odd thoughts?

All at once a huge tree shot up from the water and crushed down on the Mussante raft. They were gone in an instant.

Oh My God! Why is this happening? Is God wreaking vengeance on this town?

Victor Heiser tried to maneuver his roof raft over to where Mary was floundering in the water. Instead, he just sailed on past her carried away by the swift currents.

James was startled to find himself deep in the water. His left arm felt strange and numb. He wondered if it was broken.

I can't give up. Mary may need me. I must make it. Somehow.

He started for the surface, or at least upwards, since he had no idea where he was. Rubble kept hitting against him, scratching his face and impeding his progress. He started to swallow the muddy water.

Mary, I am sorry, I cannot make it. Please forgive me.

Just then a hand reached out and pulled him up.

Was it God?

It was Mary Mihelic. He coughed out water.

"Mary, you are here. Thank God."

"James, I thought I had lost you. Oh darling."

"We had better find something to float on. We will never last in this water long."

Mary spotted something floating along towards them.

"There! Over there is a roof or something. It will have to do."

They both swam over to the battered roof of yet another crushed house.

James crawled onto the roof first and then helped Mary.

"James what is wrong with your arm?"

"I think I broke it when the house we were in tore apart. It's fine. Where are your parents? Grace?"

"I don't know. Oh James I am so afraid."

James looked past Mary and saw a body floating in the churning waters. He remembered what Mrs. Mihelic had been wearing. He placed his arms on Mary's shoulders and turned her around. Mary cried out.

"Oh God. Oh God. Momma, My momma. Please don't leave me."

James held her tight trying to squeeze out the sadness of the sight. Her tears flowed down her face. Mrs. Mihelic was too far away for them to reach her and the distance kept growing. Mary continued to weep uncontrollably. James continued to scan the waters around the raft. The rafts bobbing up and down in the currents hindered his efforts, as did the tremendous amounts of debris floating along in the angry waters. James spotted Grace floating close to the roof raft. He gently pulled back from Mary and reached down to bring in Grace's limp form. Mary's whole body shook. Her baby sister was dead.

She took her into her arms and looked into the closed eyes. She looked so at peace, so calm. "Why James? Why did this have to happen?"

He didn't have an answer and even if he had one, he didn't think Mary wanted one just then. James continued to scan the horizon looking for danger. It was everywhere.

Gertrude Quinn was frightened as she raced along on the small mattress. A dead horse came by and caught hold of the mattress.

"Go away you dumb horse. Go!"

The horse threatened to drag Gertrude off in seconds. A tree rushed by and caught the dead animal in its branches. Slowly it pulled the horse off and away. As it moved on the poor animal bobbed up and down like some perverse rocking horse. Gertrude shivered.

I am cold. Daddy, where are you? Help. Help. Is no one here to help me? Wait.

A whole house came floating by with a man on it.

I am saved.

"Help me! Save me!"

The man on the house was clinging to what was left of the chimney. His eyes were white with fear. The house came very close to the mattress. The man did not move. He just stared at the girl while clinging to the chimney. Swiftly the opportunity and the house passed by.

"You terrible man. I will never help you!"

She shouted after him oblivious to her state and the dangers there.

Shortly thereafter, a large section of a roof, perhaps from one of the hotels in town, comes floating by. It is further away than the man had been, and as many as twenty people are aboard. Gertrude calls out again.

"Help me! Save me. Someone."

Over on the roof one man moves to answer her distress. The others pull back on him, yelling, "Don't be crazy you fool! You will only get yourself killed! Look at those waters! She is too far away."

"Be off with ya now. The child is in danger. Can't ya plain see?"

Please, let him come. Please mister, come save me.

With a great push, the man manages to break away from the restraints of the others. He jumps into the swirling waters and begins swimming towards her. Several times, he goes under. Each time Gertrude Quinn screams.

"Help me. Please don't leave me!"

He continues on, fighting the waves and fighting his exhaustion. He reaches the mattress and hangs on briefly, tired from his efforts. Gasping for breath, he eventually lifts himself aboard the fragile craft. Instantly Gertrude grabs onto him and hugs him. She clings to him as they head down stream. In the churning swirling waters the mattress spins wildly, thrashing in and out of the waves.

The Elder house on Walnut Street is hit and destroyed in an instant. Mrs. Elder cries out to her daughter, "Nannie! Oh my God. It's the end of the world." They are swept away with the house. Neither survives. Cyrus Elder remained in his brother's house only a few blocks away unaware of the destruction of his home and family. Although struck by the flood, this house survives, as does Cyrus.

Victor Heiser had rapidly moved forward, pushed by the swift currents and waves. He fought to keep his tiny raft upright.

I cannot survive long at this rate. It is only a matter of time.

The sky abruptly darkens above him.

"No!"

Looking up he sees a huge freight car about to crush down on him.

This is it. I am done.

All at once, he feels a jolt and his flimsy raft bolts forward.

"Hold on. Help me!"

The steel car crashes down right where Victor had been. The waters from the spray both propel him forward and splash over his tiny craft. The effect of the surge pushes him ahead of the major wave but even closer towards his destiny.

Where am I headed? What in God's name is going on?

He looks up from the swirling waters to see his ultimate destination. There before him looms the hill rising from the western side of Johnstown. His first observation is positive.

There, if I make it there, I can land and skidaddle up that hillside.

Reality sinks in quickly.

Only problem is I am moving so fast. Too fast. Too fast.

Mary and James trail some distance behind Victor. Like him, they are being dragged swiftly forward and towards the towering hill. Mary is in a sense of shock at having seen her mother and sister dead. She keeps brushing Grace's hair and crying. James continues to search the waters now flowing with many more bodies. People are screaming for help everywhere.

So sad. Please dear God let me see her father. He has to have survived.

James eyes stop as he spots someone off in the distance.

Is it possible? Yes. Yes, it is!

"Mary! Mary, I see your father! There, over there! Look!"

Mary follows James' pointing arm, and indeed the person looks like her father. Still, he is a good ways off from them. Whoever he is, he is not standing still. The man is in a constant state of movement. He swims through the murky violent waters, grabbing women and children alike. He places one on a rooftop or piece of a house and is off for another. James and Mary watch, transfixed by this one-person dynamo, unmindful of their pending fate. The man grabs two children in his arms and swimming only with his powerful legs manages to bring them to safety and the waiting arms of their mother. Mary did not need to see more.

It is her father, her papa. *I must call out to him, to let him know I am here.*

The buffeting continues. Mary is forced to grab hold of the tenuous raft.

No, he couldn't hear me anyway. This noise is deafening.

"Papa!"

James tries to steady their meager little raft. He looks up to see the cause of the buffeting. They are on a collision course with the mountainside.

"Mary! Hold on! Good God, hold on!"

The wave hits hard against the mountainside. Many are crushed as they smash into the hard rock and trees. The screaming is intensified as bodies are flung about as if rag dolls.

Fortunately, the main wave hits the mountainside before Mary and James' raft. Unfortunately, they find themselves now caught in the back swell. The raft spins in a circle and hurtles back towards the city to meet the still on-coming waters. Mary worries little for the dangers they are facing. She anxiously looks around, her head turning Swiftly, to locate where she had last seen her father.

Her eyes are drawn to him as if by magnet.

There. Oh Papa!

Charles Mihelic acknowledges his daughter with a slight wave. Mary starts to return the wave when a large tree, caught in the same back-wash smashes into Charles. His large back arches with the pain. He places his last bundle, a small girl onto the tree that had just crashed into him. Mary cries out, "Papa!"

Charles Mihelic turns to his daughter. Even from the distance, Mary sees the pain on his face. "Oh, Papa."

He gives her a weak salute and then slips swiftly beneath the muddy water.

"No! It can't be. Oh God, no!"

Mary moves to jump into the water after him. James grabs her by the arm and holds her back.

"Mary. Listen to me. There is nothing to be done now. I am sorry. Your father is gone. We must save ourselves."

Just then, the second wave coming through town hits the tiny craft. James and Mary are jostled and flipped like puppets. Grace's body slides off into the water and floats away. Mary is thrown to the edge and almost falls off. James grabs her by the waist and pulls her back towards the center of the small vessel. They remain there clinging to each other and to their fragile raft.

"Oh please, no, no more."

Mary reaches out straining to grab her sister. It is not to be. The swirling angry water quickly lengthens the distance between them. Mary watches for a brief while. Then she buries her face in her hands.

We are lost.

The backlash of water divides the wave and the resulting turbulence into two factions. One wave rushes south of town and roars into the Kernville neighborhood. More houses fall to this new force now unleashed. A huge oak tree pierces the Shultz' second floor and the entire house is lifted and floats along as one giant raft. The Shultz family survives.

The other portion of the wave now appeared to have a purpose. The water continues to swirl as the currents pick up speed. The wall of water pushes everything forward, toward the great stone bridge that leads from Johnstown and into the neighboring borough of Cambria City. Rubbish and the wrecked train cars pile up blocking the bridge and creating a death trap for those who follow.

"Help! For the love of God, please save us!"

The people from the newly defined shore watch with fear. The swirling water rushes by taking adults and children on a ride that will surely end in death. If they do not drown in the heavy and forceful current, then they will surely die when they crash into the mounting debris further down by the old Stone Bridge. The screams are loud and piercing the afternoon air. No one moves. The people on the shoreline watch the scene with detached stares. Some look around waiting for someone else to make a move. It is part terror and part fear yes, but also bone tired bodies that had rushed to get free of the water's deadly embrace. Once free of its embrace few had the desire to test its strength again.

All of a sudden, a blur rushes past the onlookers and dives into the swirling currents. People look up to see a dog swimming against the current and out to the desperate ones facing imminent death. They are amazed that the dog is not dragged away. Onward he swims, fighting with every stroke to make it to the helpless people. The dog swims up to a little girl. She places her arms around his broad neck.

"Nice doggie. Take me to shore."

Without any hesitation or rest, the dog turns round and heads for shore.

The crowd cheers.

"Come on dog. Come on boy. You can do it."

Again, the dog fights off the pull of the current and makes steady progress to shore. The water pulls equally hard trying to claim yet another victim in its wake. The dog does not give in and reaches the shoreline with his precious cargo.

"Good doggie. Good boy," the girl cries out. She releases the dog's neck, climbs to her feet and rushes up to the awaiting hands. The dog does not wait. He turns around and once more leaps into the rapid waters swimming heartily out to another terrified soul. Some limbs from trees and other debris hinder his progress. He changes course several times but never loses sight of his destination. A young boy, about eight years old, lies shaking on a small piece of wood. He watches the approaching dog swimming towards him. The piece of wood is all that remains of the boy's home and family. The dog arrives and the boy practically leaps onto the dog. The dog sinks under the weight and the shock but quickly rises to the surface, not losing his burden. The cheering is louder this time as the dog nears the shore. People venture closer to the edge eager to see if the dog can indeed make it to shore.

"Good dog. Good boy. Keep on coming. Yes"

This time some men enter the waters by the newly defined shore. They grab the young boy who had been carried to safety by the brave dog. Once more the dog turns and rushes back into the now raging waters. He is tired. The dog spots a young lady of about fourteen. She is larger than the other two had been but is closest to shore and to the dog. Again he dodges trees, parts of houses, and wreckage along his stated course. He swims up to the roof the young girl is sitting upon. She hesitates. She says to the dog, "I'm scared."

The dog whines but does not leave her side. Both hurtle down stream. The dog tries to climb upon the raft but cannot and slips back into the water. He whines again, imploring the girl to come with him.

"All right I'm coming! Please save me."

The girl leaps onto the dog. He once more sinks below the surface. It is but a brief moment and he is above the water. The now fully engaged crowd on shore cheers. The cheers mix in awful contrast with the screaming of the others who are dying. However, it is plain to see for those on the shore that they are seeing a true hero here today amiss the misery. This last time however, he cannot beat the currents. He is able to keep the girl above water but he can no longer fight the strong pull down stream. He keeps trying, pushing to make the awaiting shore. His legs are weak, his spirit undimmed. He makes progress but it is too little. The girl hanging on to his neck does not seem to notice his weakness.

"Come on boy. We are almost there."

A hush comes over the crowd. They watch as the strong dog fights the unyielding currents. You can almost see a look of helplessness on the dog's face. Onward, he swims no longer moving forward.

A man on shore can't stand it any longer.

"By God I will not let that dog go away like this."

Though tired he jumps in the water and wades out to the dog and girl.

"God! This current is strong. How'd you do it boy?"

He grabs the dog and the girl and pulls them to shore. The girl pats the dog on the head.

"My hero," she says and hugs the dog. Then she scampers up the hill and away from the water. The dog walks a couple more steps and then drops to the ground panting heavily. The efforts had taken their toll.

The man who had rescued the girl and the dog patted him on the back.

"Good boy. You did a great job here."

The dog tries to rise, attempting to get up once more. The man restrained him.

"Easy boy. You've done enough for today. You rest now and let us do some of the work?"

Son of a gun, I think you understand me.

He leaves the dog and runs up to several of the men standing nearby.

"Come on, we can't let this dog show us up. Look, if we make a chain, we can at least get those people close to shore in and out of that water. Come on now."

The men look around to each other and reluctantly move forward to assist. They lock arms and create a human chain reaching out to people floating by, capturing them one by one. They are so involved in the effort they don't notice the brave dog laying on the shore.

The dog watches for a time panting heavily all the while. Then slowly he lays his head down, closes his eyes, and dies. Old man Morley's dog is finally at rest.

Gertrude Quinn looks up and stares into the stern face of her savior.

"What's your name?"

He looks down at this precious child and a smile breaks on his face. He answers, "Max McAchren."

"Well Max. It is nice to meet you. I am Gertrude Quinn."

Max's gaze drops down to see a tiny hand extended in greeting. His hard rough hand engulfs the little girl's.

A scream is heard from in front of them. It comes from the roof that Max had left to swim over to Gertrude. The roof is swirling around in what must have been a whirlpool created by the wave's backlash.

"Help. Save us. Help," the people on the roof yelled. The roof keeps spinning and twisting, rocking in the rough currents. A crunching sound is heard and the roof breaks in half. Most of its passengers sink with the broken portion. A strong few manage to swim away from the current and make it to safety. Max and Gertrude watch in horror.

Max turns from the horror and spots a house on the close by hillside. The men inside are using poles to reach people close enough to pull into the shore. The mattress is too far for the poles to reach. Soon Max and Gertrude would move on past them.

One of the men on shore calls out to Max.

"Throw the child over here!"

"Do you think you can catch her?" Max calls back.

The same man answers, "We can try".

Max looks at his small charge and says. "Be calm Gertrude. I can get you there."

Gertrude did not worry. She looks up and into Max's face once more.

My hero won't let me get hurt.

"I know you can," is all she says.

Max is not as sure. The bank is a long way off and the mattress is very unsteady. He sees no other choice however, for God only knows what lay down stream.

Oh blessed lord let me make it. And let them blokes catch her.

Gertrude Quinn hugs him one last time. Max lifts her in his massive arms up over his head. As he suspected the mattress is unstable and rocks. He quickly steadies himself and with a giant heave, he throws her towards the men on shore.

Gertrude is in the air and moving as if in slow motion towards the awaiting arms.

I'm flying.

"Gotcha!"

The men catch Gertrude in their arms and gently set her down on shore. Max jostled by the heave grabs onto the mattress and holds on. He moves swiftly past the little girl and her heroes. Gertrude watches as he moves down stream. She waves and tries to catch his sight. She could not do so, as Max was now looking up forward. He was moving faster now and on a collision course with the Stone Bridge. Ahead lay only a wall of wreckage.

At least the child is safe.

Gertrude Quinn survives.

When the backlash of the wave hit the second onslaught from the town it split in two. James and Mary headed towards the old Stone Bridge. Victor Heiser headed up and into the Kernville area, away from the Stone Bridge. The water here is calmer and more stable. He spots a larger roof than his dilapidated craft.

"Mind if I jump aboard?"

"Sure if you can make it," answers a man on the roof.

Victor smiles.

Shoot, after what I have faced, this is nothing.

He leaps aboard.

Safe. I have made it.

He looks at his watch. He knew the flood had hit at exactly 4:10 PM. He chuckles to himself as he thinks of the reason that he had checked his watch at such a dangerous time. *I wanted to know how long it would take me to reach the other world.* Surprisingly the watch was still running even after the flood and the jostling.

Not even 4:20 PM yet. Ten minutes ago, my parents were alive. Johnstown existed. Now, nothing.

Several of the men on the roof gently guided it to the shoreline near the rising hill. Victor hops off and looks back towards the town.

Saved. Why me?

He notices a small piece of wood floating bye drifting along back towards the devastation. *My gosh, there's a baby on that piece of wood!* He wades out into the water and rescues the little child. He sees a note attached to her. He picks it up and reads it. "My name is Elizabeth Bingham Burdick. If you find me, please help me to find my parents."

Well little one, perhaps there is reason to hope. Yes, we will find your parents. I think I shall dub you "the flood baby".

Victor Heiser and the baby Elizabeth survive.

Mary and James are caught up in the rapids and moving towards the Stone Bridge. Mary is still much in shock from the events and the loss of her parents and sister. She stares out into the empty space. She is heedless of the screams and noise around her. James tries to steady the small raft. He views Mary with a new concern.

I need your help Mary if we are to survive. I know you are suffering. Oh dear God, will you be able to help?

Mary turns to James breaking out of her trance. She looks at him and simply says, "I love you James."

James responds, "I love you Mary."

With those spoken words, their bond is renewed. James surveys the options up ahead. All is a mass of debris. It grows larger and more massive as roofs break up and people smash into the trees, houses, railroad cars, and the other wreckage that had been carried there by the rushing waters. He notes with concern the results of roofs similar to their own. Most crumble on impact and leave the people floundering in the water. Once in the water they are caught up in the rubbish or hit by another house, roof, or tree crashing into them. Some leave their makeshift rafts and swim for one shore or the other. A few make it. Most don't make it to the shore instead drowning in the churning currents.

Even if we wanted to, Mary and I could not make the swim to shore. We are too tired and my arm is killing me. Our only chance is to stay with this piece of roof. Think. There has to be a way to get through. There has to be.

Up ahead of them and to their right James spots a lone man on a mattress. He observes him stroking frantically, attempting to move the odd craft even further to the right.

Max McAchren looks up ahead. He knows that the Stone Bridge brings only death. The wreckage and growing debris strewn there would kill him instantly. The speed of the current was too fast and the cluster of trees, trains, and wire had already blocked and clogged up the bridge. He looks off to the right and sees a slim possibility. The water that is being backed up by the bridge had created a culvert up over and around the bridge into Cambria City.

If I can catch that wave, I can make it. By God I have to.

Struggling with what was left of the mattress, he guides it for the opening. Max paddles harder then ever.

Come on. Come on.

He finds himself grabbing the ends of the mattress and barely holding on. The mattress had caught the wave. The ride is bumpy ar d even faster than the current that had been carrying him to the bridge. Several times Max is almost thrown from his craft. Up and over the bridge the mattress goes. The ride down the other side is swift and treacherous. Max hangs on for dear life.

I made it! By God, I did it.

The current on the other side, while still swift is calmer than what he had just ridden through. Max continues his ride through to Cambria City. He guides the beat up mattress to the shoreline about a mile down from Johnstown and the Stone Bridge. Max McAchren had survived.

James Peyton seeing how McAchren made the move through the culvert turns to Mary. "Mary, listen to me. We can make that opening. We must. I will use this piece of wood as a rudder. Use this other piece of wood as an oar to drive us that way."

He points to the culvert. Mary nods her head. James sticks the makeshift paddle in the water and struggles with both arms to guide their raft. They were further to the left than Max McAchren had been when he made his move. James' arms ache with the strain. The one arm, hurt earlier when the huge wave hit, was almost useless. By wrapping it around the 'rudder', he is able to leverage his weight in his attempts to guide the craft. Mary pushes her own makeshift oar into the water, and strokes, faster and faster. She cries out in anger and in pain, "Damn it! Come on you old roof! Move. Move!"

James cries out with the strain of the effort to turn the boat. Slowly the small beaten roof moves and turns in the direction they desire. Mary keeps her strange oar in the water and paddles, stroking in the same direction and with one aim, the culvert.

"It's turning. Keep going."

The progression toward the Stone Bridge is more rapid. The current is swift and strong. The bridge and death looms ever nearer. James bears down on the churning water. He yells out, "Push. Push. Make it. Come on."

James holds on to the rudder even as the water pressed against it. The roof keeps turning. The garbage and debris jammed at the bridge is almost upon them.

We have to make it. We are so close. So fast. We are moving too fast. Damn you, roof, turn! Turn!

The culvert is within sight. The pile of debris around the bridge loomed just in front of them. The roof is turning. The roof is moving towards the culvert.

Mary yells out once more, "Jesus! Please. Oh God! Help us! Have Mercy on us."

Surrounding them is death and devastation. People scream and shout for salvation. The current is moving so fast and the water swirling so violently there is no escape except for the culvert.

A tree sticking out from the debris threatens their small craft. Its roots appear to reach out to them and beckon them in. They are on a path to meet it and to be crushed in its grasp. James rushes past Mary and locks his temporary rudder onto the tree to prevent their imminent crash. A low groan is heard as the wood catches the tree. The two forces, the water and the small 'rudder' fight for dominance. James uses the tree as leverage to push the raft towards the culvert. As he pushes off, the rudder snaps. He yells and falls. James quickly finds himself staring into the muddy waters. The push is just enough, however. They have caught the wave and are bolted forward, up and towards the bridge abutment.

James clings to the raft near the edge where he has fallen. He looks back to Mary at the other end of the roof holding on in the same manner. The bumping gets rougher. James and Mary are tossed around like pieces of paper on the meager raft. Crack! The sound pierces the late afternoon air. A piece of the raft splits off and James tumbles into the water.

"Help. Oh God no. Not now."

Mary reacts immediately. She jumps from her position at the edge of the now diminished raft. She catches hold of James' outstretched hand just before he floats away. It appears as if she will just follow him into the water. The force is so strong. She manages to gain a small form of balance and grabs James with both of her hands. She cries out in pain but does not loosen her grip. The force of the water is strong pulling on James. Despite her determination, her grip begins to loosen. The water splashing over the raft makes her grip slippery. Still, she hangs on. James looks up at her knowing that if he holds on they will both end up in the waters. As if seeing into his mind, Mary screams out, "No. James, Hold on! Don't let go! Please!"

He lets loose his grip and even though Mary tries to keep hers, he is swept away and back toward the bridge. Just as quickly she and the small craft are thrust forward up and over the culvert. Mary finds herself clinging to the makeshift raft as it surges forward. The ride is quick, bumpy, and fast. Soon she finds herself in calmer waters as she sails down and into Cambria City.

CHAPTER 19

▼

HOPE

John Peyton made the long walk back to the clubhouse. He is weary from the fruitless fight and drenched by the rains that continued to pour down. Moreover, he is concerned for Fiona's health. How is she going to take this turn of events? Did she know what had happened?

He arrives back at the clubhouse to find Fiona at the door.

"It's happened. The dam broke."

"John. Where is James? My God, where is James?"

"Don't worry, Fiona. He went down to South Fork. I could not stop him. He is with Mary. He left with plenty of time to get her and head with her and the family to the hills."

"We must go. Now. Find him."

"Fiona, please. It is dusk now. The waters have destroyed everything in its path. It would be dangerous to even attempt anything in this rain and the night. It will be better to go tomorrow. First thing."

Fiona stares at her husband. She looks for the first time at what a toll the day has taken on him.

"Fine John. Tomorrow then. You're sure he is safe?"

"Yes. Fiona, James is safe. As safe as you or I."

"Let's get you cleaned up now and you can get some rest. Tomorrow, tomorrow we will go and get James and Mary."

"Yes. Tomorrow."

John Peyton washes up and takes off his now ruined clothes. He shivers at the memory of the dam giving way and rushing down the valley. As he puts on his nightclothes, he wonders about the people in the valley below, in Johnstown.

Those poor poor people. My God, what happened? How?

Even with all those thoughts racing through his mind, John Peyton soon falls asleep. He was completely exhausted from the challenges he had faced this day. Fiona does not sleep. She sits on a rocker in their room and rocks slowly back and forth. She stares at a picture of James and Janie. They are sitting on the clubhouse steps. It comforts her through the night.

John Peyton awakes with a start. He looks over to the other side of the bed and sees Fiona is not there. There is a clamoring throughout the clubhouse and more movement than usual for a Saturday morning. He dresses in a rush and charges out into the hallway to find both his wife and the cause of all the noise?

He bumps into Robert as he leaves the bedroom.

"Sorry. Oh, Mr. Peyton hello."

"Hi Robert, what in blazes is going on?"

"We are leaving, everyone. Heading to Altoona, can't get through to Pittsburgh now, all the roads are washed out, the trains can't get through either. Surely you have heard the dam has broke?"

"Yes. I knew the dam broke. But what has that to do with all this commotion?"

"Well, they say that the hunkies are going to come up here, burn us out, and rape our woman. They blame us for God's sakes!"

"Robert, first the hunkies, the local folks, aren't going to burn, rape, or otherwise hurt us. They are like us you know. In some ways better."

Robert stares at John Peyton as if he has lost his mind.

"You do what you wish sir, but I for one will not be here any longer than necessary. Where is James?"

"He is in South Fork. He went to get Mary before the flood."

"God, I hope he is safe. I mean right there with them and all. You had better get to him soon."

"Thank you Robert we shall."

John Peyton pushes past Robert clearly vexed and continues his search for Fiona. He finds her on the porch staring out at the now emptied lake. The sun is shining and the morning has a fresh smell. It would have been one of the more lovely days had not the events of the previous day occurred. Even though it is early morning, several buggies are making their way down the path towards South Fork and the train to Pittsburgh.

"Fiona, I was worried."

"Worried?"

"Yes, I didn't see you when I awoke. Why didn't you wake me?"

"Wake? Oh, I came out here in the night. I couldn't sleep. What a tragic catastrophe? We must help."

"Yes. And we will, once we find James."

"Yes. James. You said he was safe didn't you?"

"Yes, he is. Safe in South Fork. Are you ready? I will get the carriage."

"Good. Hurry. Hurry John, I must see James."

John rushes off to get their carriage from the lot in back. He worries about his wife and her fragile state. Several members wave to him as he runs and shout for him to hurry before the "Hunkies" get here. He wants to stop and tell them that their fear is ungrounded but he did not, for his fear is real.

Was his son safe? Did he stay in South Fork, with Mary, or continue his foolish mission and go into the town? Surely Mary would have stopped him. She has a good head on her shoulders.

John Peyton returns with the carriage and helps his wife aboard. He climbs up the other side and whips the horses into action. The pace is fast at first but then slows due to the number of carriages and the condition of the road around the dam and to South Fork. With the break, the usual path over the crest is now no longer available. The other roads along the back of the lake are rough and little used except by the locals and the hunters. At least five carriages are in front of John and Fiona.

"By God we will never get there at this pace," John shouts and then gives the horses a quick whip. He moves the carriage out and past the other carriages, dangerously close to the edge of the road. The others in the carriages he is passing look at him and shout.

"What in hell are you doing Peyton? You'll kill us all."

John Peyton does not hear them. He just whips the horses again and moves faster, closer to South Fork. Fiona clings to John and pulls on him to go faster. Her son is waiting. Several times the carriage threatens to topple over or to get stuck in the mud. It appears as if John Peyton just wills the carriage and the horses to keep going. The other carriages are so close that Fiona notices that she could easily step from hers to another without jumping. Not that she was about to. She urges her husband on. They pass the last carriage ahead of them and veer back onto the road skidding sideways as they make the move.

The small village of South Fork comes slowly into view. Some houses close to the edge were swept away by the flood. Indeed, the path left by the flood is very clear. Everything in its way has been destroyed. Thankfully, the Mihelics place has survived being right on the edge of the water's trail of terror. John stops the carriage. He takes a second to gaze out on the carnage left by the powerful waters. Fiona does not wait for him to get her. She jumps down from the carriage and rushes up to the door.

Why was no one coming out? Are they still away in the hills?

Fiona sees the note on the door; the one Mary had left for James the day before. John Peyton gets down from the carriage and walks over towards his wife. He sees her reading something.

Is it a note from James?

All at once, Fiona Peyton drops to the porch floor.

"Fiona," John rushes to his wife.

"Are you alright?"

He takes the note from her hand and reads the tragic news.

"Oh no. Oh God no!"

Fiona has recovered her senses but just stares ahead. John Peyton looks at his wife, then back to the note.

"Fiona, it's not what you think. I know it. I swear to you he is safe."

"You said he was in South Fork. You said he was here."

"He was supposed to be here. But just because he went to the town does not mean, I mean, oh my God."

John assists Fiona to her feet. Now she stares out at the devastation left by the flood. All in front of her is destroyed. Mud is all that is left. It's as if some giant all-powerful scythe has swept the hills. She cries softly.

"He is dead John. My son is gone."

"No Fiona. I tell you he is safe. We will find him. We will find them all! Come. We must go to Johnstown."

She looks at her husband wanting to believe. Then she takes his offered hand as he leads her back to the carriage. Fiona wonders where they are going, given the devastation she sees.

"Will we even be able to make it there? Is there anything there that will be left?"

"We will make it. I can tell you that. We will make it."

Even as he says it, John Peyton worries. Many roads are sure to be washed out and those that weren't are going to be treacherous. They start out slowly looking for roads, some of which have disappeared, wiped from existence.

It is even worse than I had imagined. These roads are barely passable.

The little creeks and streams that run through the mountains are now overflowing their banks and adding to the run-offs. Each road they travel has major holes in it. Sometimes they find themselves creating a new road because the old one has washed away. Slowly they make their way down the mountain and into the town.

Nothing could prepare them for the scene as they enter the town from the east side. Houses ripped from their bases and settled against each other. Whole streets completely gone. St. John's church gutted and in ruins. Fiona starts shaking involuntarily. John Peyton scans the horizon. He sees signs of life everywhere. Some people seem to be just wandering around aimlessly while others appear to be rushing off on some mission or search. He looks for evidence of James and Mary but can't locate them.

The carriage can't go any further. A twisted railroad car and a large house crumbled in ruins block the road. It would have been fruitless to try to pass anyway since there was not any semblance of road or street left. John Peyton helps his wife to the ground.

"Come Fiona, let's begin our search."

She follows her husband but she is lost in thoughts of the devastation before her. Her son is surely dead. Mud is all about them, the residue of the flood. The waters have receded from most areas although parts of the town still have to contend with pockets of high water. Sometimes John stops to help Fiona over a fallen tree as they made their way down the remains of Main Street. All around them, there are signs of the massive destruction brought by the waters.

John grips Fiona's hand.

"Look, there. It is Mary! I tell you it is she!"

Fiona looks off to where John was pointing. The woman is young and about Mary's size. She is hunched over and has a blanket about her shoulders. She does not look at all like the confident young woman who had helped Fiona with the last dance. That happy time is now a long distant memory.

John can't hold himself back any longer. He releases Fiona's hand and rushes up to the young woman.

"Mary. Mary it is you. Where is James?"

The woman he addresses looks at him strangely. She tilts her head as if trying to recall where she may have met him.

"It's me, John Peyton, James' father. Don't you remember me? Where is James?"

She does not reply at first looking beyond him to the slowly approaching Fiona.

Fiona's eyes lock onto Mary's. A strange transference occurs and Mary is snapped back to reality. She blurts out.

"He is dead. James is dead."

She starts to cry. Fiona rushes to her and holds her close.

"Cry my dear. Cry. We will all cry. For a long time."

"He is not dead."

They turn to see John Peyton standing there tall, his legs spread, his voice strong.

"I tell you now, and I know it. He is not dead."

Mary tells them the story of the flood from James arriving at the Hamilton's house. The deaths of her family, the many escapes, and the final conflict at the bridge with the awesome force of the water, all is told in a torrent of words. She finishes with the tale of the fire at the bridge and the screaming people. After that, she remembers little, except walking into town and finding them here.

"You did not actually see him die then, did you?"

"Mr. Peyton, I saw him go under and away from me. He couldn't have survived. Oh God."

She begins to weep uncontrollably. John places his arm around her and spoke gently. "Mary, you've been through a lot. Take heart. There is still hope for James. I can't tell you both why I feel this way, but I do. I believe that James is alive."

Mary and Fiona find themselves both wanting to believe. Fiona worries at getting Mary's hopes up once more should they be dashed. However, she also realizes that hope was all they had left.

John Peyton realizes that action is needed and starts to make plans saying, "First we have to get you cleaned up little lady. Let's see if we can find some place where there is some fresh water. We have some clothes back in the carriage."

"No. Please. I am fine, really. I do not want to waste any time. James may need me if…"

She stops short of saying "if he is alive".

"No. You go with Fiona now. Fiona, help her clean up and get her dressed in something better. I will search for James and your family."

Mary starts at the mention of her family.

All dead now. Why am I here? Why did I survive?

Fiona places her arm around Mary and leads her back to the carriage.

John watches them move away, then says, "I will meet you at the carriage in about two hours."

He looks to Fiona. She then turns and shouts over her shoulder, "Yes, John, please hurry. Please find our son."

He hates to let them go off alone but he has his reasons. First they will be focused and that will keep their thoughts from the tragedy that is all around them. Second, it will give him time to check out the morgues and see if he recognizes James or any of Mary's family. It doesn't take him long to find one of the morgues.

It is the Adams Street School. The school has taken water damage but generally withstood the floods well. Bodies are being placed there for review and for claiming by survivors. Each is being documented as to clothes and as to where the body was found if known.

So many bodies, so much death.

The stench of death and filth is everywhere. John places his handkerchief to his nose to keep the smell from gagging him. He finds himself crying often, seeing little children there, often clutching a doll, or a toy.

How am I ever going to find anyone here? This is hopeless, utterly hopeless.

He moves on to each body and stares wondering what story this person or that could tell if alive. Some bodies are unrecognizable, either

burned by fire or torn apart by the flood. He examines these more carefully. He has to be sure, to know, whether James is among them.

He finds Charles Mihelic first. He looks as he had in life, strong and
bigger than most men do, and strangely at rest. Close by Charles he
sees Jennie Mihelic. She also looks serene, as if asleep. She is covered
with a blanket as her clothes had obviously been turned to rags in the
raging waters. He signs some forms that the personnel at the morgue
place in front of him. The forms acknowledge him as the claimant and
that he will take care of burial arrangements. He moves on noticing
that the time is passing and he will have to head back to Fiona and
Mary.

He comes upon one body that resembles James from a distance. As
he moves closer, he is able to see that the young man is not his son. His
heart beats faster now. He worries that he perhaps he has spoken too
hastily and maybe gave Fiona and Mary false hope.

By the time he nears the end of the morgue he is shaking. He still
has not found Grace nor any sign of James. He steps up to the man at
the door who had given him the forms.

"Excuse me, are there other morgues around here?"

"What?"

"Are there other morgues around?"

"Oh yes, at least three, one in Cambria City, one up in Kernville,
and one in Millville, I believe. This is the main one here."

"Thank you."

"You're quite welcome. Did you find everyone you were looking
for?"

"No. I am still looking for a young girl, about fourteen, brown hair,
green eyes."

The man perused the charts in front of him for a while. John grew
impatient. He wanted to leave and get back to Fiona and to Mary.

"Here is one like that. Come, let's see if this is her."

John Peyton follows the young man up to a body of a young girl.
He wonders how he had missed her when he had passed this spot pre-

viously. It is Grace. She was very muddy and almost unrecognizable. He sees the bracelet on her wrist, Janie's. It's still there. His hands shaking, John Peyton takes out his silk handkerchief and clears the mud from her face. He bends down and kisses her cheek. John Peyton fills out some more forms. His hands shake and the tears flow.

"Sir. Can I do anything for you?"

"No. I'm fine. Thank you so much for your help."

John Peyton hesitates. He turns and looks back over at the many bodies laid out in this morgue.

"Excuse me sir, is there someone else you are searching for?"

"What? No. No, that is all."

"Well then if I could ask you," He looks down at the completed form. "Mr. Painter, if you would please leave. We have many to assist here now."

John thought to correct the man's mispronunciation of his name, but did not. He just wanted to get away from this mausoleum of death.

"Yes, of course. Thank you again. We will be back later for the," John stopped short of saying 'bodies'.

It seemed so final and so cold to him.

"Fine sir."

The young man turned to assist another dazed and troubled person. It was going to be a long day.

John gathers himself together and wipes away the tears from his eyes. He looks up and down the street, for what he does not know. Perhaps a glimpse of his son, perhaps anything that would speak of hope in the devastation before him. Then he turns away and walks back, at a quick pace, to where the carriage and the ladies are waiting.

He observes them there sitting on a step of a devastated house facing the Main Street. Curiously, the house had been crumpled but somehow the porch and steps remained intact. Fiona and Mary look weary but resolute.

Why did I not see this before? They are so much alike. Why was I so blind? Oh God, please forgive me.

He walks up to them slowly. His weariness is evident. They rise to meet him.

"I found your family Mary. They are in the Adams Street School. I signed the necessary forms. We can take care of the burial and the other arrangements for you."

"Thank you," Mary nods and begins to cry. She starts out slowly but then her emotions take full force. She sobs and breathes as if her very life was being driven from her. John Peyton hugs her trying by his body to give his strength to her. He then says, "It will get better, Mary. It will. We will help you through this sad tragic time."

Fiona clasps her hand in Mary's, looks into her face and says, "From this day forward, Mary, you are a member of our family. I know we can't take the place of your wonderful parents. But we will be there for you. Always."

Mary cries harder. Fiona cries. She closes her arms around Mary and John. Fiona cries out, "It's not fair. Why? Why did this have to happen?"

John Peyton holds them both. Soon he too gives into the despair and cries, silently, tears running down his cheeks.

Time stands still. The bustle of the town and the people around it seem to vanish. There is only this moment. There is only these three people standing together in a desolated town. Crying and letting out all of the pent up pain, the despair, the anger, the culmination of too many trials.

John Peyton leads the ladies back to the steps. He sits Mary and Fiona down and stands facing them. He draws a deep breath trying to get his emotions in check. It is difficult.

"We're all tired. It's been a long two days. Let me get you both back to the clubhouse. I can then return and continue to look for James."

No one answers him. Fiona sits with her head down, still crying. Mary stares out ahead and over John Peyton's shoulder. At first, she is just staring out; wondering at the massive devastation that has taken place. Her glance turns west down what had been Main Street. It is quieter now as dusk is setting in. The cool breezes of a gentle wind give little hint of the torrential rains that had fallen the night before. She looks further on, down near the other end of town. She sees a lone figure is approaching. He is limping badly but something about his gait is familiar. Whoever it is he is covered in mud and had obviously been through the worst of the flood. Her heart starts to beat wildly.

Is it possible? Please, lord God; do not give me false hope. It can't be, yet I can see. James!

John Peyton looks at Mary Mihelic and sees the change in her appearance.

Good God, she is losing her senses again. We must get her to the clubhouse. Now.

He reaches to grab her but she pushes him away and runs down the street. He turns to see where she is going. Fiona looks up to see what has happened. Mary is running down the street towards something. What is it? Then, Mary finds her voice and calls out, "James! James, it is you, it is you!"

The person down the street looks up to see a woman rushing towards him. He stops. Then he hears her voice yelling to him and he breaks into a slow run. He has little energy left to move faster. They meet in the middle of the Main Street and embrace. Mary ignores the mud and the dirt covering his face. Her James is alive. He's alive. She kisses him all over his face and hugs him close to her.

"I love you James Peyton. I love you!"

Softly James replies, "I love you Mary Mihelic. I always will."

Fiona and John Peyton hurriedly find their way to the young couple's side. Fiona is crying uncontrollably now and John holds her close to him. John Peyton fights back his own rush of emotions.

Thank you God! Thank you!

Mary reluctantly lets James go. He hugs his mother.

"I'm back mother. It is a miracle but I am back. When I got swept away at the bridge, I flowed back into the debris and started to go under. The current was so swift. All of a sudden I was picked up and cradled in this tree, actually the roots of a tree. The force knocked me unconscious. The next thing I know I'm somewhere near Nineveh still stuck in that tree. It took me a long while to make it back here once I was free."

He breaks off his hug of his mother and faces his father. So much had passed between them. John Peyton stands back, not knowing what to say, or to do. He looks to the ground grasping for words to express the feelings in his heart. He finds none. Tears roll down his cheeks and he says the only words that are needed, "I am sorry son."

James grabs his father and hugs him tightly.

"I am sorry too, dad. There is much to be sorry for. We must go on."

"Yes. Yes James. Now we will leave this place. We will go back to Pittsburgh. Back to where we belong. Let's put this place and its memories behind us."

James stiffens and he moves back from John Peyton. He grabs Mary's hand.

"Father, do what you wish. Mary and I are staying. We are going to help this town rebuild. We must."

Mary squeezes James' hand affirming his words. John Peyton looks at his son at first stunned and then with a growing sense of pride. He nods his head and then slowly and with meaning he says, "You are right son. Your mother and I will stay also. Together we will help this town rebuild. We will make it better than before. We can do it."

The four of them lock arms and walk down the street to a new beginning, a new Johnstown.

"As He swore to your fathers when the flood destroyed the land,
He will never forsake you,
He will swear to you again."

—*Though the Mountains May Fall*
By Dan Schutte

Bibliography

Beale, Reverend David J., *Through The Johnstown Flood By A Survivor.* Hubbard Brothers, Philadelphia, 1890.

Connelly, Frank, and Jenks, George C., *Official History of The Johnstown Flood.* Journalist Publishing Co., Pittsburgh, 1889.

Degan, Paula & Carl, *The Johnstown Flood of 1889 The Tragedy of the Conemaugh.* Eastern Acorn Press, 1984.

Dieck, Herman, *The Johnstown Flood.* Philadelphia, 1889.

Gallagher, Jim, *Johnstown Flood.* Chelsea House Publishers, Philadelphia, 1999.

Heiser, Victor, M.D., *An American Doctor's Odyssey.* W.W. Norton and Co., New York, 1936.

Johnson, Willis Fletcher, *History of the Johnstown Flood.* Edgewood Publishing Co., Philadelphia, 1889.

Law, Anwei Skinsnes, *The Great Flood Johnstown, Pennsylvania, 1889.* The Johnstown Area Heritage Association, 1997.

Livesay, Harold C., *Andrew Carnegie and The Rise of Big Business.* Harpers-Collins Publishers, New York, 1975.

McCullough, David G., *The Johnstown Flood*. Simon and Schuster, New York, 1968.

McLaurin, J.J., *The Story of Johnstown*. James M. Place, Harrisburg, 1890.

Reynolds, Patrick M., *The Johnstown Flood and Other Stories*. Pennsylvania Profiles, Volume thirteen, The Red Rose Studio, 1989. A book for children, illustrated.

Sanger, Martha Frick Symington, *Henry Clay Frick: An Intimate Portrait*. Abbeville Press, New York, 1998.

Slattery, Gertrude Quinn, *Johnstown and Its Flood*. Wilkes-Barre, 1936.

Newspapers

Frank Leslie's Illustrated Newspaper, no. 1761.-Vol. I,LXVIII.J, New York—For the Week Ending June 15, 1889, a reproduction copy.

Johnstown Daily Democrat, Souvenir Edition, Autumn 1894, a reproduction copy.

Johnstown Tribune Democrat, July 1889, reprinted July 15, 1919 and January 2, 1969. Article on Elizabeth Bingham Burdick, "the flood baby".

Johnstown Tribune Democrat Commemorative Edition of the 100th Anniversary of the Johnstown Flood of 1889.

Johnstown Tribune Democrat, Sunday June 3, 2001, *Clubhouse Concept,* Article describing plans to revive South Fork Fishing and Hunting Clubhouse and remaining Cottages in St. Michael PA.

Washington Post, Tuesday May 30, 1989, Page A-3, *Johnstown Flood Survivor Recalls the Wall of Water 100 years ago,* Survivor, Elsie Frum interviewed at age 106.

Videos

A Victorian Summer. The Story of the South Fork Fishing and Hunting Club.
Obtained in spring 2001 and available from the 1889 SFHC Historic Preservation Society, St. Michael PA.

The Johnstown Flood. The Johnstown Flood Museum Film.
Produced by Guggenheim Productions Inc. Washington D.C. in conjunction with MetaForm Incorporated New York, N.Y. 1989. 26 minutes, Academy Award Winner.

Web-sites

http://www.nps.gov/jofl/home.htm
National Park Service Johnstown Flood National Memorial.
http://www.jaha.org/flood/main.htm
Johnstown Flood Museum.
http://smoter.com/flooddam/johnstow.htm
Copy of article that originally appeared in Civil Engineering (May 1988) pages 63-66 in edited form. Article and website produced by Walter S. Frank.
http://prr.railfan.net/documents/JohnstownFlood.html
Pennsylvania Railroad site dedicated to the Willis Fletcher Johnson book reprinted in almost its entirety.
http://www.photolib.noaa.gov/historic/nws/nwind14.htm
NOAA Photo Library. Pictures of the 1889 Flood as appeared in the book, *History of The Johnstown Flood*, Willis Fletcher Johnson.

Visitor Sites

National Park Service Johnstown Flood National Memorial
Johnstown Flood National Memorial
733 Lake Road
South Fork, PA 15956
information desk telephone:
(814) 495-4643

The Johnstown Flood Museum
The Johnstown Flood Museum
304 Washington Street
Johnstown, PA 15901
For more information—Johnstown Area Heritage Association at
(814)-539-1889

1889 South Fork Fishing and Hunting Club Historic Preservation Society
P.O. Box 219
St. Michael PA. 15951

0-595-26172-8